LIQUID MOON

BRUCE EBERTS

Liquid Moon
Copyright © 2021 by Bruce Eberts

Tellwell Talent
www.tellwell.ca

ISBN
978-0-2288-7195-8 (Hardcover)
978-0-2288-6984-9 (Paperback)
978-0-2288-6985-6 (eBook)

Acknowledgement

The benefit of writing an acknowledgement for a second book
is you get to thank all those people who read and supported
you through your first! A big thank you to the readers
who contacted me with praise, constructive critiques and
thoughtful questions regarding my debut novel, Drip Castle.
Indeed the interest was the impetus to write Liquid Moon.

Thank you to all the beta readers who stepped forward to
read Liquid Moon and provided feedback on improvements
I couldn't possibly see with the myopic vision that so often
develops with reading your own manuscript too many times.

Thank you, once again, to Stuart for the great
art work and Jefferson for the editing.

A thank you to my hometown area of Northwestern
Ontario for the memories. This includes the towns of
Ear Falls, Cochenour, Red Lake, Balmertown and all
the other towns in between (I wonder how many people
will spot the reference to Dryden in Liquid Moon).

Thank you to my family (which includes our new Labradoodle, Sadie) who excused a second round of inexplicable vacant looks at the dinner table which they intuitively understood as hot flashes of plot-itis.

Family support and forgiveness for writer self-indulgence is hard to beat!

For my Mom and Dad

Thanks for the courage

Prologue

December 22, 1971

Pat Galverson sat on the log bench of his plywood lean-to and poked the bonfire with a long stick. A flash of bright embers rose up, but they were quickly extinguished and carried into the night on the blowing snow. He looked out onto Yars Lake, but he was lucky to see more than a few feet of snowshoe tracks beyond the light cast by the fire. He stood and stroked his white beard as he watched the snow swirling overhead. He looked back at the warm glow of his cabin window, lit by the hanging lantern. Should he check his ice-fishing hole one more time? He pulled back his tan leather mitt to check his watch: 7:40 pm. Storm or no storm, he decided one more look couldn't hurt for the reward of some fresh pickerel for the morning's breakfast.

Strapping on his oval snowshoes and grabbing his six-volt square flashlight, he began a memorized march out onto the lake. Fifty feet out, he slowed his pace.

"What the hell?" he asked himself. "That a plane?"

He looked up into the darkness of the falling snow, trying to use his bush pilot's ear to decipher the sound. *That ain't no Norseman or Beech*, he thought. He continued to walk, concentrating the whole time on the drone of the plane to gauge its direction. Reaching his ice-fishing hole, he squatted down to check the line. Then he suddenly stood.

"Shit, that plane is circling!" he said as he looked up again.

Vainly, he searched for the flicker of navigation lights, but he could see nothing. Almost immediately, he was distracted as, to his right, the sound of the plane's engines became more distinct. He eyes widened as he spotted the bright white landing lights.

"Jesus living Christ!" he yelled as a twin-engine Cessna burst into view through the blowing snow.

The plane roared just a hundred feet over his head. He ducked instinctively and then turned to watch in shock as the Cessna came down on the snow-covered lake. It skipped off the lake and then came down with force, but the wheels did little to support the weight of the plane on the snow. The fuselage lurched wildly as the plane's left wing clipped a snowdrift, and then it flipped onto its roof before sliding another hundred feet. It finally slammed into the rocky shoreline of Yars Lake. Pat watched in stunned silence as a small fire erupted from the right engine.

"What the fuck! What the fuck is this?" he yelled, already adopting his best snowshoe-racing gait to rush to the crashed plane.

When he reached the plane, he shielded his face from the heat of the engine fire and made his way around to the cockpit. Here he found the right side of the plane torn open and the pilot lying sideways, suspended by his seatbelt. Blood was dripping from his head onto the snow. Pat came close and kneeled under the hanging pilot. Grabbing the collar of the pilot's leather jacket, he pulled him back and used his flashlight to try and examine his injuries.

"Buddy...you okay?" he asked.

He shone the light on the pilot's face and then took a deep breath as his eyes dilated in sudden realisation.

"Fuck...Rick! Is that you? Are you okay?"

Rick Torrison looked back at his former boss from Brown Airways. His breathing was shallow from a punctured lung. "Pat, take it. Take all of it," he rasped.

Pat yanked out his fishing knife to cut the seatbelt straps. "Take what? What the fuck are you talking about? I'm going to get you out of here, Rick. You're going to be okay. Hold on!"

He cut through the straps and pulled Rick from the wrecked cockpit of the burning plane. Rick cried out in pain as Pat struggled to drag him down the shoreline. Once he'd reached the forest's edge, he gently laid Rick down and took off his wool toque to place under Rick's head.

"Rick...Jesus Christ! What the hell are you doing out here with that plane? Is there anyone else on board?"

As Rick turned to look at Pat, his head wound became clearly visible in the flickering light of the plane fire.

"No one," Rick struggled to reply. "Just gold."

Figuring Rick was disoriented from the crash, Pat unzipped his parka and used his knife to cut off a strip of his bush shirt. As he placed it over Rick's head wound, he hastened to reassure him. "Don't worry about any fucking gold, Rick, here or anywhere else. I'm going to check the rest of the plane. Be right back!"

Pat retrieved his flashlight from the snow and headed back to the plane. By now, the flames were beginning to die down, and he could reach the passenger area. He shone his light through the open space left by the broken back door but saw nothing other than a compartment half-filled with snow. He turned to go back to Rick when his eye caught the glint of firelight reflected off an object in the snow. Stepping forward, he leaned down to examine the half-broken crate.

"You've got to be fucking kidding me," he said under his breath.

He looked up again and then shone the flashlight at the cargo door. Now he could see a number of other crates half-buried in the snow. He rushed back to Rick.

Pat put the flashlight down and kneeled beside Rick, whose eyes were now closed. He placed his leather mitt on Rick's shoulder.

"Rick! Rick, wake up!"

Rick slowly opened his eyes and stared up at Pat. He took a laboured breath and struggled to speak.

"Save my mom, Pat. Save her with that gold."

"What the fuck are you talking about, Rick? Where did that fucking gold come from?"

Rick coughed, and blood seeped from the corner of his mouth. He slowly blinked his eyes.

Pat grabbed hold of Rick's leather jacket. "Don't you die on me, Rick. Don't you dare die on my fucking lake!"

Rick reached up and grabbed Pat's arm as his eyes slowly began to close.

"Fucking MS!"

Chapter 1

NONDISCLOSURE

"Hello?"

"Milt?"

"Shit, not fucking you! What time is it?"

"It's one am…well, midnight your time but one here."

Milt sat up on the side of the bed. "Christ almighty, Berts, can you not call at a decent hour if you are going to call at all!"

Kristen rolled over in bed and placed her hand on Milt's back. "Who is it, babe?"

Milt covered the phone handle. "It's a crank caller. Don't worry about it, hon. Go back to bed. I will explain tomorrow."

Milt threw the covers off and reached for his grey sweatpants. He cradled the phone with his chin as he pulled them on.

"Fuck, Berts, why are you calling me?" he whispered. "You know, this borders on harassment." He looked back to make sure Kristen was asleep, and then he headed for the kitchen.

"I received another fax, Milt, and this person is asking a lot of questions. And they seem to know a lot more than anyone should off the street."

Milt walked into the kitchen and took a glass from the cupboard. He opened the fridge, grabbed a jug of cold water, and poured himself a glass as he continued to speak. "What the fuck does that mean? You made a fortune on the back of my dead friend's plane crash. Why the fuck am I talking to you about anything?"

"Easy, Milt. I've got you on speakerphone. Don't want to wake my own family." Milt could hear the sound of a bottle hitting the rim of a glass. "Now, this affects you as much as me. I have no idea who this person is or where they're getting their information. And you're right. I could just go ahead and write a second book and say, fuck you. Deal with it. But the reporter blood runs too deep in me. I make an effort for the facts, Milt. The complete story. For your dead friend Rick and everyone else in Tear Falls."

Milt sat down at the kitchen table and rubbed his forehead. "Oh, Christ, the virtuous reporter. The suspense is killing me, Berts. Fuck…okay, I'm listening. Talk!"

"Good!" Berts said. "But I'm thinking it might be better for me to fly up there and we have a face-to-face and discuss this at the NearNorth over a few drinks."

"You're going to fly all the way up from Hamilton to discuss what, exactly? Another kook who thinks they know where the gold is? I'm fifty-three years old now, Berts, and it's been twenty-two years! Twenty-two fucking years since the crash, and you are still listening to these assholes with their conspiracy theories? I'm really starting to think you need some professional help! And if you had any sense at all, you would be writing about the missing Chad DeMello story. Or does that not make enough money for you!"

Berts laughed. "You still think he's out there, don't you. Some legend of the north. You don't think he would have had enough of black fly lunches to decide to call it quits by now? Don't think so, Milt. And not sure why you are so hung up on that fucking kid, anyway. Someone who tried to take your head off. But I'll leave that one with you. Let you write your own book."

"Yup, you do that." Milt replied. He rested his forearm on the table. "So, what is it, then? What do you have for me, smart guy. Give me your best writer spiel. What's this mystery person asking, and what have they told you that has you drinking and calling me at midnight…oh, sorry…fucking one o'clock?"

"Okay, let me start by asking, how well did you know Rick? I mean, outside of work. His family, his relationship with his mother? What happened to his father?"

"Did we not go over this twenty years ago? We were best friends. You know that, so don't waste my time. What are you getting at? What the fuck is this person saying about Rick or me?"

"This person thinks Rick's father took his own life. Well, took it in the manner of purposely driving recklessly on a snowmobile after some heavy drinking. I have some notes here that say the tree he hit was in the middle of a clear-cut logging area. Not another tree in sight. Did you know that? Did Rick tell you that part of his father's death?"

Milt took a deep breath as he stretched his neck in discomfort. "Does it really matter? And why would they even be phoning and telling you this? This is probably just someone who wants to stir up trouble. Could be anyone in Tear Falls who wants to start a rumour if they know you might pay for good information."

"That would make sense if they did want me to pay for, as you say, good information, but they don't. My anonymous faxes are more interested in details about Rick and the crash. I just can't tell which is more important to them. Did Rick have a girlfriend back then? Any serious relationship you knew about? How about extended family that could be poking around for more details on his death and family years later?"

"Not that I'm aware of. There was a girl named Tracy Rellis, but that seemed to be more her than him. And extended family? Nope! Never saw any of them other than a few flower bouquets from distant relatives at his funeral." Milt rose from his chair. "You know what? I think I need a real drink! Don't know where this is going, but knowing you, I better be prepared."

"You know me well, Milt!" Berts laughed as Milt placed the phone down.

Milt walked to the fridge and took out a beer. He came back to the table and purposely twisted off the beer cap near the phone speaker so Berts could hear the hiss. "Okay, that's better." he said with a grin as he sat down. "Yeah, I can't think of anyone who would be bent on looking him up over twenty years later or the crash. His eighty-one-year-old mom is still managing over at the nursing home with her MS. She has some dementia now, but I've never heard her once mention any family contacting her or Rick having a girlfriend."

"But who takes care of her, Milt? Who is paying for all her medical bills if she has no family?"

Milt leaned forward and picked at the label on the beer bottle. "Why? What's that got to do with anything?"

"Because this person seems to think it might be you. Is it?"

"And so what if it is! Why is that any of your business or anybody else's?"

"I'll get to that," Berts replied. "If you would care to answer the question."

"I help out here and there, but as I have always said, small towns look out for each other. Tear Falls helped out with a fundraiser at the time of Rick's death, but she also has a trust fund set up by an unknown benefactor. So, obviously, someone has come through for her. Can't tell you anything further than that because I don't know. Her lawyer said it's private legal shit. I can make decisions about her care if she can't, but that's it."

"But this unknown benefactor, that wouldn't be you?"

"I just fucking told you, I help out where I can. End of story!" Milt sat back. "Okay, I've answered your questions. Now answer mine. If this person doesn't want money for a juicy story, what do they want? Fill me in. What's the big fucking mystery?"

"Like I said, they want to know what I found out about Rick's life while writing the book. Everything leading up to his plans to steal the gold. Anything extra about his father and the health of his mother. Even you, Milt. They want to know more about your friendship with Rick and what you knew about the gold."

Milt laughed. "Oh, fuck! Here we go! I don't think you have family or an old girlfriend on the line. I think maybe you have another reporter or writer on your hands!" Milt smiled as he took a drink of his beer. "Maybe it's my turn to make some money on all this crap you write. What's their number? I think I'll give them a call."

"I wouldn't bother. For all of what this individual is asking, if they were a reporter, they would have contacted you long ago. And there is never a name on these faxes. Only the letter B. I've seen numbers printed at the bottom. A few are Southern Ontario, and a few are from up there, so I'm reasoning there has to be some sort of connection. Nope…there is another angle here, Milt. Just not sure what. Otherwise, they wouldn't have negotiated with me for what I know."

Milt couldn't help but smirk. He pushed his chair back, rested his beer in his lap, and placed his crossed feet up on the table. "Man, it sounds like someone is turning the table on you, Berts. This is getting good! What's this person have on you that you would have agreed to do that? They have some compromising pictures of you at a fucking strip club or something?" Milt laughed as he took another drink.

"It's not what they have on me but what they have on you, Milt, that has me interested."

Milt sat up. "What the fuck is that supposed to mean? Don't start fucking me around with another bullshit story from somebody thinking I knew of Rick's plans to steal the gold. Had my fill of that crap! You should know better by now."

"Nah…nothing about you stealing the gold. But how about a document dated June 6, 1973. Also signed by one Conrad Reese, mine manager of the Stinson Gold Mine, Tear Falls, Ontario."

Milt stood up with a start. His beer bottle toppled over on the table as he threw the phone down. He took a few steps away from the table and brushed his hair back with both hands. "Fuck!" He stared at the phone.

Berts voice called out over the receiver, "Milt! I'm a reporter, not the fucking police. Pick up. I just want to talk about this."

Milt took a deep breath as he grabbed the phone. "Okay, what the fuck are you trying to do to me, Berts, ruin my fucking life? Who the fuck is this person? Where are they getting this information? Or maybe it's you. Maybe you're making all this shit up so you can write another book on my back instead of Rick's! You know, Kristen was right when we first met you and she said you were an asshole!"

"Milt, calm down. Just calm the fuck down! It's a nondisclosure agreement, not a fucking arrest warrant. And all I have is the last page. Just the signatures. I don't even know what this is all about, although I have my suspicions."

Milt paced the room. "You think this is a joke, Berts? How about David DeMello trying to kill me over trying to find the gold. You think that's a joke, too? People have been murdered over this. Gone missing! And now you have my nondisclosure agreement floating out there from some fucking Watergate Deep Throat? I'm not saying anything to you until you find out who this is and what they want! Fuck you! And fuck your books!"

Milt clicked off the phone and threw it on the table. It slid off the far side and smashed to the floor, scattering the battery and cover lid across the room.

Milt turned at the sound of a sigh and saw Kristen leaning in the kitchen doorway in her underwear and a white top.

"That sounds a little bit more than a crank caller," she said. She walked into the room, picked up a tea towel off the stove handle, and threw it on the puddle of beer dripping from the table. Then she stepped over to the counter and leaned back with her arms spread across the top. "So…I guess this is one of those…how can I phrase this…'what the fuck is going on' moments?"

"That was Chris Berts, hon," Milt said, shaking his head. "He's got a hold of my fucking nondisclosure agreement with the Stinson Mine."

Kristen slowly inhaled. "Really. Okay, well, considering it nearly caused us a divorce over you not telling me until fifteen years after you signed it, what's it matter that Berts has it now? That's not your fault. It didn't come from you."

Milt rose from his chair, walked over to the broken phone pieces, and picked them up. "That's not the point!"

"Then what is the point, Milt? Enlighten me on the lawyer talk of nondisclosure agreements, because it isn't necessarily at the top of my reading list these days."

Milt placed the battery back in the phone and snapped the cover shut. "The point is, I don't want the fact that I found the gold and collected the reward money being broadcast all over Tear Falls! We just bought the Abby last year. I don't need people coming in and ordering the breakfast special with a side of 'how much did you get? Why didn't you tell anybody?'" He walked over to the table, set the phone on it, and righted the tipped beer bottle. "And another thing…" He walked over to the fridge and opened the door.

"Better make it two." Kristen said.

Milt took out two beers. He twisted off the caps and handed one to Kristen.

"What about the DeMellos, or even Fritz Rinestein, Kristen? You think they are going to take kindly to hearing this news if it gets out? They'll be pissed! Probably send a fucking hit squad up here from prison."

Milt walked over to the table, sat down, and took a long drink of his beer. "Fuck, I hate that Berts."

Kristen came over and sat close to Milt. She folded her arms and leaned on the table. "Alright, enough, Milt. Nobody is sending any hit squads to Tear Falls, and who gives a shit if the story comes out that you got the reward money for finding the gold? You have done nothing wrong. In fact, you have only done right! Does anybody know you paid off Trent Campbell's kid's wheelchair with that money? Or that you helped out with Rick's mom's care at the nursing home? How about that story, Milt. Let shitface Berts write about that. Fucking stick it to him, babe!" Kristen placed her hand over his. "It's going to be okay."

"Yeah…stick it to him…" Milt said, staring across the room. "But…fuck… How the hell did someone get my nondisclosure agreement to give to Berts?" He turned back to Kristen. "And why would they be digging into Rick's past and the gold now?"

"What?" Kristen replied. "Now you are really confusing me. Berts has someone else feeding him information? On his reporter payroll?"

"No, no…" Milt replied. "Or at least, that is not what he is telling me. He said some anonymous person said they had my nondisclosure. Wanted to trade it for what Berts knows about Rick and his family and the crash from writing his book. He also said they mentioned something about Rick's dad's death. Said it might have been…I don't know…a fucking suicide?"

Kristen put up her hands. "Okay, now you are starting to freak me out! You know I have tolerated your Chad DeMello theory and your makeshift crime lab in the basement, even if you are the only one on the planet that thinks he is still alive. But Chris Berts has been trouble since the day we met him. And I don't think this lost gold shit is ever going away. There is always going to be someone somewhere that is going to think it's still around. Maybe it's a good thing if people know you found it. Maybe it will finally put an end to the speculation about you and the gold."

Milt took a deep breath. "Yeah…maybe. But maybe you were right when you said we should just get the fuck out of Tear Falls. Probably should have done it long ago." Milt shook his head as he stared at the table and took a drink.

Kristen leaned back. "Whoa, whoa! We're not going anywhere. You… Let me correct that. We have too much tied up in this town to be chased out by Berts or any other asshole that decides they want to try and get rich finding gold or stirring up another story about Rick or you. Not going to happen, babe! Besides, Rick's mom needs you, Milt. That is your legacy to Rick. You know you could never leave her to fend for herself."

Milt chewed his lip. "I don't know about that. She seems to be doing okay. She certainly has enough money coming in through her lawyer for good care. But I guess my visits help so you may be right."

"It's not a maybe. I am right!" Kristen reached over and squeezed Milt's hand. "Hey, maybe Berts paid someone off at the Stinson Mine just to try and get you to talk, and this so-called person is just bullshit. You know what he is like. Anything for a buck. Wouldn't put it past him. I suggest you call Abigail in the morning. She'll know how to put a stop to this pretty quick."

"She's retired, Kristen. She doesn't want any part of this crap anymore. And Christ…what about the boys coming for a visit this summer? Welcome home, boys, and by the way, your dad is in the newspaper again!"

Kristen stood, stepped behind Milt, and started giving him a massage. "Okay, someone is way, way overthinking this. And I've been told lawyers never retire. Why don't I call Abigail in the morning myself and at least have her point us in the right direction?" She leaned forward and gave Milt a kiss on the top of his head. "'What'd ya say, Mr. Gold Hero! Come to bed, and we'll discuss it more?"

"Sounds like I have no choice," Milt said, leaning back and giving Kristen a kiss with his head tilted back. "And you're right. Why would I trust Berts. Fuck'im and his fucking stories. This one is going nowhere!"

Chapter 2

ALL SALES ARE FINAL

"Silas, do you want to take this file or not? Silas? Silas… are you even listening?"

"What…yeah, I'll take it. Where is it?"

"It's down in Port Larch."

"Port Larch! That's an hour's drive from Toronto!"

Ethan Chaste shuffled some files in front of him and slid one over to Silas. "Yours now. Scenic Woods retirement home."

Blessing Lee looked over at Silas and smiled. "Late night?" she mouthed.

Silas took the file, placed it in the tan shoulder bag by his chair, and looked back up. "You bailed," he mouthed back.

"That's it for now, guys," Chaste said. He passed out Starbucks coffee gift cards to all the sales staff around the table. "It's just before ten. The morning rush should be gone next door. Enjoy a coffee on me, everyone!"

Conceited prick, Silas thought as he stood and put on his grey wool dress jacket. He looked over at Blessing, who had already donned her red designer winter parka. "Care to explain yourself over coffee?" he asked, holding up his gift card. "I'm paying!"

"You're a generous soul, Silas." Blessing said, smiling back. "Sure, why not?"

Silas and Blessing made their way through the revolving doors of the office building and came face to face with a cold Toronto March wind.

"I swear Toronto streets are designed to act as wind tunnels," Blessing said as she pulled her hood up.

"It's a conspiracy!" Silas said, placing his hand over his mouth to shield his face from the wind. "It's all to get you to buy that expensive jacket you have on."

Blessing looked over and saw Silas's dimples rise from the smile he concealed beneath his hand. She shook her head as they reached the door of the Starbucks and ducked inside.

"The usual?" she said as she unzipped her parka and placed it over the back of a tall wooden stool by a table near the window.

"Too early to drink, so I guess," Silas answered.

Silas sat down and stared out the window. He watched with empathy as pedestrians passed, engaged in their own thermal-retention fight with the cold wind. The sight sent an uncontrolled shiver down his spine, causing him to look back at Blessing in anticipation of her return with his hot coffee.

Silas Agro was twenty-six years old and a '91 Kin grad from the University of British Columbia. He felt he was typical of someone two years past graduation. His job was low paying, he had lots of debt, and, much to the delight of his Greek-born parents, he lived at home. He had literally stumbled into his current job at Morrow Medical, tripping over one of their wheelchairs and spraining his ankle at a job fair, which had served as good an introduction as any to speak with one of their sales recruiters, Ethan Chaste. Their talk, while he waited for medical attention, was long enough for an informal interview, and Chaste contacted him with a job offer a week later.

Blessing returned to the table and set a large black coffee in front of Silas and a latte in front of herself.

"Can't believe you drink that straight up." she said, sitting down. "Must be close to what they give for an enema in the hospital."

"Maybe, but I imagine it's a lot healthier than adding coffee to your sugar," Silas replied. "Why didn't you show last night?" He sipped his hot coffee.

"Wanted to get my own sales numbers in order. Last day of March is the year-end, my dear friend. Have to look good for that promotion they're going to offer me." Blessing said with a wink.

"You think your job is more important than a night of drinking with your miserable cohorts? You have your priorities wrong, Ms. Break Up the Party Girl!"

Blessing laughed. "Would have been the same old routine, anyway. Complaints about Chaste, complaints about pay and bonuses. Oh, and let me guess, Kyle suggested the strip club at around…I'm going to say midnight, right?"

Silas leaned back in his chair with his hands in his pockets and watched as Blessing snapped open her briefcase and began removing file folders. "No. You are totally wrong, I will have you know. At least on Kyle. He suggested the strip club at 10:30 and was gone by eleven. Guy's an asshole, anyway."

Blessing smiled without looking up from sorting her files. "Should have known."

Silas kept silent, knowing there was not much use in continuing the conversation until Blessing was finished. He watched patiently as she made a few notes in the various files.

Silas had met Blessing the first day he started at Morrow Medical. She was assigned to him for the obligatory meet and greet tour. He shook hands and nodded to countless staff, but few names registered as he concentrated on his attractive guide. Blessing was twenty-eight years old, five foot seven, and had straight, shoulder-length black hair. Her facial features reflected a mixture of her Canadian-born European mother and Japanese-born father, who had met while she was on a government posting to Japan. After three years at Morrow, Blessing was already in charge of their large corporate medical accounts, but she was always willing to visit her roots by helping junior staff with their single-sale customers.

Blessing put the files back into her briefcase and looked up. "Okay…done! Now, how are your numbers this month? Because I can probably give up one of my small corporate accounts and still make my own target. Open to the offer?"

"I don't need charity. I'll get it done." Silas reached over and closed the top of Blessing's briefcase. "C'mon, Blessing. Really, how long are you going to slave away at Morrow Medical, anyway? You, the woman with the business degree who could fire her resume onto Bay Street with a t-shirt gun and still get ten offers."

Blessing gently removed Silas's hand from the top of her briefcase. "Why would I trade my top corporate sales job at Morrow and go to the bottom of the ladder down the street? Just more stress and more people like Chaste. Besides, I wouldn't have time for the important things in life, like saving your ass in our next company volleyball game." She picked up a spoon and gave Silas a grin as she scooped foam out of her latte.

Silas responded with a shrug of indifference and glanced around the room.

"Oh, c'mon, Silas. It isn't all that bad. I know Chaste can be a jerk, but you are doing okay. Something else will come along. Just be patient!" She sat back and crossed her arms. "Okay, forget about work, then. Let's talk about something different. Let's talk about your next big trek. When, where, and with whom, Mr. Survivor Man?"

"Probably in a few months, the spring. Where? To be determined. And with whom?" He turned back and leaned over the table. "Well, with you, of course."

Blessing responded with a flat smile. "Right, and I'm sure Mark would go for that."

Silas lifted his hands. "Hey, adventure-minded male simply seeking platonic trip with like-minded female."

"Not when like-minded female has a not-so-like-minded fiancé," Blessing remarked. "Next choice?"

"Well, he is in England, studying to be what, again?" Silas asked. "A professional student?"

"It's called a master's in architecture, shithead! And he will be back at the end of next month."

"Oh, defensive, I see!" Silas retorted with a grin. "Okay, I tried. Don't burn me at the stake." He took a sip of his coffee. "Most likely, your brother, Ben, then. He enjoyed the last one, and I still have lots of spare gear for him." He looked over at another table where a man's sleeve had retreated to reveal a Rolex.

"Want to make sure this trip is a good one. Maybe document it with a night-vision camcorder for a TV special. Make a million bucks, pay off my parents' mortgage, and buy one of those." He nodded in the direction of the man's watch.

Blessing glanced over and raised her eyebrows. "Well, maybe you should start with that file down at Port Larch first to get a down payment. What's it for, anyway?"

Silas took the file out of his carrying bag and opened it. "Well, the guy was born in 1935, and it says he wants to buy a four-wheel scooter. Guy must be in rough shape because that only puts him at fifty-eight." Silas looked up from the file. "Fifty-eight and already in a retirement home? Remind me to never get old." He closed up the file. "Should be an easy sale."

"This guy, this easy sale, he have a name? Did they at least give you that?" Blessing asked.

"Yeah…it's…" Silas opened the file again and ran his finger across the top of the page. "His name is Marty. Marty DeMello."

***

Silas drove the Morrow Medical van up the Scenic Woods retirement home driveway and parked in the visitors' area. He shut the engine off, took out his cell phone, and dialled his voicemail to see if he had received any messages from the occupational therapist who was to meet him for the assessment with Marty DeMello.

"They're always late," he said to himself as his phone reported no messages. His attention was broken by a white BMW pulling up beside him. He looked over to see a young woman talking on a cell phone. She made eye contact with him and put her gloved finger up to signal him to wait.

Dressed to the nines, he thought as he looked over. *How much do they pay these therapists?* He was lucky if he could pay for his ride-sharing membership every month, let alone BMWs and designer clothes. He reached over to the passenger seat, picked up his carrying bag, and placed it on his lap. He stared straight ahead and through a large bay window of the retirement home. One by one, the residents were dutifully guided in by home workers. Many struggled to propel wheelchairs or take slow, unsteady steps with a cane or walker. He observed workers pointing residents to various tables, and although he could hear no words, he could see the staff's facial expressions demonstrating their obvious impatience. Once the residents were seated, a worker pushed a cart to the various tables and set out boxes of games, puzzles, and cards.

Silas chuckled, as few of the residents seemed to take interest and continued to talk. He shook his head. *Is this what I have to look forward to in my later years?* he thought. He reached over and grabbed his ID badge out of the glove compartment. "Lord help me!" he said as he placed it around his neck.

A knock on the van window startled him out of his thoughts. He turned to see the occupational therapist smiling and tapping her file. "Ready?" she asked.

Silas opened the door and stepped out. "Yeah, hi! I'm Silas Agro." He reached out to shake her hand.

"I'm Bianca Cortini, occupational therapist from TS Health." She handed Silas her business card.

He looked down at the bordered card and ran his fingers over its embossed print. "Great! Thanks for the card. Do you mind if I email you my contact information? We actually did away with the business card stuff. Some environmental thing from head office."

He pushed his homemade business card out of sight and deep into the side pocket of his carrying bag.

"Okay, no problem. You brought the scooter I asked for?"

"Yeah, it's in the back of the van. I'll get it ready and unload it. Why don't you go ahead and get out of this cold, and I will meet you at the room."

"Sure," Bianca said. "Room 41!"

"Thanks. See you there!"

Silas unloaded the electric scooter and drove it through the automatic doors of the retirement home. He paused on the welcome mat and hopped off the scooter to wipe the tires.

"Where you going with that smart-looking machine?" a walker-using resident asked as she ambled up to Silas.

"Person in here is looking to buy one," Silas replied while circling the scooter and continuing to wipe off the tires.

"Let me guess. It's either Borton or DeMello. They are the only ones in here with the money to buy something like that."

Silas looked up. "Really can't say, ma'am, but I suppose, if you see one of them riding around on it, you'll have your answer!" he said with a smile.

He jumped back on the scooter and headed for room 41. He was starting to think this could be an even easier sale than he had planned.

Silas parked the scooter outside the room and gave a soft knock on the door. "Hello," he called out.

"Come in, Silas," Bianca replied.

Silas opened the door to see Marty DeMello in a wheelchair, facing Bianca, who was sitting opposite him in an armchair, holding a notepad. Silas took a quick glance around. Marty DeMello's room was like most he had seen in retirement homes. The room itself was not very large. There was a bathroom to his immediate left as he walked in and a bed up against an indented wall just beyond the bathroom entrance. Beyond the bed was a small living area, where Bianca and Marty DeMello were sitting.

A small back window with a screened partition let air and light into the room. What Silas didn't expect was the decrepit-looking wooden bookshelf that ran the length of all three walls, filled with books.

"Hello, Mr. DeMello. I'm Silas Agro." Silas walked over to shake hands with Marty, but he was immediately intercepted by his cane.

"Sit down and shut up until we are done, son!" Marty DeMello said. "I know you're anxious to sell, but this young lady is more important to me than listening to some two-bit bullshit sales pitch!"

Silas took a few awkward steps back and quickly found a seat on the bed. Bianca cast him an empathetic smile as she continued her conversation with Marty.

"So, you see, Mr. DeMello, the government should help you pay for seventy-five percent of the cost of the scooter. You just have to pay the remaining twenty-five percent."

"Well, will they, or won't they?" Marty replied. "I want my goddamn scooter now! I can't wait for the government. I will probably be dead by the time they make a decision." He looked over at Silas and once again raised his cane. "How much, Mr. Salesman?" he asked.

"Well, that depends," Silas replied.

"Depends on what!" Marty DeMello snapped back. "On how clean my ass is? Speak up, son!"

"Yeah, sorry." Silas stood, quickly opened his carrying case, and handed Marty DeMello a brochure. "On what model you get. And any extras we add."

"Just tell me the price on the most goddamn expensive one you got. With all the extras!" Marty demanded.

"Ballpark…with all the bells and whistles, I would say close to five thousand dollars. But that gets you everything! For that, you would have the Cadillac of scooters to drive around here." Silas did his best to smile. He looked over at Bianca for reassurance that he wasn't overstepping his bounds.

"Done!" Marty replied.

"Okay…" Silas said. "But there—"

Bianca interjected. "Well, Mr. DeMello, you don't have to rush into anything. I'm sure Silas can work out some arrangement for you to have a rental scooter so you can see exactly what the government will pay for."

Marty reached over and placed his hand on Bianca's. "I know you are just trying to help, Bianca, but as you can probably imagine, I don't trust government programs all that much. I've suffered enough from their bullshit over the years. I don't need their help." He turned back to Silas and raised his voice. "You get me that scooter as fast as you can! A cheque will be waiting here for you for six thousand dollars or whatever it goddamn takes to buy it. I'll even throw in a tip for you if Bianca here says you are worth it!" he said with a laugh.

Bianca smiled. She glanced over at Silas as though expecting a closing sales pitch, but he remained silent and simply responded with a submissive nod. Bianca turned back to Marty. "Okay, Mr. DeMello. It's your decision. I will make a note on the paperwork that you are going to handle the purchase privately with Silas. I will check in with you once you get it. You seem like you can take care of yourself from here." She turned back to Silas. "You okay with that, Silas?"

"Yeah, by all means." he said. "We'll definitely work something out. I will bring back another scooter model next week."

"Good." Bianca stood and placed her file into her bag. Then she reached out and shook Marty's hand. "Any questions, you call me, Mr. DeMello." She turned back to Silas. "Meet you out in the lobby once you are done with Mr. DeMello?"

"Absolutely. Just a few things for Mr. DeMello to sign, and I will be right out."

A few minutes later, Silas came out into the lobby and spotted Bianca sitting on a leather couch in the waiting area.

"Nice, easy sale?" she said with a smile as he approached. He sat down on a leather chair opposite her.

"Can't complain." He smiled back. "Left him with the scooter I had. Interesting guy, and I see he is quite the reader. Must be why he doesn't trust the government. Probably too many conspiracy books." He laughed and handed Bianca a brochure on the scooter he was going to deliver.

"Or the fact he spent eight years in prison," Bianca said as she perused the brochure. She handed it back to Silas. "Looks nice. Definitely much more than the government would pay for. Just tell me when it arrives so I can make sure he is safe using it." She stood to leave.

"Hold on! Prison?" Silas placed the brochure back in his bag. "Really? For what?"

Bianca laughed as she zipped up her jacket. She wrapped a designer scarf around her neck and donned a pair of brown leather gloves. "You'll have to ask him, Silas. Client confidentiality, you know." She picked up her leather carrying case off the couch. "Call me when it's in. Thanks for your help!" With that, she turned and walked toward the front entrance.

"Thanks for the reassurance!" he called after her. Bianca smiled and gave him a wave as she pushed open the lobby door and left the building.

"Fuck…the guy was in prison. That's all I need," Silas said to himself as he gathered up his paperwork and placed it in his bag. "I'll probably be the first salesperson to have a scooter jacked." He zipped up his bag and headed back to his van for the hour-long drive home.

***

Silas returned a week later to the Scenic Woods retirement home and once again looked through the front window as he parked his van. He observed the same group of seniors sitting around tables, staring at the same stack of puzzle boxes and games. "I can't take this," he said and exited the van. He shook his head as he watched the residents inside peer out at him while he unloaded the new scooter. *How bad can it be when the arrival of a medical van is the day's attraction?* he thought.

He drove the scooter through the doors of the home and down the hallway to Marty DeMello's room. Then he got off the scooter, softly knocked, and listened.

He could hear Marty DeMello's loud voice through the door. "I don't give a fuck how old he is! Kick him out if he doesn't pay!" There was a pause, and then Marty said, "Yeah...who is it?"

Silas quickly removed his ear from the door. "It's me, Mr. DeMello, Silas. I have your scooter!"

"I'll call you back," he heard Marty say. A moment later, Marty called, "C'mon in, son! Door's open!"

Silas opened the door and propped it open. He pressed the hand controls on the scooter and guided it into the room. "Here you go, Mr. DeMello. A JX-6000. The BMW of scooters!"

"BMW. I don't want any German shit. I want a Cadillac." Marty said with a laugh. He rose from his wheelchair and, with the help of his cane, took a few steps over to the scooter and sat down. He examined the controls and moved the wheels with the steering handle. "Where was this made?"

"Made in the US." Silas replied.

"Good! I don't want any Japanese shit, either. I'll take it!" Marty said, looking up at Silas.

"You don't want to take it for a test drive, Mr. DeMello?"

Marty slid off the scooter seat and hobbled back to his wheelchair. "Nope! Leave it here and take the other one. Come and check on me in a few weeks. I'll pay you now, but if there is a problem, I'm giving it back to you and getting a full refund. You have a problem with that?" Marty didn't allow for a reply. He sat down and pointed with his cane. "Now, go over there and get my chequebook out of that drawer, and I will give you the money."

Silas complied and brought Marty his cheques. He picked up a book for him to write on and handed him the itemized bill for the scooter.

"Five thousand three twenty-six," Marty read as he wrote. "Let's make it an even fifty-five hundred." He tore the cheque off and handed it to Silas. "Little tip for ya! Do some fucking good with it and take Bianca out for a nice dinner."

"Uh…well, I can't do that, Mr. DeMello," Silas said with a smile. "It's against company policy."

"What, taking a good-looking girl out for dinner? Fuck your company policy. You want to follow the rules or get laid."

Silas laughed. "No, taking a tip is against the rules, Mr. DeMello, not going out for dates. But I appreciate the gesture. So, if you wouldn't mind just making another cheque out for the original amount, that is more than enough for me. I get a good commission off the sale."

"Okay," Marty replied as he filled out another cheque. "Fucking stupid if you ask me. Can't say I understand your generation."

Silas nodded with a smile. He scanned the bookshelves as he waited for the second signed cheque. He recalled Bianca's comment about Marty DeMello's prison time. "You've read a lot of books, Mr. DeMello."

Marty handed the second cheque to Silas. "No, I just have them up there for fucking show." He laughed at Silas's blank face. "Of course I read a lot. Let's just say I had some time on my hands before coming here." He closed up his chequebook and handed it to Silas to put away. "You like reading, son?"

"I enjoy reading real-life adventure stories," Silas said over his shoulder as he put the chequebook in a drawer. He turned back. "I have a passion for hiking and exploring on my days off when I can."

Marty DeMello pressed down on the arms of his wheelchair, and Silas instinctively reached over to help him stand. "Well, then I have the book for you!" Marty replied. He took a few steps toward the bookcase and pointed his cane at the right shelf. "Go over about the middle of that shelf and look for an orange-coloured book. It will be well worn."

Silas walked over to the shelf and ran his finger along the book spines. "Title?"

"*The Torrison Treasure*," Marty replied. "Written by an asshole named Chris Berts."

"Oh...okay," Silas replied, chuckling. "Here it is!" He took the book down, but when he held it out, Marty pushed his hand back. "I have read that shit enough, but you may like it. It's about some lost gold up north."

Silas looked at the book cover. "Really? True story?"

"True as they get with a good dose of bullshit." Marty said, laughing. "But sometimes those are the best kind. Read it and tell me what you think." He sat back down in his wheelchair. "We done?"

Silas turned his attention away from the book. "Yeah...yeah, Mr. DeMello. We're done." He pulled out a clear bag with some paperwork in it and placed it on the seat of the scooter. "Here is the manual for the scooter. I will check back with you in a week. Thanks for the sale, Mr. DeMello. I will be leaving the other scooter for another resident to try here if you don't mind."

"Why would I fucking mind." DeMello replied. He lifted his cane and pointed at the book in Silas's hand. "Make sure you have read that before you return. Part of the deal of this sale!" he said with a grin.

Silas smiled back, and then he held up the book as he turned to the door. "Will do, Mr. DeMello."

Silas returned to Morrow Medical by 4 pm and quickly headed to his cubicle. He sat down with a big smile. "Hey!" Blessing said over his cubicle wall, surprising him. "Why the big smile?

Something or…maybe…someone I should know about?" She flashed him a grin.

Silas grinned back and stuck out his Bugs Bunny Pez dispenser. "Care to celebrate with me? I just sold a JX-6000 today…no questions asked! Even got a free book out of it!" Blessing reached forward with an open hand and took the candy. "Yeah…what book?" she replied, popping the Pez into her mouth.

Silas handed her *The Torrison Treasure*. "Courtesy of a one Marty DeMello. Says it's about some lost gold. I have a week to read it as part of the deal." He laughed.

"Cool!" Blessing replied as she examined the book cover. "Sounds like you might have a sale and your next adventure trip planned. You still going to try and drag my brother along?"

"Actually talking to him this weekend. According to rumour, there is a party at your parents' place Saturday night. We'll talk options."

Blessing sighed. "Ben always thinks a party is his reward for taking care of my parents' place when they are away."

Ethan Chaste's head appeared above Silas's cubicle wall. "Hey, Blessing," he said. "Wanted to speak with you about the Disall corporate account." He flipped through some papers. "These numbers are looking pretty good. Nice job! Have another one I would like to discuss with you in my office if you are interested."

Blessing glanced at Silas with a smile as she said, "Sure!"

"Oh, hey, Silas," Chaste said, looking down. "How are things with you?"

"Good…good. Got some good sales lined—"

"Fantastic," Chaste replied, cutting him off. "I will meet you back in my office when you are ready, Blessing." He turned and walked away. "Love these numbers!" he said, holding up the paperwork over his shoulder.

Silas leaned back in his chair and peered around the corner of the cubicle to see Chaste enter his office. "That guy is the very definition of narcissism."

"Yeah, well, that narcissism is in charge of your next promotion, so just think of your best Bugs Bunny cartoon to keep a smile on your face when he talks."

"Good one!" Silas reached up. "Book, please? Since you have no interest in adventure trips and getting rich."

"I'll get rich the old-fashioned way." Blessing said. "Even if that goes through a narcissistic prick," she added, raising her eyebrows as she handed the book back to Silas. "Fill me in on the plot later. My promotion awaits."

Chapter 3

NINE YEARS

Oakey walked into the Abby Cafe and carefully wiped his work boots on the welcome mat. His curly brown hair recoiled as he removed his hat and scanned the restaurant for an open seat. He was happy to spot a vacant booth by the window, perfect for stretching his legs out, read his paper, and keep an eye on his logging truck parked outside.

He walked over, sat down, and smiled as he surveyed the dated restaurant. *Are all these small-town Northern Ontario diners stuck in the '50s or just this one in Tear Falls?* He took the menu from between the steel napkin container and glass sugar jar and glanced over the breakfast specials. Quick bite, and he figured he could get at least two loads delivered to the pulp mill and still be back on the reserve by 7 pm.

He looked up to see an older man with a full head of grey-streaked black hair approach with a cup in one hand and a coffee pot in the other. The man placed the cup in front of Oakey and began pouring. "You know, we don't often get your kind in here."

Oakey kept a stern face. At five foot nine, he was shorter than most other men, but he wasn't intimidated by anyone. "And what kind is that?" he asked, exchanging glares with the man. "The kind that has a job and money to pay for this?" He picked up his cup and examined its contents. "This white man's bullshit coffee?" He readied himself for what he knew would come next.

The man broke out in a smile. Oakey stood and gave Milt a handshake and a big hug. "How have you been doing, Milty?"

Oakey said with his trademark high laugh. "You're looking good! Even with that cook's apron on. How's the Abby treating you?"

Milt laughed. "Yeah, well…surviving on the crumbs, as they say in the restaurant business." Milt reached for a cup from a nearby empty table, and the two men sat down. "And how about you, my friend? You look like you lost some weight. You throwing those logs on the trailer yourself? Haven't seen you in a month!"

"More like carrots and water in the truck, Milty. Doctor's orders. Just turned fifty. Want to enjoy my retirement years hunting and fishing, not bent over with arthritis. But what am I talking about…look what you do with a little bit of severance money. You go ahead and try and relive your youth by buying this Elvis-wannabe restaurant."

Milt poured some sugar into his coffee. "Hey, I would have given Rennet Mine their money back and bought the CEO coffee for life if he would have kept the mine open. You see the number of houses for sale in town?"

Oakey shook his head. "Yup, it's a shame. Guess everyone's severance money is running out. Hard to get anything to compete with those high-paying Rennet jobs." He took a sip of his coffee as he watched Milt stare blankly out the window. "And how are you doing?" he asked, trying to get a read on Milt's face. "You and Kristen going to be okay? I mean, this restaurant thing working out?"

Milt turned back to Oakey. "Yeah, yeah…" he replied, refocusing and taking a quick drink of his coffee. "Sorry…mind has been on other things. But don't worry about the Abby. We still get the main highway drive-throughs. We're a tourist attraction. Iron ore might have run out, but not good food in a vintage diner!" He smiled.

Oakey paused and stroked his chin. "Okay…if you say so, buddy." He pushed his newspaper on the table over to Milt. "And speaking of tourist attractions, you read the latest?"

Milt picked up the paper, took out his glasses from his apron pocket, and read the front page. "Santtini. Now, why do I know that last name?" He laughed. "Seems even his kid thinks the gold is still up there." He read further down. "And it looks like this Mead, our new sergeant, has taken full credit for their rescue, even though I heard they walked out on their own." He peeked over his glasses. "How long has he been with us now, Mead?"

"She…" Oakey said. "I believe she has been here a few months."

"She! Ah…a woman in uniform. I was always a sucker for that." Milt handed the paper back to Oakey and sat back. "He or she, it doesn't really matter, does it? Headlines help them get that transfer out of Tear Falls they all so desperately want. They're all the same, Oakey."

Oakey set the paper aside, and as he spoke, his usually high voice went low. Milt knew it was his way of saying he was serious or about to lose his temper, but it was hard to believe it was the same person talking.

"Milty, the Santtini kid, and the others came back because they reported pieces of their gear were stolen on the third night." Oakey sat back and stared.

Milt took off his glasses and stroked his hair as he looked over at the paper on the table. He turned back to Oakey. "I'm not going there, Oakey. But nice try. Not going to feed into that conspiracy shit anymore. Nobody has believed me about robberies up there over the years or the people that have gone missing, and a new sergeant certainly isn't going to believe it now."

"She is new, Milt. You never know. She may have an open mind." Oakey raised his eyebrows.

Milt sat back and let out a breath. "Nah…I'm finished with them. Singh was the only good one in the bunch. Every sergeant since then has chalked it up to misadventure, even though that doesn't make sense. And bodies? Well…apparently, they all fell down hundred-foot abandoned mine shafts, are lying at the bottom of Yars Lake, or were eaten by bears." Milt shook his head. "Nope, Mead will be like the rest of them. Don't rock the boat. No budget for a search. But maybe I don't blame them. The older I get, the crazier it seems even to me." Milt gazed around his restaurant. "Just as crazy as me buying this fucking restaurant, I suppose."

Oakey leaned in on the table. "Okay…you are fucking crazy for buying this restaurant. I grant you that. But humour me. How old would Chad DeMello be now? If it was him, how many years would he have been living in the bush?"

Milt tapped his finger on the side of his coffee cup. "Well, he would have been close to eighteen when he came at me with a tent pole, so yeah, after nine years, he would be twenty-seven." A tight-lipped grin spread across Milt's face as he took a moment to stare up at the ceiling.

"What's so funny about that?" Oakey asked, mirroring Milt's grin. "Am I missing something?"

Milt looked back at Oakey. "Ah, it's all crap, Oakey. Always was. Let's forget about it. I'm not sure being locked up with you in the nuthouse is worth it. I don't trust anybody with the last name Santtini, anyway. Probably just making it up to get the attention. No different than his old man."

"I won't argue with you on that!" Oakey replied.

"About Santtini?"

"No, about a good-looking Indian bunked up with an old white man," Oakey said with a smile. He sipped his coffee. "Bad combination!"

"Well, isn't this sweet. A little male bonding in the middle of the breakfast rush." Kristen stood at the end of the table with her hands on her hips, smiling.

Oakey rose from his seat and grinned as he gave her a hug. "How are you, Kristy? And don't tell me I'm stealing your husband—or should I say employee—from his kitchen duties."

Kristen laughed as she sat down beside Milt and gave his head a stroke with her hand. "Well, I guess even a husband deserves a break." She turned back to Oakey. "So, what brings you into the Abby, Oakey? I thought all logging truck drivers did breakfast on the road."

Oakey took a deep breath and shifted his gaze to Milt for support.

Taking his cue, Milt reached across the table and grabbed the folded newspaper. "Well...Oakey thought he would share this headline with me." He handed the paper to Kristen.

She took a moment to read the front page, and then her smile disappeared. She looked up. "Okay...really, you two! Have you not had enough of this crap?"

"It's just a theory, Kristy," Oakey said. "Stupid one at that, but still just our theory." He braced for her response.

Kristen's face became tense as she turned her anger to Milt. "He's dead, Milt. D-E-A-D...dead! Stop trying to make Chad DeMello into some fucking Tear Falls human bigfoot. You know, you are getting worse than Berts!" Kristen stood and shook the paper. "Let people think what they want, but you have no need to feel any guilt with his disappearance. And I would say you have enough on your mind without going on another fugitive wild-goose chase!"

"I was just—"

"Just what, Milt...just what? It's been...nine years! Chad DeMello tried to take your head off before running off into the bush, and his uncle tried to shoot you dead. Is that not enough to put this behind you? Or do we have to relive this shit every time a new sergeant comes to town to talk about some assholes who ran into trouble looking for the gold!"

Kristen turned to Oakey. "And you...you are a great friend, Oakey, and my husband owes you his life. But this is not healthy. You have to stop! How about doing that for me? For all of us who had to live through this shit." She threw the paper onto the table and turned back to the kitchen. "Burn it, Oakey!" she said over her shoulder. "Do us all good!"

Oakey said to Milt, "You know, you could have waited until I at least had eaten my breakfast. Who knows what will come out of the kitchen now?"

"Yeah…" Milt replied, staring at Kristen as she disappeared through the swinging kitchen door. He turned back to Oakey. "She's pissed! But I'm thinking I do need to pay our new sergeant a visit in the coming days. You know…a little introduction of the police to a local business is not a bad idea. What do you say you come with me as backup?"

"Not a chance." Oakey replied. "I just make the recommendations. Not a participant." He stood. "But maybe before you announce your plans, can I get my breakfast to go? Might be in my best interest."

Chapter 4

SANGRIA

Silas sat in the restaurant and looked over his paperwork for the month of March. *How did Chaste come up with these numbers for my sales? They are way too low!* He took a large drink of his draft beer, flipped open his cell phone, and hit the pre-programmed number.

"Hey," he said as a woman answered. "What are you doing?"

"I'm shopping in a fit of depression," Blessing replied. "Why, where are you? I hear a crowd."

"I'm over at Shork's, trying to determine how Chaste screwed up my year-end sales numbers. Care to help me figure this out when you have time?"

"You know what? I'm actually not too far from you. I could use a drink anyway. I will be there in fifteen."

"Even better."

Minutes later, Blessing walked up to Silas's booth at the back of the restaurant. "You looked shell-shocked," she said as she slid into the booth seat opposite him. "Or maybe sales-shocked is a better word."

Silas looked up from his paperwork and was surprised to see her long, dark hair pulled back in a ponytail. She had no makeup on and was wearing a blue sweatshirt underneath a three-quarter-length black windbreaker.

"You sure you were out shopping?" he asked. "This looks to me more like your moving-day garb."

"Yeah, well, it's been that kind of day. Let me see those sales."

Silas passed over his yearly summary sheet and sat silently. He was transfixed by Blessing's profile as she looked things over.

She looked up. "Well, these look pretty good. You should get your bonus. What are you worried about?"

"It doesn't exactly agree with Chaste's numbers." As Silas handed Blessing another spreadsheet, the waitress brought over a glass of sangria and set it in front of her. Blessing smiled as she looked at the drink. "Sort of rushing my summer there, aren't you?"

"Ah…it's April. It will warm up soon." Silas leaned forward, crossing his arms on the table. "I need this bonus, Blessing. My mom and dad got another notice from the mortgage company. They—or maybe we—are in big trouble. I heard her crying the other night and arguing with my dad about it. One more, and I think they'll be coming for the house."

Blessing looked up from the paperwork. "Really? Wow, that really sucks. Anything I can do to help?"

"Finding me my bonus in those numbers would be a great start."

Blessing passed the paper back to Silas. "Yeah, well, his numbers are off for your Sevan Hospital account. That's a big chunk of your commissions. Do you know why?"

"Why?" Silas pushed Blessing's glass of sangria closer to her. "Because he gave half of those commissions to Felk. Darren Felk! That little ass-kissing, shit-sucking sycophant whose uncle owns Disall. Your biggest corporate account."

Blessing wrapped her fingers around the stem of her glass. "But that doesn't make sense. Even for Chaste, he can't randomly assign commissions to different people. You did all the work."

Silas sat back and smiled. "He can when Felk brought Disall the brochures on Morrison, shook a few hands, and gave out a few fucking pens. Even though I did all the follow-ups and sales for the next eight months." Silas took a drink of his beer. "That's how Chaste will justify it, Blessing. I know him. He will say I would never have had the sales if dick Darren had not done the introductions. Felk has the connections, plain and simple."

Blessing clenched her hands together. "Wow! I don't know what to say, Silas. I mean, if that's true…and crap…the Disall account is mine. I get a lot of big sales from that company. I feel terrible."

"Oh, c'mon, Blessing. It's not your fault. I'm sorry that I even brought it up." Silas took a book from his brown leather carrying case and threw it on the table. "Forget about that shit. Hey…I finished *The Torrison Treasure*." He pointed at the book. "I bet old man DeMello will be pleased when I visit him in a few days. Seal my scooter deal."

Blessing picked up the book. "Ah, yes. I remember you showing me this. Any good? Mind if I borrow it?" She flipped it over and read the back cover. "Wouldn't mind some diversion right now."

Silas sat back and rested his arms on the back of the booth. "Shit, I'm sorry, Blessing. I haven't been a very good listener, have I." He leaned forward, gathered up his paperwork off the table, and stuffed it back in his bag. "Okay, you have my full attention. What's up? Why the need to support the retail industry tonight?"

Blessing placed the book aside. "Oh, not much. Just that my fiancé has decided he needs to stay in England this summer to finish his thesis. And that puts him back just a week before our wedding in September. So…. guess who has to do all the summer wedding planning and who just shows up?" Blessing picked up her glass. "So, here's to last-minute wedding planning. Cheers!"

"Shit, that's a bummer." Silas replied. "Anything a single guy who knows nothing about weddings can do to help?"

Blessing laughed as she placed her drink down. "Well, there is an offer that is hard to refuse!" She wiped her mouth with a napkin, trying to hide a grin. "No…no…don't worry about it, Silas. My sister and bridesmaids are up to the task."

Silas nodded. "Okay…I get it. But don't say I didn't offer." He pointed at the book. "If you have time, it's a story about a guy who stole a plane full of gold up north and then crashed it. Way back in 1971. Supposedly, the gold went missing from the plane, or at least, that is what this Chris Berts, the author, says."

Blessing reached over and flipped through some of the book's pages. "Hmm…Interesting. So, someone took this gold from the plane when it crashed? That's the gist of the story?"

Silas took a drink of his beer. "Actually, that is the interesting thing about what he writes. The police and the mine that owned the gold said it was all recovered. But this Chris Berts guy basically says that is all bullshit. The gold is still missing."

Blessing laughed. "Oh, I get it. I'm going to guess it's just waiting for an adventure-minded person like yourself to find it."

Silas shrugged and smiled. "Could be. And maybe with your brother, Ben." He leaned forward. "You know there was over five hundred thousand dollars worth of gold on that plane. I did the math. That would be worth almost two and half million today."

"Uh…Silas…I would think you would probably have to give it back. Not finders keepers."

"Uh…I think I know that, Ms. Honesty." Silas replied with a smirk.

"Smart-ass!"

Silas leaned back. "Okay, so I do the right thing, as you say, and turn the gold over after I find it. But if this Berts guy is right, there is always a reward for finding lost treasure. That could go a long way to helping my parents out of this shitty mortgage mess and maybe have a little left over to pay off my student loan. Not a bad deal."

"Speaking of which, what are you going to do?" Blessing asked, staring down and swirling her drink.

"About?"

Blessing looked up. "About your parents' shitty mortgage mess. C'mon, Silas. Shouldn't you be concentrating on that instead of some sort of…I don't know…lost gold story."

Silas finished his beer. He pushed the empty glass to the end of the table and stared out at the gathering bar crowd. "Yup. I guess you're right, Blessing." He turned back to her. "It is all screwed up. But what can I do? My dad isn't getting any better. In fact, he is only getting worse. I've got my student loans to worry about, my mom won't take my money, and now I'm scared to look at the front door in case I see a fucking bailiff letter! Maybe a lottery ticket would be a better idea."

Blessing sighed. "I'm sorry, Silas. I'm not trying to get you down. I'm sure it will work out. But maybe you're right. A little treasure hunting this summer to take your mind off all of this could be a good thing. I certainly could use something to take my mind off a crashing wedding."

Blessing took another drink and then looked down at her watch. "Well, I'm sorry, but I have to go. Screwed-up wedding or not, I'm going to keep shopping."

She stood, zipped up her jacket, and then leaned over the table. "Word of advice?"

"I'm listening." Silas replied, raising his eyebrows.

"Go see Chaste. Let him know how hard you worked to get those sales. Negotiate! Give him that Silas charm I know so well." She winked as she picked up the book and placed it under her arm.

"Yeah…right. I think that charm only works for certain people."

Blessing laughed. "See you at work, and let me know how it works out, Iacocca."

As she headed for the door, Silas yelled after her, "Make sure you read that book!"

Chapter 5

JOCELYN
E. MEAD

Milt sat in Sergeant Mead's office and rested a folded newspaper on a shoebox. He leaned over and took the weighted gold-coloured nameplate from her desk. "Sergeant Jocelyn E. Mead," he read aloud. *At least they don't waste money on nameplates*, he thought.

He looked out into the lobby and saw a young, attractive officer with a notepad in her hand, talking and directing another constable. "Times are a-changing," he said to himself. "Oakey is going to be pissed he didn't come with me."

"Mr. Tonkin!" A tall female officer with brunette hair tied in a bun said, startling Milt as she hurried into the room. She placed some files down and then quickly extended her hand across the desk. "Sergeant Jocelyn Mead. How are you?"

"Good…." Milt replied as he shook hands with the sergeant and did a double-take of the female officer out in the lobby. "Thanks for meeting with me."

"More than happy to. Always ready to get to know the community I am policing."

Milt waited as the sergeant sat down and sorted through her files, marked with multi-coloured tabs. He estimated her age to be mid-forties. Certainly tall and fit and, by the look of things, extremely well organized.

The sergeant took out a pad of paper and a pen from her desk drawer and looked up. "So…what can I do for you?"

"Uh…well…" Milt was already struggling with his words as he stared at the sergeant's twitching pen. He held up the paper he was carrying. "I was just reading this article from the Tear Falls news. The article on the men who made that camping trip up to Yars Lake and had to hike out when they lost half of their supplies. Or…stolen, as they report." He laughed nervously.

"Yes, well aware, Mr. Tonkin," Mead replied.

There was an awkward silence. Finally, Milt leaned forward in his chair and said, "Well…don't you find it interesting they reported only specific things were taken from their site?" He unfolded the paper and placed the open article on the sergeant's desk. "This one kid, Kent Santtini here, says all their wallets with their money were still in a pack they left inside their tent." He ran his finger down the print. "And here it says their tacklebox was opened but only the line was taken. All the expensive lures were left." He looked up. "Is that not an odd thing for a thief to do? You would think he would ransack the place, not just take specific things."

"He—or maybe it's a she—also took all the batteries out of their tape players and flashlights, according to the young men's statements." Mead set her pen down. "Is this why you came to see me, Mr. Tonkin? To discuss a stolen-item list from a campsite robbery?"

"Yeah…well…no. What I was going to say—"

"Is that you think this thief might be this long, lost kid Chad DeMello," Mead replied with a smile.

"Well…. yes… that is exactly what I was going to say! How did you know that? You know his story?"

Mead sat back in her chair and clasped her hands together on her lap. "Mr. Tonkin, the DeMello case, the plane crash and missing gold, Sergeant Singh…it's all practically mandatory reading for any new detachment commander starting in Tear Falls." Mead pointed at the flagged files on her desk. "Even you, Mr. Tonkin. I've done my homework. It's all in there, along with the unsolved disappearance of Chad DeMello. I find the story fascinating, to tell you the truth."

Milt sat up, placed his elbows on the armrests of his chair, and pressed his fingers together. He was already impressed. "Wow, never had any of the other sergeants research the story or me." He opened the shoebox balanced on his lap. "Okay, then...so... what do you think?" Without waiting for an answer, he took out newspaper clippings. "Because, if you look at the investigations of the people who have gone missing the last few years, they all have similar elements."

Milt arranged the articles on Mead's desk and pointed at the first one. "If you read this one, it's this accountant from Montreal that Sergeant White investigated in 1985. Campsite barely disturbed other than rope and a hatchet they said he bought from the Riley hardware store." He pointed to the second article. "And two years later, the geologist from Winnipeg, all his .306 bullets were gone, but the gun was left. Nothing else was taken. And what about—"

"The retired teacher two years ago that said he was robbed up there?" Mead interrupted, pointing to another clipping. "Investigated by Sergeant Waun. Apparently, he wasn't even camping at Yars Lake but just stopped off on a canoe day trip to explore and look for the gold. All that was taken was a fishing rod and bucket."

"Exactly!" Milt replied. "And I can only think of one person that would act like that. Chad DeMello was obsessed with living off the land out in the bush. He would see it as a sense of pride to take only what he needed or could use."

"So, would it be your contention that this Chad DeMello was also responsible for these people's disappearances? Because that is a little more serious than a robbery. If you have evidence on that, Mr. Tonkin, I would definitely like to know."

"Well, I think the two go hand in hand, wouldn't you say? Makes sense. If you have done all this research, you would know

Chad DeMello is more than capable. These disappearances have his trademark written all over them. Maybe they surprised him as he was robbing their sites. Maybe there was an unfortunate confrontation."

Mead leaned forward and folded her arms on the desk. "What they have in common, Mr. Tonkin, is they were all amateur, out-of-town treasure-seekers who went missing while looking for the gold. They all had little knowledge of the terrain or the risks. We have no evidence of possible confrontations with anybody, let alone a person from a nine-year-old case. And therein lies the problem."

Milt shifted uncomfortably in his chair. "Fair enough, but let me ask you something. And I know what the reports state, what people say, about these people going missing. Stories on possible drownings, misadventure with mine shafts, bears…you name it, and everyone has a theory. You think those make more sense than mine?"

"Mr. Tonkin. You have it all wrong. I work on leads. Credible leads, not stories or speculation." She tapped her index finger on her stack of files. "These reports all point to exhaustive searches to try and find the people that went missing, including your friend Sergeant Singh's report on trying to find Chad DeMello. They found no evidence connecting Chad DeMello to anything beyond him being missing and presumed dead like the rest of them. There is very little left to investigate. So, to answer your question, until you can bring me solid evidence, your theory is just like everyone else's, speculation."

"Evidence…?"

"Yes."

"Like bodies?"

"Yes, like bodies. That would be a good start. But I would also settle for clothing, personal items. Even a sighting of a live body if one is to think there is even a remote chance this Chad DeMello is still alive. Of course, you know what we are dealing with here."

Mead pointed at a local map pinned to the wall. "We are talking about a huge area of dense Northern Ontario bush with some of the harshest conditions one can imagine. With all your fifty-three years of living here, do you really think someone could be out there all this time and survive? Never be seen?"

"Forty-eight," Milt said.

"Pardon me?"

"I said, forty-eight. I know you can look up my driver's license, Sergeant, but I moved here when I was five. But I see where you are coming from."

Milt sat back. "And to clarify where I'm coming from, my whole purpose for being here today was simply to show you a pattern in the disappearances and campsite robberies, a connection that points, in my humble opinion, directly to Chad DeMello. And yeah, you are right, it's a long shot. But I don't see anything else coming to light, including bodies, that might explain what happened to these people. It might be that the Santtini kid and his friends just got lucky with a few things going missing."

Mead stood up. She walked over and looked at the map. "Appreciated but not good enough, Mr. Tonkin. No, I would say Chad DeMello is long gone. Just like the gold." She turned back to Milt. "Or are you one of these people that believe the Stinson Mine never recovered the gold?"

Milt smiled. "No, I think you can firmly put me in the Tear Falls camp that says they have."

"Really?" Mead said. "All of it?" She walked back to her desk and sat down.

"Wouldn't think otherwise," Milt replied.

Mead nodded. "Well, that's good to hear. It's just too bad more people are not like you and would stop taking the risks of going to look for it."

"In all honesty, Sergeant, I don't think it matters what I or anyone else says about the gold. I would imagine the conspiracy theory will last long after I'm gone. In fact, some people make a good living at peddling that crap. But if you have all these files on me and know how everything went down in eighty-four, you would know the gold and I don't mix. Nearly got killed and lost a best friend over it. Someone I pretty much considered a brother. There will always be people in this town that will think it's out there or I had some sort of knowledge about the plane being stolen."

"You're referring to Rick Torrison, your friend who stole the plane."

"Yup!" Milt replied. "We grew up together. Worked together. Was there for him when his dad died. Still help take care of his mother, who had to go into the nursing home here in Tear Falls."

"Yes, that's very nice of you to help out your friend's mother after his death. I think someone in the community mentioned that to me when I inquired about the crash. But let me ask you, do you think your friend Rick would have wanted you to have put his mother in a nursing home?"

"Well, I think you hit the nail on the head, Sergeant. That's exactly the reason Rick felt he had to steal the gold in the first place. He wanted to take his mother to a hospital in Tijuana where he thought they might be able to cure her. Wanted nothing to do with her going into a nursing home, but there was really no choice after his death."

"None?"

"None that made sense."

"I see. Well, that's very laudable of you, Mr. Tonkin, for taking on the responsibility of her care. Good for you."

Milt smiled. "Am I missing something here, Sergeant? You don't seem convinced. You have a concern about our local nursing home in Tear Falls?"

"I have a problem with all nursing homes, Mr. Tonkin." Mead picked up the files and stacked them in front of her. "Dangerous places, in my opinion, especially for those you care about. I've investigated a lot of abuse, even a suspicious death here and there.

Nobody deserves to spend their final days in what I see are old-people warehouses disguised with a few nice drapes and a smiling director. Very rarely have I come out of one with a good feeling. But just an opinion based on my line of work."

"Interesting…okay…sounds like you have had a lot more experience with them than me, but I think you might be wrong about the one here in Tear Falls."

"I doubt it, but it's your call as her caretaker." Mead replied. "I'm not here to interfere in people's family affairs."

Milt brushed his hand across his chin as he stared at Mead. "Right…okay." He sat up. "Where are you from, Sergeant, if you don't mind me asking?"

"I'm from Southern Ontario. Last posting in Chatham, to be exact."

"Fascinating."

"Oh, and why is that? Some connection between Chatham and Tear Falls?"

"No, just that most sergeants posted to Tear Falls travel in the opposite direction. They head for the bright lights of Southern Ontario pretty quick when they get the chance. Just a little unusual. But hey, we're glad to have you."

Mead broke out in a wide smile and leaned forward. "I didn't get into trouble, Mr. Tonkin, if that is what you are thinking," she said in a loud whisper. "Sergeants can have all sorts of reasons for choosing small towns for police work. I just happened to choose Tear Falls. That's not unsettling to you, is it?"

"I wasn't—"

Mead raised her hand. "No need to explain. Just a point of clarification for you to tell anybody over at your restaurant if they happen to ask."

"Ah…got it!" Milt replied. "Understood."

"Thank you." Mead pointed at the files on her desk. "So, back to our issue at hand. I'm not sure if the police have anything more to offer you. I will take a look at these files further. Even one unsolved disappearance is enough to pique my interest. It may not be Chad DeMello, but I'll be surprised if there is anything more to be uncovered unless someone comes forward with new evidence. Most of this is long gone from the news cycle."

She picked up the stack of files, took out an elastic band from her top drawer, placed it around the files, and laid them back on her desk. "So, I understand being a proud owner of a new restaurant in town must mean you are a busy man, Mr. Tonkin." She smiled and sat back.

Milt understood the message and knew the meeting was now over. "Busy is the way you want to be when you own a restaurant, Sergeant." He collected his clippings, placed them in his shoebox, and capped the lid. Then he stood, took a step forward, and extended his hand. "Thanks for your time."

"More than welcome. Sorry I can't be of more help." Mead stood and shook Milt's hand.

"Sure thing," Milt replied. He headed for the door and then turned. "Oh, I do have one more question. What, under the law, constitutes harassment?"

Mead came around her desk and sat on the corner. "Well, that depends, but in general, it comes down to someone actually fearing for their safety or well-being. Every case is different. We take all complaints of that nature seriously. Is there something you need to report?"

"No, not yet. But if they ever come up with a law about unwanted phone calls after midnight, let me know, will you?"

"I can certainly do that, Mr. Tonkin." Mead smiled and walked back behind her desk. "You have a great day."

"Thanks," Milt said. "And hey, stop by the Abby when you can. Coffee is on the house. We're never too busy to thank our police in Tear Falls!"

Chapter 6

EVIDENTIARY

Silas arrived at the Scenic Woods retirement home and parked in his usual spot. He looked at his watch, which read 9:30 am. He was in plenty of time for his ten o'clock appointment with Mr. DeMello, but he was already nervous. He had met with Ethan Chaste the day before and boasted of this sale as part of his case for Chaste to revaluate his year-end bonus. The last thing he wanted to do was return a beat-up, high-priced scooter to the company inventory. He picked up his coffee and carrying bag, took a deep breath, exited the van, and headed for Mr. DeMello's room.

"Mr. DeMello?" he said as he lightly knocked on his door.

"He's on the back patio!" A person called out from down the hallway. Silas turned to see a man in a dark blue suit and patterned grey tie walking towards him. As the man came closer, Silas noticed a pin on his lapel of the home's logo. "Can I help you?" the man asked as he reached Marty DeMello's door.

"Was looking for Mr. DeMello. I'm his sales rep from Morrow Medical. Was just going to do a follow-up on the scooter he purchased."

"Oh, so you're the one responsible for that chaos." the man said with a laugh. "I'm Gerry Freestan, executive director of BD Homes, the company that owns this place. I was just meeting with Mr. DeMello." He pointed in the direction he had come. "If you go down this hallway and turn left, you will see a door to the outside. He is at a far-back table, sitting on your machine and taking in the sunshine."

"Thanks," Silas said.

"You're welcome," Freestan replied. "And give him some training on that thing before he kills someone!" he yelled over his shoulder as he walked away.

Silas walked through a side door onto an open-air patio and spotted Marty DeMello sitting on his new scooter near a table at the back. Marty had a cigarette in one hand and a foam cup in the other and was staring off into the distance.

"Hello, Mr. DeMello!" Silas called as he approached, weaving his way past empty tables. "I'm a little early. Hope that is okay?"

Marty put his finger to his lips as Silas arrived at his table. "Shhhssh...up there." He pointed. "A hawk is looking for its breakfast."

Silas quietly sat in a chair and shaded his eyes as he looked up. "How do they turn their heads like that?" he asked in a whisper. "It's like they have no neck or something."

There was a bang from the patio door as two other residents came out, scaring the hawk away.

Marty turned with a start. "Fucking noisy people!" he said. He looked at Silas. "Special vertebrae in their neck. Lets them see who's coming in any direction. Could have used that in my life!" He laughed. "Now, what can I do for you, son?"

"Well..." Silas set his coffee down and took out his sales paperwork from his bag. "Just making sure the scooter is to your liking and everything is okay." He placed a sheet of paper on the table and took out a pen. "And if so, if you can just sign at the bottom of this page, we are all good."

Marty ignored the paper and turned his head to look for the hawk again. "You read that book I gave you?"

"Oh...yeah...of course!" Silas said. "I just don't have it with me, but I will make sure I drop it off soon. Very interesting story. Thanks for lending it to me."

"I didn't lend it to you, son. I gave it to you! I told you, I've had my fill of that book."

"Oh, right…thanks."

"And…?"

"And…?"

Marty turned back to Silas. "And…do you believe it? Are you going to go look for it? You said you were the big adventurer. Gold treasure not enough for ya?"

Silas let out a laugh. "Funny you should mention that, Mr. DeMello, because I actually did give it some thought, but this town where the gold is, this Tear Falls, it's in the middle of nowhere in Northern Ontario. You ever looked it up on a map? I already figured it's at least a two-day drive from here."

"Looked it up?" Marty replied, grinning. "I fucking lived there! Whole reason I spent time in jail! And don't bullshit me, boy. I know you know I have spent time in prison."

"Well, it was mentioned, but that really is none of my business, Mr. DeMello. Really, I just want to make sure you get the right scooter. Help with your independence."

"My independence." Marty repeated with a laugh. He leaned over and put out his cigarette in an ashtray on the table. "Conspiracy to commit murder!" He looked up. "Framed so the cops could get their big fish up there. Eight years in the can, all because I was looking for that same gold in that fucking book ten years ago. Just got mixed up with the wrong people, that's all."

Silas's eyes went wide. "Wow…really…I'm not sure what to say, Mr. DeMello."

"Good! Then listen, because I have a business proposal for you." Marty took out a mickey of Southern Comfort from his sweatpants pocket and poured it into his cup. "I lived in Tear Falls when that gold in that book was stolen. Went looking for it for years with my twin brother." He reached over and offered to pour some of the liquor into Silas's coffee.

"No…no…I'm good." Silas replied with a smile, placing his hand over the top of his coffee.

"Suit yourself," Marty replied. He capped the bottle and put it back in his pocket. "We knew the cops and the mine up there were bullshitting when they said they found it back in '72. That's why that Berts asshole wrote the book I gave you. Thirteen years later, in eighty-four, my brother and I got a tip. Found out a couple of high school kids of a friend who knew the guy who stole it were going on their own search. But things didn't go as planned." Marty reached for the cigarette pack on the table and took out another cigarette. "Went a little awry, as they say." He paused to light his cigarette, and he took a long drag before continuing. "My brother and I and my son followed them up to Yars Lake, where the plane crashed. Raining like fuck that weekend. Found these Tonkin kids holed up in a cabin. We were just going to ask them a few questions." He turned to Silas. "You know, like a share-the-wealth sort of thing, right?"

"Right." Silas replied with a nod.

"But then their old man shows up. Mr. Milt Fucking Hero Tonkin. Fucking guy wants us to leave his sons alone and says he can show us where the gold is. So, off he goes in the bush with my brother to find it at this old mine. Next thing I know, my brother has been shot in the back by some fucking Indian!"

"Shot?" Silas exclaimed. "Your brother? Why?"

Marty took a drink of his liquored orange juice. "Because this injun fucker named Oakey said he was saving Tonkin from my brother. Said my brother was about to shoot him! Cop who was there agreed. Let this Oakey guy off scot-free. But the fucking cops never liked us DeMellos anyway, so that wasn't any big fucking surprise."

"Wow, Mr. DeMello! Your brother was okay, though? He survived?"

Marty chuckled as he tapped some cigarette ash into the ashtray. "You ever seen what a .306 rifle does to a moose, son? Brings him down with one fucking shot if done right."

"Not really. Seen hunting shows but never knew what kind of gun they used."

Marty leaned in and stared at Silas. "Well, it's what was used to shoot my brother. That answer your question?"

"Jesus! Really sorry to hear that, Mr. DeMello." Silas looked down at his coffee, trying to think how to properly phrase his next question. "I'm a little confused, though. Why did you go to prison, then? Your brother was the one that was killed."

"Shit, you can think!" Marty said, grinning. "Because they said I was mixed up in bringing too much weed into Tear Falls. I was supposedly part of an international drug-smuggling network headed up by this bastard Fritz Rinestein." He poked his cigarette at Silas. "You can look all this up on the internet." He took another drag and then put out his cigarette. "This Fritz fucker tended to have people he considered a liability to operations go missing. He's the guy who owned the plane that had the gold on it. But he didn't give a shit about gold; he gave a shit about all the money he could make while smuggling drugs with it on his planes! But don't get nervous about me, because I never killed no one. They just lumped me in with the rest of them. Apparently, it was in my best interest to plead guilty to the conspiracy shit, or so my fucking lawyer told me." Marty took out his mickey of Southern Comfort and poured several more ounces into his empty cup. He set the bottle on the table

"Sure, I tried to make a few extra bucks here and there selling, but I lost a hell of a lot more than I gained." He held out his aged hands. "And now I can barely hold onto toilet paper, let alone a fucking gun." He raised his cup. "A drink to old age, son!"

Silas raised his coffee cup, trying to keep a steady hand. He watched as Mr. DeMello down the contents of his cup.

"Ah…that's good medicine!"Marty said. He pulled the sales paper closer to him and looked it over. "So…let me ask you something." He motioned for Silas to pass him his pen. "What do you get for this sale? What's your cut?" He signed the paper and pushed it back to Silas.

"Basically, a three percent commission on everything I sell," Silas said, picking up the paper and folding it. "And year-end bonus. Well, most of the time, if I hit the company sales targets."

"So, we're talking maybe a few hundred bucks here?" Marty asked.

"Yeah, a few hundred is a good estimate."

"And how many sales a week? What are you pulling in a month?"

"Oh, I don't know, Mr. DeMello." Silas placed the folded paper into his bag. "Not going to get rich, I guess, but it's not a bad job. You know about sales, Mr. DeMello?"

Marty moved his scooter forward a few feet and then signalled for Silas to come around the table. "Come over here and help me to this chair. I don't have my cane with me."

Silas stood and helped Marty into the chair. Marty leaned back with his hands folded in his lap. "That's better. Now we can talk eye to eye. Maybe not sales, but I do know business, and I did say I have a business proposition for ya, didn't I? You have time, now that I have signed for your fucking commission?"

"No, no, I have time," Silas said, thinking he didn't have much choice.

"Good. Then listen up!" Marty leaned forward. "My son, Chad, that helped us go look for the gold back in eighty-four, well, he went missing that same day. Ran off into the bush after a little run-in with that fucking Tonkin guy. Cops tried to find him. Friends went looking for him. Nothing! After a few months, the cops called the whole thing off. Left my wife crying on our doorstep while I rotted in fucking jail. Fucking cop bastards!"

"So, you lost a brother and son all on the same day?"

"So I'm led to believe." Marty pointed across the table. "Hand me my cigarettes and lighter there."

Silas passed them over, and he waited patiently as Marty lit another cigarette.

"But I don't believe it. Cops were more than happy to give up on my son. Nope. I think my boy is still alive up there, living off the land." Marty waved his right hand in a wide arc. "Like Robinson Crusoe in the great white north!" He smiled as Silas's forehead furrowed. "You don't believe it, do you? You think this old, grey-haired man is going crazy."

"Well…" Silas chose his words carefully. "It is a long time, Mr. DeMello. I guess we're looking at nine years if we are talking 1984 when your son went missing. That's an awful long time to be out in the wilderness on your own."

"It ain't about the time, boy! It's about the survival skills!" Marty said with a rising voice. He pointed to his head. "What matters is what's up here! What you do with it! My son knows everything there is about surviving in that fucking bush for fifty years if need be! Get it?"

Silas sat back, startled. "I'm sorry, Mr. DeMello. I wasn't trying to offend you or your son." He nervously looked down at his watch. "And to be honest, I probably should head out, or I'm going to be late for my next appointment."

Marty grinned. "Take it easy. I know I can get a bit bitchy about the whole issue. Don't take it personally." He placed his hands flat on the table. "But here's my offer, and I want you to think about it really carefully the next time you are sweating your nuts off, wondering whether someone is going to sign for a sale. I need someone to go up there to look for my son. Some fresh legs and eyes on the ground. No baggage, no attitude, no bullshit! Just an open mind. A treasure hunter, as you say. The only difference is you are looking for a person."

Silas shifted in his chair, doing his best to hide his discomfort. "Oh, I don't know, Mr. DeMello. I'm not that kind of explorer.

Sure, I like to go to out-of-the-way places to hike and camp, but search and rescue, that's a little out of my league."

"It ain't a rescue, son. You just have to find him. Make contact. Confirm to me he is alive. Give him a message from me. Pretty simple, really, especially if there is a nice reward attached to it."

"Mr. DeMello, I don't—"

"Hundred thousand dollars!" Marty said as he slapped the table with his hand. "And ten thousand just to go up there! Help you pay for your expenses. Anything left over after a week of searching, you keep." Marty sat back. "That kind of money is worth a lot of fucking scooter sales, son!"

"A hundred thousand dollars!" Silas said, trying to control his voice. "You're going to pay a hundred thousand dollars for someone to look for your son?"

Marty DeMello laughed at Silas's outburst. "The hundred is only if you find him, boy. Prove to me he is alive."

"Shit…" Silas said under his breath as he stared down at the table. He looked up. "But where do you get…" He stopped himself. "That's a lot…well, a lot of money, Mr. DeMello. But why me? For that kind of money, you could hire your own helicopter and a whole search team."

Marty leaned forward. "Shit, have you not been listening to me? My son is a survivalist. He can smell people like that a mile away. He don't trust them! Just drives him further into the bush." He shook his head. "It's all been done. What do you think the cops were doing all those years ago." He gave his finger a hard tap on the table. "And I have had people go out and look for half of the money I am offering you. Flying around with bush planes, fucking heat sensors, and dog-tracking bullshit. All I got was my name in the papers, pissing off my other brothers, who are still up there. Nope, I need a different approach."

Marty emptied the last of his Southern Comfort into his cup and drank it. He waited for a response from Silas, but he could tell Silas was having trouble taking in everything he had said. "Ah, fuck it! Don't worry about it. I knew you were just an old person's pussy salesman. Carry on with that shit. I'll get somebody else."

He went to grab his empty bottle of Southern Comfort, but it slipped out of his hand and smashed to the floor. "Shit! Fucking useless old hands!"

Silas glanced around the patio and noticed other residents looking over.

"Fuck! Help me back to my scooter, boy. I don't have any more time to waste on you out here. I have some fucking important calls to make!"

Silas rose and helped Mr. DeMello back to his scooter. Then he leaned down and started to pick up the glass pieces. "Fucking leave it!" Marty yelled. "Least they can do in this fucking place for what I pay them."

Marty backed the scooter up, and Silas jumped aside as he drove forward. He stopped beside Silas. "You give my offer some thought the next time you cash one of those hundred-dollar commission cheques. And before you start thinking my reward money is from some criminal activity, you take a closer look at that cheque I gave you for this fucking thing. Now, clear me a path!"

Silas swung chairs aside as Marty drove by.

"I will!" Silas shouted after him. "And thanks...thanks for the sale!"

Chapter 7

SHUFFLEBOARD

M ilt parked his pickup truck in the gravel lot of the Tear Falls Legion Hall and looked down at his watch, which read 8 pm. He knew the Legion closed at eleven, but the hall was rarely more than half full, and three hours would be ample time to have some refreshments and fit in a few games of shuffleboard.

He stepped out of his truck and shook his head as he saw Oakey's truck parked out front with his quad strapped in the back cargo box. He was usually the first to arrive at any of their get-togethers, but he already knew why Oakey was here early. He wanted to grill him about his meeting with Mead. Milt drew out his wallet from the inside pocket of his green nylon jacket and checked its contents. He wanted to make sure he had enough drink money to survive his impending interrogation.

The Legion Hall was one of the few bars in town where the older people of Tear Falls could visit and not expect a fight. It was long in tradition, with the queen's picture above the second double-door entrance and various wartime pictures and military insignia adorning the walls inside. The decor consisted of plain, round wooden tables accompanied by worn, heavy spindle-backed chairs. A padded oak bar ran along the majority of the back wall and had a large rear opening to accept readymade kitchen orders from behind. The kitchen did double duty, serving the large hall attached to the backside of the building for weddings, socials, or other large town gatherings. Of particular interest to Milt and

Oakey were the shuffleboard, pool table, and refurbished jukebox that still only required a quarter a play.

Milt pushed open the second pair of doors and immediately spotted Oakey sitting at a table near the bar. A small bowl of peanuts and an untouched glass of beer stood in front of him as he intently watched two men throw coloured discs on the shuffleboard across the room. Milt smiled as he noted Oakey was wearing a white collared shirt, new jeans, and shined-up black work boots.

"You expecting someone else?" he said with a smile as he approached, "or are you just looking good for Julia over there behind the bar." He took his jacket off and draped it over the back of his chair.

"Looks better than that black t-shirt you're wearing!" Oakey quipped back. "What the fuck is Tesla Tales?"

"Ah, some video game my son has been working on for the last ten years, but hey, I like the shirt, so I'm wearing it." Milt replied as he sat down.

Oakey pointed at the shuffleboard table. "You ready? Because I get the green rocks. Slide better than the reds."

Milt twisted in his chair to look over at the shuffleboard. "You think so?" He looked closer. "Who is that playing over there? Is that Mike Reed and Glen Puans?"

"Yup!" Oakey replied. "And I don't think either one of them is over fifty. Little young to be on our Legion stompin' grounds, wouldn't you say?"

Milt turned back. "Ah...as long as they have money, I guess. Hey...isn't Pauns a chemist or something for the town? I may have to talk to him later."

"Official water tester is all I know," Oakey replied. He sat back and locked his hands together in his lap. "So...?"

"Shit, that didn't take long. Can't a man even get a drink?" Milt peered over at the bar.

"Yeah, you're right!" Oakey said, laughing. "A little Labatt truth serum never hurt." Oakey waved at Julia behind the bar and signalled for another beer as he pointed to Milt. He leaned forward and rested his arms on the table. "Okay...now start with the important stuff first."

"Ah...basically struck out. I brought my shoebox—"

"Oh fuck your shoebox! I said the important stuff first! Is she good looking?"

Milt laughed. "Should have known. Yeah, not bad, really. Tall brunette. Pretty solid. Could probably kick both of our asses." He paused as Julia arrived at their table. She placed a glass of beer in front of him and then shots of tequila rimmed with slices of lemon in front of both men.

"You're a mind reader, Julia. Thanks!" Oakey said.

"You're welcome, Oakey." Julia replied with a smile. "Everything on a tab for the night?"

"Absolutely!" Oakey said, grinning. "Just make sure it says Milt at the top!"

Julia laughed as she set some napkins down and headed for another table.

Milt eyed Oakey. "You know, she is twenty years your junior," he said as he pulled his shot glass closer.

"A man can dream, my dear friend. A man can dream." Oakey raised his shot glass. "To Rick!"

"To Rick!" Milt replied as both men downed their tequila.

Oakey took a sip of his beer and then grabbed a handful of peanuts and sat back. "Okay...now, where were we. Oh yeah, solid, good-looking sergeant. Not a bad start. Now, give me the boring parts. How long before she started laughing."

"No laughs, actually. She had done a lot of research on the whole thing. Had a stack of flagged files on her desk about Rick's crash and the gold. Search files for Chad DeMello. I was impressed."

"So, a solid-looking sergeant who has done her research. Sounds good so far! Then what?"

"Then nothing. Went south. She kept going on about no evidence. No bodies, no discarded personal items. Not enough there for the cops to do anything now. Basically, I got the impression she thought I was a crazy local wasting her time. Just like the last sergeant." Milt filled the palm of his hand with peanuts. "I did find out one thing about her, though. She doesn't like nursing homes."

"Yeah? Why is that? She have to bust some eighty-year-olds selling illegal Geritol somewhere?" Oakey said with a grin.

Milt tried not to choke on his peanuts as he laughed. "Nah, we just got into Rick's crash and me taking care of his mom over at the nursing home. She actually seemed disappointed in me that I had her in there. Sounds like she has had some bad experiences with homes."

"Well, she could be Rick reincarnated. But hey, it might not be a bad thing if the nursing home here knows a cop might do an inspection on them from time to time. Could think of worse things for the police to do."

"True… and I don't think our meeting was a complete waste of time. I imagine she is at least thinking about what I said."

"Thinking you are crazy man, more like it!" Oakey said with a chuckle.

"Maybe that, too, asshole!" Milt replied. "You know, though, her whole point about the bodies, she's right. How is it they have never found anything? Like nothing, as far as I know. I don't even think the newspapers have ever mentioned signs of a struggle or blood. And I guess even if my theory is right about Chad, why is there no other evidence other than a few things missing from these people's campsites?"

"Yeah, I've thought about that, too."

"Really? You've never said that before. Why don't you tell me these things, you cryptic bastard." Milt took a drink of his beer.

"Okay, so, what have you thought about? Spill it! What's your Perry Mason take?"

"I prefer Cannon."

"What?"

"Cannon. You know, the big fat guy with the Lincoln. More my style."

"Okay, whatever! Fuck, just tell me what you're thinking!"

"Okay...calm down!" Oakey brushed some peanut dust from the table with his hand. "Let's just say Chad DeMello is still alive, robbing the campsites for supplies as you say. Does it really make sense he would march some people off into the bush to get rid of them? For what reason? The guy hasn't been seen in nine years! Murder would only bring him more attention."

Milt leaned on the table. "Because maybe people did have a confrontation with him. The guy is probably scared shitless he is going to jail if they ever find him. It's his way of getting rid of the evidence. What's he got to lose?"

Oakey sat back. "Still doesn't explain why the cops haven't found any clues of a struggle or fight. Can't believe these people walked off willingly with some crazy fucker who comes out of the bush."

"So, you are on Kristen's side now? Mead's side?"

Oakey put up his hand. "See, I knew you would get pissed. I'm not saying it's not Chad. I'm just saying whoever is doing this is pretty good at getting rid of the bodies and covering their tracks. And at least Mead had a half-decent conversation about it with you. That's more than you have ever gotten out of any of the other sergeants. You should be singing her praises."

"Ah, shit...I don't know, Oakey. I think all these sergeants want out of Tear Falls as fast as they come in. I can't see Mead being any different. I'll bet you my truck she is gone within few years after a couple of speeding tickets and shooting a bear."

"Probably! But I'll take your truck bet." Oakey glanced over Milt's shoulder. "They're sitting down. Looks like they're finished. Let's grab the table!"

The two men quickly picked up their beers and the peanut bowl and headed for the shuffleboard.

"What do you want to talk to Pauns about, anyway?" Oakey asked as they walked over.

"Chemistry. What else?" Milt replied.

"Of course… I was about to say that!"

Oakey nodded to Mike Reed and Glen Pauns and placed his beer and the peanut bowl down on a small side ledge bordering a window beside the shuffleboard. "All done?" he asked the two men.

"All yours, Oakey!" Mike replied as he and Pauns stood and pulled their jackets off the backs of their chairs.

Milt finished his beer and placed it on the window ledge. "Hey, Pauny, before you go, I have a question for you. He walked over. "You're a chemist, right?"

"Technician. Why?"

"But you have an idea how things break down, decay?"

"Sure, I took carbon dating in school, but I don't use much of that crap working for the town. You trying to figure out what you can re-serve at your restaurant?" Pauns said with a laugh.

Milt laughed back. "No, I was thinking more along the lines of bodies. How they decay or decompose and how long it takes."

"I don't fucking know, Milt. You need a pathologist or someone for that. I just do tests for the town to make sure your customers don't die drinking your table water at the Abby."

Mike Reed cut in. "Why you asking about that, Milt? Dom Santtini causing you problems over at the Abby again?" He grinned.

"Nope, he's not worth killing. I just had the stupid idea of going in to talk to our new sergeant, Sergeant Mead, about the people that have gone missing up at Yars Lake, and she kept talking about bodies. Actually, the lack thereof. Wanted to get her opinion on the story before she requests her transfer out of Tear Falls like the rest of them."

Oakey leaned forward and whispered in Mike's ear, "She didn't buy into his Chad DeMello theory. Maybe thinking my friend here is a bit crazzzzy…"

Mike laughed as he glanced at Oakey, and then he turned back to Milt. "Well, who knows about Chad DeMello, Milt, but you are wrong about one thing."

"Yeah, and how is that?"

"Mead! She ain't going nowhere. Unless she intends to sell the Halgren place after fixing it up."

"What are you talking about?" Milt asked. "She bought that old bungalow? I thought the OPP provided housing for sergeants."

"They do. That is what that nice house on Aspen Street is for, but I guess she turned it down. Wanted something on the lake. I've been doing some electrical for her to get it back in shape. You know that house has all the big doorways and shit. Even a small elevator to the basement. Someone was thinking ahead!"

"Fucking waste of money if you ask me." Pauns chimed in. He zipped up his jacket and placed an unlit cigarette in his mouth. "I'm going for a smoke, Mike." He headed for the door and then turned back. "You know, though, come to think of it, Milt. You know who you could talk to about that shit is Rob Krylic over at the MNR. That guy is pulling road kill off the highway all the time, and I heard he has been in on the searches for those missing people up at Yars Lake. He probably knows a little bit more about things decomposing."

"Krylic? I thought that fucking guy spent all his time in his government office, looking good in his ministry uniform and tie."

Pauns chuckled. "Yeah, he is a freeloading asshole. Won't argue that! But I do know he is up in the Yars Lake area quite a bit. Had him check Chuck Newlan and me out for hunting licenses up there last year. Asked us a hundred questions. I think he is scared someone is actually going to call him out for not doing his job. Thinks he's personally responsible for catching every fucking person illegally hunting or fishing in Tear Falls. He'd ask for a tadpole license if he could."

Milt smiled. "Yeah, I don't really know him that well. But it sounds like he could take a few more deep breaths from the air up there."

"Try telling him that." Pauns replied. "Guy's fucking uniform goes to his head." Pauns reached the entrance and opened the door. "You guys have a good night!"

"Take it easy, Pauny!" Milt said. "And thanks for keeping my customers from dying!"

Paun's hand went up as he headed out of the building. Milt looked back at Reed. "You sure Mead bought that house? This isn't some Good Samaritan project by her and the cops to make them look good in Tear Falls? Donate it back to the community or something?"

Oakey cut in. "Don't mind me, Mike, but I'm going to go over and put some tunes on that '70s music machine and celebrate winning a new truck!"

"What the fuck is he talking about?" Mike said with a laugh as he watched Oakey head for the jukebox.

"Ah…don't worry about him. He's delusional." Milt said. "So, when did she buy that house? She never mentioned any of that in the meeting I had with her. She have a family? Married?"

Mike buttoned up his ball jacket. "Fuck if I know. Her cheques don't come with a resume. Why all the questions, anyway? You interested?" He laughed. "Last I heard, you were married to a pretty fine-looking woman over at the Abby."

"Still am. But fuck, Mike, you know our sergeants don't stick around Tear Falls. Just surprised one of them may be actually thinking of staying awhile. Or seems to be."

I think she is divorced, to be honest." Mike replied. He put his hand into the side pocket of his ball jacket. "But who knows." He took out a ten-dollar bill and left it on the table. "You never heard that from me, right? I don't care if she builds a new fucking house as long as I'm getting the business." He looked over Milt's shoulder with a smile. "Ah...good song choice, Oakey. Jerry Doucette!"

Milt stared in the same direction to see Oakey dancing his way around Julia.

"Well, I gotta go, Milt!" Mike reached out and gripped Milt's hand for a shake. "Later! And hey...maybe you should be giving our new sergeant free coffees at the Abby. She may stay around long enough to see you finally find Chad DeMello." He smiled and gave Oakey and Julia a wave as he left for the door.

"Yeah...thanks for the recommendation. I will...I'll do that!" Milt called out after him.

Oakey was still dancing as he made his way back over to Milt. "Man, that Julia can move those hips!" He said with a grin. He took a closer look at Milt. "You okay, buddy? Don't worry. I'll lease your truck back."

Milt didn't respond. He walked over to the shuffleboard and slid a rock down the table. "Oakey, you know who originally built that house that Mead bought?"

"No fucking idea. Stephen Hawking?"

Milt turned back to Oakey.

"Rick's fucking dad!"

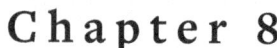

Chapter 8

WHY DO YOU ASSUME?

S ilas lay on the bike path bench and closed his eyes. He breathed the fresh air and smiled as he absorbed the May sun, which was finally delivering warmth after a cold Southern Ontario spring. He felt a nudge on his foot and repositioned himself, but then he felt it again.

"Wake up, Armstrong! Time to deliver on your promise!"

Silas opened his eyes to see Blessing straddling her mountain bike and leaning over her handlebars. "Ready?" she asked, smiling. Silas raised himself onto his elbows as Blessing turned her head to gaze up the trail. "It's not a bad grade. I'm thinking maybe four to five kilometers to a lookout."

Silas gently stretched his cheeks with air and then exhaled. Blessing had on tight black spandex biking shorts with purple side stripes. Her top was of bright white cotton with a multi-coloured band running across her chest and a forward-leaning cyclist icon to the side. A vented red and white bicycle helmet was secured to her head, with her ponytail extending neatly out the back.

"Something doesn't belong here." Silas said, looking down at his black Colin James rock t-shirt and tan cargo shorts.

"It's not the clothes, hiking guy!" Blessing said. "It's the pedalling legs in them!" She swung her bike around and started up the hill. "C'mon! Let's go! We need to get you in shape for your explorer trips!"

"Son of a…" Silas grabbed his mountain bike from where it leaned against the end of the bench and hopped on. He pedalled fast to catch up.

"You know, you could humour me and give me a push to start." he said as he came up alongside her, breathing heavily.

"No gimmes! You have to earn this hill." Blessing replied. She continued to stare straight ahead. "Speaking of earning, how did it go with Chaste?"

"It didn't," Silas replied, concentrating on the path ahead of him. "He said for me to send him an email and explain in not so many words how my numbers differ from his. It still comes down to the Sevan Hospital account and Darren Felk. It's dead in the water as far as I'm concerned. I'm sure Felk has gotten his own bonus because of it. There is no way Chaste is going to backtrack on that."

"Go above him?" Blessing asked, turning to face Silas.

He returned the glance. "What, are you some sort of career masochist? To who! Dave JoJoe? That guy is worse than Chaste! Probably wind up with a fucking pay cut if I talk to him." Silas turned his attention back to the trail. "I don't see any lookout."

"It's coming," Blessing said with a smile. "And I thought hikers were in good shape. Want me to slow down?" She gave him a wink.

"Slow down?" Silas yelled. He rose from his seat and pushed hard on the pedals. "You're messing with the wrong Tour de France mountain climber, woman!"

Blessing laughed as she switched gears and sprinted to catch up.

Minutes later, she had coasted into the lookout area, parked her bike against a black concrete-supported steel rail, and was taking off her helmet just as Silas came around the corner. He swung one leg over his seat and glided up to her with both feet on one pedal. "Old habit from grade six." he said with a smirk. He parked his bike beside hers, and the two made their way over to a bench overlooking the city.

Silas draped his arms over the backside of the bench and squinted as he looked up at the bright blue sky. He spotted the vapour trail from a barely visible plane. "You ever wonder where those people on that plane might be going. What they might be doing?"

Blessing shaded her eyes and looked up at the plane. "That's what you think about when you see a plane up in the sky?"

"Sure. I think it's a great thing to ponder. Who knows, there could be a couple flying off for their honeymoon, all smiles. Might be another person down in the dumps, going to a funeral. Or maybe there is a tense businessman looking out his window right now that has just embezzled millions of dollars and is making a run for it!"

Blessing laughed. "Well…maybe not a plane, but you know what I do wonder about?"

"No, not really, if you don't like my plane ponderance, but tell me anyway."

"Knew I should have biked solo." Blessing said. "What I wonder about when I'm stuck in a traffic jam on the freeway is where all the people around me are going!"

"Why do you assume they are going anywhere?"

Blessing raised her eyebrows and gave Silas a doubtful glance. "Right. They are just out in traffic to aggravate the rest of us. Makes sense."

"Ah…you see! This is where your assumptions fail you. My parents often say they are going for a drive. When I ask them where, they say nowhere in particular, just a drive. I imagine you and Mark will do that after being married for thirty years. I think it's inevitable with older couples."

Blessing smiled. "So, that is what married people have to look forward to in their later years? Driving aimlessly around neighbourhoods?"

"That and maybe throw in some Parkinson's and losing your house." Silas said, staring off at a busy highway in the distance.

"Coming to realize there is a lot of bullshit that goes with getting older."

"There is bullshit at any time, Silas." Blessing said. "Let me assure you of that." She shifted forward, placed her hands on the bench, and sat up. "Still bad news on the house front?"

"When isn't it bad news? My mom is saying she and I may have to move in with my ninety-year-old grandmother."

"What do you mean, you and your mother? What about your dad?"

Silas took a deep breath. "She is thinking of one of those government nursing homes for my dad. He is just getting too much for her to handle. I told her to wait and let me look into some hired help. I think if we can just get someone to visit during the day, I could do more for him at night."

"Silas, if your parents can't afford the house, how are they going to hire extra help? Am I missing something here? How are you going to pay for that on top of your student loans?"

Silas rose from the bench and stood in front of Blessing. "Well…" He held up his hands. "Guess what? I have a plan. A good plan!"

"Okay…well…plans are always good. What is it? You're getting a second job?"

"Sort of… It's contract work," Silas said. "Now, don't freak out, but you remember that guy that gave me the book about the gold story, *The Torrison Treasure*? The guy I sold the scooter to? I gave you the book."

"Yeah, I remember. Sorry, still have to read it."

"Don't worry about that. Well, it turns out the guy is part of the story!"

Blessing gave Silas a confused look. "Okay, you're losing me. What are you talking about?"

"This guy, this Marty DeMello, he went looking for the gold back in eighty-four with his brother and son. They got into a shootout with some other guys, and his twin brother was killed, but his son took off into the bush. Now Marty is offering a hundred-thousand-dollar reward for someone to find him and ten grand just to look. This is perfect for me!"

Blessing's eyes widened. "Silas, what the hell are you talking about? You sell a scooter to some old guy in a retirement home, and now he wants to hire you to look for his lost son way up north in the bush? Uh…I would say there is something very strange about that."

Silas sat back down on the bench. "I know. I was thinking the same thing, but I started looking into it on the internet and at the library. His story checks out. And he's got money. That part I know for sure."

"Yeah…and how's that? His cheque didn't bounce for the JX-6000?"

"Because, my MBA friend, he owns the retirement home he is staying in. Well, him and his brothers do. Before he left, he told me to look at the cheque he gave me for the scooter. It said 'Brother DeMello Homes Inc.' He owns the whole fucking building and a few others as well."

"Money or not, it still seems strange, Silas. Didn't that crash happen years ago? And why you? Why not the cops?"

"Same question I had." Silas paused as he rubbed his neck. "But…I guess it might have something to do with the fact that he is an ex-convict." He looked at Blessing and forced a smile.

Blessing stared back. "You are bullshitting me, right? You want to get into a money deal with a convict? Silas, I know things are tough with your parents and the home, but now you are just starting to sound fucking crazy! Who knows what this guy is involved in for offering you a deal like that. And what if something goes wrong? You want to be in debt to a criminal? Give me a break!"

Silas placed his hands in his lap and stretched his legs out. He took a deep breath. "They're going to lose the house, Blessing, and my dad is going to have to go into one of those shithole nursing homes. And you know what? He doesn't stand a chance in there. He knows it, and my mom knows it. They would basically be saying their goodbyes at the door if it comes to that. I can't let that happen. At least not yet."

Blessing sighed. "Jesus Murphy," she said, looking down. She raised her head and gazed out over the city. "I don't know, Silas. I just think it seems…" She shrugged and stood. Then she walked a few steps and turned around. "You know what? Never mind what I think. You are going to go up there and look for the gold anyway, aren't you?"

Silas looked up. "Yup. I would say it's a done deal. And putting the crazy stuff aside, it's still a cool trip."

"Okay, well, if you are dragging my brother into this, you get everything in writing. You need to get a contract for all of this shit and that it's all above board. And make sure everyone knows where you are going and that this Marty guy knows it!"

"I was going to do that. I was going to set—"

"And I want to read it over," Blessing said, pointing at him. She turned and headed for her bike. "Let's go!" she yelled over her shoulder. "We can discuss it more over the next twenty kilometers!"

"Twenty?" Silas replied as he jumped up from the bench. He hopped on his bike and pedalled after Blessing. "I'm sure we can fit it in ten!"

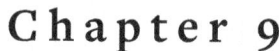

Chapter 9

UNIFORM BREAKFAST

Milt parked his pickup in front of the pumps at the White Moose gas bar and then looked at his watch. It was only 5:45 am, but Tear Falls was far enough north for daylight to already be sneaking above the treetops. He took a moment to sip his coffee and enjoy the view of the mid-May sun breaking the horizon. He heard a tap on his window. "Hey, we don't open until six on a Saturday! Go drive around for fifteen minutes." the man said with a smile. "I'll make more on the fill-up when you get back!"

Milt laughed as he opened the truck door. He gave Harry Tartiak, the gas station owner, a hard handshake. "How are you, Harry? And don't bullshit me on the sign saying six o'clock. I know you're here by 5:30 every morning, even on Sunday."

"I'd make that five." Harry said with a grin. He unhooked the gas handle from the pump and began filling Milt's truck.

Milt walked around the truck, leaned on the cargo box, and waited patiently as Harry watched the digital numbers on the pump change.

Milt enjoyed his fill-ups at the White Moose. Harry would always come strolling out, sporting his signature broad smile and grey-blonde moustache and goatee. His hair was a chaotic, tangled mess of the same colours, but it seemed to suit his easygoing nature. Harry had been running the gas station ever since he had purchased it off a large chain over twenty years ago and renamed it the White Moose. He believed the gas company that owned the station had it all wrong. They wanted people in and out on self-serve and stuck an uninterested attendant in a booth to accept people's money through a small glass window. Harry wanted to talk to people, to "shoot the shit with them," as he would say. Pretty soon, he would know them well enough that they were more than happy to come back to finish a conversation or start a new one—and of course, to buy more gas and maybe a thing or two in his convenience store. Milt knew there were few people in Tear Falls that Harry didn't know, so he decided to ask him for an informal character reference.

"Hey, Harry, how well do you know Rob Krylic over at the MNR? How old is he?" Milt yelled out across the back of the truck. He heard the familiar clunk of the pump cut-off valve as Harry topped up the tank.

"He was a grade below me," Harry said with his back to Milt. He placed the gas handle back into the pump, grabbed a brown paper towel from a side dispenser, wiped his hands, and turned around. "So, he must be around forty-five. He was on our junior high school basketball team. Not sure why, though. The guy is barely five seven and couldn't play worth shit, but I guess Strott put him on the team only because we were always short players."

"But a good guy or a bonehead?" Milt asked.

Harry leaned on the opposite side of the truck. "Why, you have a bear to get rid of or need a permit to plant trees in front of the Abby?"

Milt laughed. "Nope, I just heard from Glen Pauns that he has been in on the searches for the people that have gone missing up at Yars Lake. Just wanted to pick his brain a bit on what he knows about the area. Why it might be that they never find any bodies."

Harry shrugged. "Don't know about the bodies, but Krylic has always been a little bit odd. He lives with his dad out at Nancy Point, but I don't think he has ever had a good home life. I think there was a lot of fighting at home. Father is a drinker. Big gambler, too! I know his mother left in high school. Pretty sure his dad put a lot of pressure on Rob to make something of himself. He wanted Rob to be a cop, but he never made it in. Guess the MNR was the closest he could get to having a vehicle with lights and carrying a sidearm—even though it's a tranquilizer gun. Probably best because he's not much good at making business decisions."

"Business decisions? Thought he was a lifelong MNR guy," Milt replied.

Harry came around to where Milt was standing. "That's his day job but not his dream. He bought the old D and B property a number of years ago. Thought he could make it into some sort of souvenir gift shop and gas bar. Hasn't exactly worked out that way, though."

"Jesus Christ." Milt said. "I thought the whole reason that place has sat empty is because the foundation is sinking. Krylic owns that property?"

"Lock, stock, and barrel," Harry said. "Oh, he has tried to pump concrete under that building. Thought he could fix it. But the place is built on a fucking swamp. Wouldn't be surprised if it sinks clear through to China."

"That place was owned by old man DeMello, right?"

"Yup! He even took back the mortgage on it for him. That is why Krylic is in a whole heap of trouble with it. He owes DeMello, and I hear his own dad, a shitload of money. There is no way any MNR salary is going to pay for that debt."

Milt took out his wallet and handed Harry some bills as the two men headed for the store entrance.

"Fuck…talk about some bad luck!" Milt said.

Harry opened the door for Milt. "Sure is," he said as the two men stepped into the store. "And I would be careful about talking to him about the missing people up at the Davidson Mine and Yars Lake."

"Oh, and why is that?" Milt asked.

Harry walked behind the counter. "Because he's got this stick up his ass about what these people hunting for the gold are doing in giving Tear Falls a bad name. The missing people, campsite robberies. Heard he is always stopping out-of-towners and grilling them on where they are going. Rifles through their belongings like they are smuggling in the gold, not looking for it. Treats that area like his personal property. If you ask me, he is the one giving Tear Falls a fucking bad name!"

Harry rang in Milt's money.

"Wow...never knew all that shit. Guess I should be coming in here more often, Harry."

Harry handed Milt his change. "Hey, if you're buying, I'm talking!" he said with a smile. "Let me know how you make out if you do talk to him. I've found him to be pretty antisocial unless he thinks there is something in it for him. Maybe make him feel all important and police-like. He likes to think he wields some power around here. Oh, and another thing, don't call him Bob. Might be some kind of childhood trauma, but he freaks out on you with a twenty-minute lecture on the origin of the name Robert." Harry gazed out the window as the pump bell went off. "Ah, this is going to be a good day! That's Dan Freschuck out there with his dually. Double tanks on that monster. Gotta go, Milt!"

"Yeah, no problem." Milt said, placing his change in his wallet and sliding it back in his inside jacket pocket. He called out as Harry reached the door, "Hey, thanks for the info, Harry!"

"You're welcome, Milt! And tell Krylic he should be coming to the White Moose more often for fill-ups. We give free windshield washer fluid to law enforcement." He winked as he dashed out the door.

At the Abby, Milt pulled in around back, jumped out of his truck, and rushed in the back door to the kitchen. He grabbed his apron from a hook and tied it on as he approached Jamie, who was flipping eggs on the grill.

"All under control, Jamie?"

"Busy as all hell for 6:15. Few of them were lined up before six!"

Milt looked out through the kitchen server window and saw Kristen and some waitresses clearing tables and taking orders. "That's what the start of fishing season does, Jamie. I don't recognize many locals out there."

"Yup! That American money can buy a lot of breakfasts," Jamie replied.

Milt pulled some orders off the hanging clips on the top side of the serving window and read them over. He reached around Jamie, picked up a stainless-steel pitcher, and poured pancake mix onto the hot grill.

Kristen burst through the swinging kitchen door, carrying a tray stacked with dirty dishes. She looked at Milt as she headed for the dishwasher. "Glad you could make it, Mr. Owner! Let me guess, Harry had more business advice for you." She lowered the heavy tray down on the counter and turned to Milt. "I hope some of it was to show up on time."

"Sorry, hon. You know Harry—always has something to say. Let me get those dishes."

"Not to worry. Finish the pancakes and then come out front. I'll come back in after taking a few more orders and help Jamie. You have a customer who has been asking about you."

Milt turned his attention back to the pancakes. "Oh, c'mon! Oakey is back in here again?"

Kristen walked to the kitchen door and pushed it halfway open with her backside. "Actually, this customer is wearing a police uniform, and she is pretty darn good looking." She raised her eyebrows at Milt as she exited the kitchen.

"What…?" Milt quickly stepped over and reached to stop the swinging door from closing. "Who is—"

"Hey, Milt!" Jamie yelled. "Don't let these pancakes burn!"

"Yeah, sorry, Jamie!" Milt jumped back to the grill. He removed the cooked pancakes and placed them on a large plate. "Here," he said, handing the plate to Jamie. "This should take care of a few orders." He untied his apron, threw it on a nearby counter, and brushed his hair back.

"Jesus Christ, Milt." Jamie said, looking over. "If you're going to get arrested, nobody gives a shit what you look like!"

"Asshole!" Milt said, giving Jamie a sharp look.

Milt walked into the dining area and over to the young woman tending the cash register at the end of the bar. "You see the police in here, Di?"

Diana looked up from sorting receipts. "Not that—"

"She's sitting over by the door, Milt," Kristen said as she walked up to him from behind. She pinned another order to a clip. "She is taking up a whole booth for a coffee near the door. Hope this is all good news."

Milt turned back to Kristen. "She is probably just here for PR. I did offer her a free coffee if she stopped in."

"I bet you did," Kristen said, turning her back to Milt and heading through the swinging door back to the kitchen.

Diana looked at Milt. "You're not in trouble, are you, Mr. Tonkin? I mean with the restaurant, not your wife."

"I hope not." Milt replied. "On both counts." He spotted Mead and headed in her direction.

As he approached her booth, she greeted him with a big smile and raised her coffee cup. "Decided to take you up on your offer. Hope you don't mind?"

"No, not at all," Milt said. "Coupon without an expiry. On the house."

An awkward silence fell as he stood and watched her drink her coffee.

"Care to sit down for a moment?" she said, gesturing to the booth seat opposite her. "I just didn't come in for this great coffee. I've brought something."

"Yeah, sure," Milt said, sitting down. "But I have to get back to work here in a minute. Busy time, as you can see." He looked nervously over his shoulder, trying to spot Kristen.

"I get it! This won't take long, but I thought you might be interested." Mead reached into her carrying case on the booth beside her and withdrew some stapled papers. At the top was an Ontario government crest and the title "Ministry of Long-Term Care."

"What's this?" Milt asked as Mead handed him the papers.

"It's a ministry compliance report on Ontario nursing homes. Cites the most common violations over the past five years. I could have gone back further, but I thought that would be enough to give you an idea."

Milt tried to smile. "Yeah…well…thanks for doing that. I'll look it over."

Mead sat back. "Milt… You don't mind if I call you Milt, do you?"

"No…most people do."

"I just think you should keep a good eye on Rick's mother. On her care. I know I would if it were one of my family members."

"Sergeant—"

"No need to thank me," Mead said, putting up her hand.

"Right…okay. I guess I just wanted to say that I really appreciate you doing this for me. And don't take this the wrong way, but to be honest, I have never heard or seen anything that concerns me over at the Tear Falls nursing home for her care." Milt looked down and flipped through a few pages of the report. "In fact, it's all been good."

"That's great. Let's hope it stays that way. Just a friendly reminder from your local police to always be vigilant, Milt. We have to look out for our seniors." Mead closed up her file case and picked up her hat. She moved to the end of the booth and stood. "Well, I have to go. Sorry for the quick visit, but I just wanted to drop off that paperwork. And thanks for the coffee. When I have more time, I will make sure to order off the menu. All these people in here can't be wrong."

"Yeah, stop by anytime," Milt replied as he stood. He reached out and shook Mead's hand. "And thanks for the report. I will make sure I read it."

"More than welcome." Mead turned to leave and then turned back. "Oh, by the way, Milt, I have given all those files I had on the missing people up at Yars Lake over to a Constable Devon. I've even briefed him on your Chad DeMello theory. You know, you have really got me thinking about a lot of things."

"Yeah…well…" Milt nodded as he searched for an appropriate response. "Glad to be of assistance." he finally said. "And when I get more evidence, I'll be in touch, Sergeant."

"You do that, Milt," Mead replied as she waved goodbye with a smile.

Chapter 10

NAZARETH

Ben parked his black pickup truck in the visitor area of the Scenic Woods retirement home and shut the engine off. He looked at Silas. "You sure we're going to come out of there alive? This guy is not going to dispose of us down some fucking laundry chute, is he?"

Silas reached into the back seat and grabbed his carrying bag. He opened it and checked the contents. "You know, you have some serious problems."

Ben stared at Silas. "I have some serious problems? I have the problems...really?" Ben looked through the windshield at the front entrance of the home. "You want to do a deal with a guy who has been in prison. You're the one with the problems. This is nuts."

Silas pulled out a piece of paper and looked it over. "What are you worried about? You're six foot two and play football, and didn't you take that self-defense course at one time?"

"It was a self-awareness course." Ben replied, placing his keys in his jeans pocket.

Silas glanced over at Ben. "Look, the guy is fifty-eight years old and can barely walk because of arthritis. Smokes like a chimney. Do you really think he is going to come after two fit twenty-six-year-olds? Relax." He held up the paper he was reading. "I've got an ironclad contract right here. This is all on the up and up. We're going to get paid for going on a cool trip. I've never been up in that area of Ontario, anyway. I'm looking forward to it."

"Yeah, but why you, Silas? Blessing is right. That part, I don't get. Why not some of his criminal buddies or someone from up there?" Ben shook his head. "I just hope you know what you are doing. What we are doing."

Silas put the paper back in his case and snapped it shut. "Like I said before, he has done all that. He doesn't want the attention. Trust me; this is going to work out. Even if we find squat, we make ten grand. That can go a long way to keeping my mom and dad in their house."

Ben placed his hand on the truck door handle. "Alright. Let's go see what he has to say. But I want half up front before we go. Probably take ten thousand in gas just to get there."

Silas grinned as they exited the truck and headed for the front door.

The two men approached Marty DeMello's room and knocked. They could hear him talking loudly.

"I'm not paying for a goddamn water break that ain't on our property!" Marty said. "Fucking city's problem! Let's see if they want to argue a lot line when the papers find out a senior can't have a fucking shower. Fuck 'em!"

"Sounds like a nice guy so far," Ben whispered to Silas.

"He's just a good businessman," Silas whispered back. "Give him a chance." He knocked again.

"It's open!" Marty yelled. "Gotta go. Business meeting," he said into his cell phone as Silas and Ben entered the room. "Welcome back, Silas and newcomer. Have a seat!"

Silas and Ben sat down on a small couch opposite Marty, who was sitting in an armchair. Ben eyed a stack of books and papers on the coffee table.

Marty sat back and stroked the front of his neck. "So, this is your partner in crime you were telling me about."

Ben looked at Silas with raised eyebrows.

"Yeah, this is Ben Lee, Mr. DeMello."

"Sure his name isn't Bruce Lee?" Marty said with a laugh.

Silas smiled. "Nah. He's faster than Bruce Lee and smarter. He has agreed to go with me up to Tear Falls for the search. I would like to have a partner. Hope you don't mind."

"Not at all, son. You can take as many people with you as you want. Just don't come back on me with any partner bullshit fights over money."

"Not to worry," Silas said. "Ben and I are good friends. We've already arranged to split it fifty-fifty." Silas pressed on the steel latch of his carry case and released the strap. "Speaking of arrangements, Mr. DeMello, I did bring along a small, one-page contract for you to look over. Just outlines the terms of some of the things we have discussed." Silas pulled out the paper he had been reading in the truck and handed it to Marty. "You can add or strike out anything you want, but I thought it was a start."

Marty reached across and took the paper. He scanned it for a minute and then placed it down. "Mind if I smoke?" he said, leaning towards a side table and taking a cigarette out of a package.

"I don't think—"

"Sure, no problem," Silas said, cutting Ben off.

"Open that window there, son." Marty pointed at Ben. Then he put the cigarette in his mouth and lit it with a lighter he took from the pocket of his sweatpants. He picked up Silas's paper and looked it over as he took a long drag of his cigarette and exhaled. "So…this is your contract. Fifty percent of the ten grand up front, one week of searching, hundred grand on proof of one Chad DeMello being alive…" Marty rested the cigarette on the ashtray on the side table. He handed the paper back to Silas. "I'm sorry, boys, but I'm not interested in your contract. Not befitting of a man of my background to have a contract like that." He sat back and stared solemnly at both men.

Silas looked at Ben and then back at Marty. "I…I'm sorry, Mr. DeMello, but there has to be something in writing with the terms we agree on. I know you are probably used to a handshake on these things, but we need something more formal."

Marty leaned forward. "Handshake? Who said anything about a fucking handshake!" He reached into the stack of documents on the coffee table and pulled out a thick bundle of papers held together with a heavy staple. He threw it over to Silas, who caught it in his lap. "There's your fucking contract, son! Twenty-six pages drawn up by my lawyers. Tells you everything you need to know and do to collect the money. You sign that, and you fucking work for me."

Silas picked up the bound paperwork. "Wow. I wasn't expecting—"

"Expecting what?" Marty interrupted. "An ex-convict entering into a legal fucking contract?" He laughed as he reached for his cigarette, and then he took another drag. "You can read that shit over when you get home. Bring it to your own lawyer if you want, but I will save you some time and go over the main points buried in that legal fucking jargon everyone pays for."

Marty put the cigarette out, sat forward, and started counting on his fingers. "One, you don't say a fucking thing to anyone in Tear Falls about how you are there to search for my son. You can say you are looking for the gold, on a fishing trip, trying to find the fucking Loch Ness monster, I don't give a shit! But if one word comes out from up there or anywhere that you are looking for Chad, the deal is off. I don't need any fucked-up reporters coming around to my family or me. Understand?"

"Absolutely," Silas replied as Ben nodded in agreement.

"Two, you accept all the risk! Includes everything that can fucking go wrong. That means everything from getting crabs from fucking some skank at the NearNorth to having a boulder fall on your fucking head. It's your trip, your risk."

"Yeah, we expected that," Silas said.

"What's the Near—"

"Sshh," Silas said, waving his hand at Ben. "Anything else, Mr. DeMello?"

"Yeah, if you find him, if you find any evidence he is still alive, you are going to send a fax to my lawyer. No communication to me. All through my lawyer. Got it?"

Silas looked at Ben, who shrugged. "Yeah, I guess so. Like to read through this contract first, if we could, before we sign anything."

Marty ignored the comment and lit another cigarette. He reached forward, took out another piece of paper from the stack in front of him, and pushed the rest of the pile aside. He unfolded the paper, revealing a large map, and placed it on the table. "Now, let's make sure you know what you are fucking getting into before you sign anything. This is a map of the Tear Falls area."

He pointed to various landmarks. "Here is Tear Falls, and here is Yars Lake. It's about a forty-mile drive up the Bitman logging road and about an hour hike in. Over here is the Davidson Mine, where everyone thinks the gold was stashed by a man named Pat Galverson. He's the old fucking recluse who found the crashed plane but disappeared long ago and is most likely fertilizer for a nice pine tree up there. Last sighting of my son, Chad, was here, at the start of the trail to the Davidson Mine and the Galverson cabin. I'm figuring he wouldn't have strayed far from this area. He had gone up on his own lots of times before he went missing. Almost a second home for him on weekends."

Ben and Silas studied the map as they listened. Ben spoke first. "So, this happened in eighty-four, when your son went missing, and he was how old?"

Marty sat back. "Eighteen, so, yup, he would be twenty-seven now. I imagine close to you boys in age. Maybe that's the connection I've been looking for. Someone who might think like him, act like him even after all these years in the bush. I know the cops and anybody else I've hired have been fucking useless!"

"Useless in that they have come back empty-handed?" Silas said.

"That's my fucking definition. What's yours?"

"No, that makes sense," Silas replied, trying to soften his tone. "I get it." He looked back down at the map.

Ben sensed the tension and intervened. "You know, your son must be quite the outdoorsman to live on his own for over nine years, Mr. DeMello. Did you teach him all that?"

"Like I was telling your friend here, he is a self-taught survivalist. Yeah, shit, I taught him how to aim a rifle straight and set a snare trap, but the rest was from his own reading. His own doing." Marty leaned forward with his hands clasped together. The smoke from his cigarette between his fingers drifted over Silas and Ben. "I'm telling you he is alive up there. And I will bet you an extra thousand dollars I'm the only one from Tear Falls who believes that's fucking true." He smiled. "But I guess that's not the point, is it, boys?" He put his cigarette out. "The point is…" He jabbed his finger at Silas and Ben. "You're going to get paid good fucking shit just to look for him, and if you're any good at it, you'll hit the jackpot with some proof he is alive."

Silas quickly nodded in agreement. "Hey, we're in, Mr. DeMello. Don't worry about that part." He picked up the contract. "I'm sure there is nothing in here we can't agree on."

"You agree to all of it or give it back," Marty replied. He picked up the map and folded it. Then he moved the stack of papers back to the centre of the table and placed the map on top. "This is all yours to take with you with the contract." He slid the pile towards Silas. "Be fucking smart and read this stuff before you sign my contract. Got it?"

"Yeah," Silas said, looking at the side of the stack of files, trying to decipher the contents. "We'll read all of it."

"Good." Marty picked up his cell phone. "Now, I have some calls to make, if you don't mind."

"Oh…right. Okay." Silas said. "Guess we'll come back later when we have gone over everything."

"That's the fucking idea!" Marty replied, raising his eyebrows. "You boys are fast learners. This may work out after all."

Silas picked up the stack of papers, and then he and Ben stood. "Thanks, Mr. DeMello. We'll get back to you."

"You have one week, son. You call me. And you have to be up there in June. No fucking around, or I look for someone else."

"One week," Silas repeated. "We'll have an answer." He and Ben headed for the door

"And one more thing!" Marty yelled.

"Yes?" Silas said, turning around.

"Get to know Nazareth!" Marty said with a grin.

"What is—" Ben tried to ask.

"Never mind!" Marty said, cutting him off. He waved his hand. "Get the fuck out of here. I'll explain if you sign."

Ben gave Silas a surprised look, and then the two men left the room.

As Silas drove the truck back home to Toronto, Ben flipped through the papers Marty DeMello had given them.

"What is all this shit?" he said, holding up the various papers and examining the writing. He looked over at Silas. "You know, my mom said this was a crazy idea. Didn't like it."

"Oh, fuck. You told your mom? What did your dad say?"

"He was against it, too, until I told him about the money," Ben said, laughing.

"Well, as long as everything is clearly spelled out in that contract. He's not asking us to rob something; he's asking us to find his son. Seems like a pretty noble cause, if you ask me." Silas nodded at some of the papers Ben was sorting. "Well...what's in there?"

Ben started placing stapled documents on the dash. "Got a few police reports. One here from Millenguard Search and Rescue out of Winnipeg, a lot of newspaper articles." He glanced over at Silas. "This guy has drawn a lot of attention. How come we've never heard about this?"

"Probably because Southern Ontario news ends an hour north in Barrie. Who knows? I didn't even know about the big gold heist until he gave me the book."

"Yeah, I would like to read that," Ben replied.

"Ask your sister," Silas said with a sardonic smile.

Ben reached the middle of the stack and picked out a sealed envelope stapled with a piece of paper. "Here's something." He pulled off the paper and began reading it. "Looks like a list."

"Of…?" Silas asked.

"Says Line Inventory," Ben said. "And it's got some interesting shit on it." Ben started reading the list out loud. "Eighteen twenty-ounce glass preservative jars, eighteen multi-coloured pens, eighteen photographs with signature area, eighteen plastic army men, bazooka stance, eighteen grape jawbreakers, seventy-five feet snare wire, Nazareth times eighteen, sterilized needles times eighteen, one bottle of Southern Comfort, sixty ounces."

"What the hell?" Silas said. "We going to be doing some artwork on this trip? That's pretty fucked up."

"That's pretty fucked up?" Ben asked. "Are we on the same planet, Silas? You said I was the one with the problems. And you know what, I think you're right. This whole thing is royally fucked up! We got a guy who has been lost for nine years, stolen gold, talk about some Nazareth religious shit, and now this bizarre list. How can it get any more fucked up than that?"

Silas shrugged. "I don't know. Maybe check what's in the envelope, for starters."

Ben began to open it. "Probably another list…or…" He took out a wad of hundred-dollar bills. "Or fucking cash! Jesus Christ!" He fanned the bills out. "Silas! Look at this!"

"Told you!" Silas said, trying to look at the bills while keeping his eyes on the road. "The guy has money! Lots of it!"

"Watch the road!" Ben replied.

"How much?" Silas asked, still trying to look at the money. He moved over to the slow lane.

"Looks like a few thousand!" Ben said. "You know what? Pull into that Tim Horton's up there. I'm going to make sure."

Once they were inside, Silas brought back two coffees and two Boston cream donuts as Ben leaned back in his chair and read over the contract.

"Where's the money?" Silas said as he sat down.

"Stuffed in my front pocket," Ben replied, still looking down and reading. He placed the contract aside and picked up his coffee. "Half of what's in there is all about what we do if we find him dead or alive, evidence, communication. He even lists people not to talk to up in Tear Falls. For a criminal, he sure covers all the bases."

"So, he is a picky convict. So what?" Silas said, taking a bite of his donut. "Let me see the money."

Ben stretched out, removed the envelope from his pocket, and handed it to Silas. "You know you are getting blinded by all this dough. I don't know if that's a good thing."

"Oh, and you're not?" Silas flipped through the bills in the envelope. "Look, if it makes you feel any better, I will bring the contract to my mom and dad's lawyer. Let him look it over." Silas handed the envelope back to Ben. "Maybe that is what part of this money is for? Not just what's on that list."

"If we have this type of money flying around, I would highly recommend the legal advice." Ben put the list back into the envelope. "Are you going to ask him about this?" He placed the envelope back in his pocket. "Because, if anything deserves an explanation before we sign, it's that."

Silas finished his donut and licked his fingers. "Why would a lawyer know anything about a list? We'll just ask DeMello about it if we end up signing. Probably some shit he wants brought up to a craft store or dropped off to someone. Let's go. The sooner we are back, the sooner I can call my parents' lawyer about this."

Chapter 11

MNR

Milt was washing the Abby's large industrial kitchen sink when Diane pushed the swinging door open and called out, "Milt, you have another uniformed visitor here to see you."

Milt looked at his watch, which read 3 pm. *Right on time*, he thought. "Yeah, no problem, Diane. Bring him a coffee, if you don't mind."

"Sure thing."

As Milt placed the sink sprayer down, took off his apron, and hung it on a hook, Jamie took a bag of frozen fries out of the kitchen freezer. "Another police visit?" Jamie said, dumping the fries into a bin of hot oil with a loud hiss.

"Nah...MNR. I like to change it up a bit, Jamie, keep everybody guessing why I'm in trouble," Milt replied.

Jamie scraped the grill with his flipper. "Well, you are doing one hell of a job!"

"Thanks, Jamie," Milt replied with a wink as he left the kitchen.

Milt came out into the dining area and spotted Rob Krylic sitting on a counter stool, looking over a menu. He had on a short-sleeved light green shirt with tan pants and black work shoes. A red-handled tranquilizer pistol was holstered on his belt, and the words "Ministry of Natural Resources" were clearly visible on a patch sewn on his left shirt sleeve. Milt spotted a MNR hat lying on the stool beside him. He approached with a smile.

"Hey, Rob!" He removed Krylic's hat from the stool and went to sit down.

"Hey, do you mind sitting on my right side?" Krylic said. "I hate talking to people on my left."

"Uh…yeah, sure," Milt said, carefully placing Krylic's hat back on the stool and moving around to his right. He sat down and signalled to Diane for a coffee. Then he turned back to Krylic and extended his hand. "Well, thanks for coming in, Rob. I know you are a busy guy."

Krylic shook Milt's hand. "You bought yourself a nice place here, Tonkin. Rennet severance or someone must have been good to you."

"Ah, Landry sold it to me in good shape. Abby has a good reputation. Just hope I can keep it that way."

Krylic looked around the busy restaurant. "Still, nice to be your own boss, though, eh? You get out of it what you put into it. Yup…I'd say it's the way to go if you ask me. But it takes a lot of fucking money to get something up and running." He set the menu down. "Now, what can I do for you? You got a wildlife problem? Complaints about unlicensed yanks coming through here?"

"No…no," Milt said with a smile. "None of that. I just wanted to ask you about the people that have gone missing up at Yars Lake over the years."

"Yars Lake?" Krylic said, raising his voice. "Why would I know anything about that? That's a police matter!"

Diane placed coffees in front of two men and raised her eyebrows at Milt. He gave her a fake smile and pulled his coffee closer. Then he turned back to Krylic.

"For sure, I know, Rob, but you spend time up there as part of your job, right? The cops would be stupid not to come to a person like you for help. It's not like they have had much success finding anyone so far."

Krylic took a sip of his coffee. "Damn right, I know the area, but the reason they don't find anybody is because there is nobody to find. But they won't listen to a MNR uniform. They never have! All their search dogs and helicopters are just a big shitshow to say they have done something. But in the end, they know I'm right. They just won't admit it! Or they are too worried about their own ass to do something about it."

Milt nodded as he reached for the sugar jar. Krylic blocked his hand. "That crap is bad for you, Tonkin."

Milt pulled his hand back. "Yeah, you are probably right." He took a drink of his black coffee. "Okay, so you have lost me here. What do you mean when you say they know where they are? I've always wondered why no bodies have ever been found. I don't ever recall the police or the newspapers giving an explanation for that."

"Fuck, Tonkin! Doesn't matter what the police or the papers say. Think about it. These out-of-towners are amateur fortune hunters. And where do they think the fucking gold is? Inside all those tunnels and shafts at the Davidson Mine. They come here with a few maps and a flashlight stuck to their head and figure it's a cakewalk in there. If they didn't fall down a shaft or get buried under a rockslide, they probably got lost and starved to death."

"So, the cops never searched the tunnels and shafts dug out around the mine up there?"

Krylic drank his coffee. "Never! They said it was too dangerous even if they hired someone who knew what they were doing. Oh, they poked their heads in one or two shafts and shined a flashlight in some open areas in the rock face, but actually go in? Fuck, no! Bunch of chickenshits! One cop said he didn't want to get lost in there. I told him to bring some fucking twine. He didn't like that." Krylic laughed and took another sip of his coffee.

"Shit, I never knew that about cops," Milt replied, shaking his head. "Guess that is not a bad theory, though."

"It's not a theory," Krylic said. "You got a better one? No other reason they can't find any bodies. I just told that to our new sergeant there…what's her name…?"

"Mead," Milt said. "She actually came to talk to you about it?"

"Yeah…Mead. No, I bumped into her downtown, near the library. Told her the same thing when she started asking. Waste of police time."

"That's interesting," Milt replied, brushing aside some sugar that had spilled on the counter.

"Interesting?" Krylic said. "It's the truth. And I just asked you a question. What is your theory, if you don't like mine. And spare me any fucking bigfoot stories."

"Chad DeMello," Milt calmly replied.

Krylic laughed as he shook a finger at Milt. "You know, I had a fucking feeling you were going to say that. What is it there, Mr. Milt? You have some vendetta against the DeMellos now for what they did to you? Want to string up that son-of-a-bitch kid if you find him? Would love to help you with that, but the sad news is that bastard is dead. Better to go after the old man or one of the brothers for the shit they have caused in this town."

Milt shook his head and smiled. "Nope…no revenge here, buddy. That's done and gone with. Just wondering, if you have spent so much time up there, you might have seen something. I have my reasons for thinking he might be still alive, even if it is farfetched."

"Hey, if that will keep these out-of-town assholes from coming here, I will be glad to help you spread the rumour. They're giving Tear Falls a bad reputation. Never liked that." Krylic leaned towards Milt. "You know, when I get a chance to stop their vehicles, I tell them it's not their fucking gold anyways. Belongs to Tear Falls now. Fucking Stinson Mine has taken enough from us as it is. Sure as hell ain't going to some fucking person from out of town."

Milt nodded, recalling Harry Tartiak's stories. "Yeah, well, it's not really the Stinson Mine's fault or anyone else's. It was my friend Rick who stole it in the first place. The mine did say years ago they found it. I would guess it's more like fucking asshole authors writing books and starting rumours it's still out there that are causing the problems."

"Yeah…the story that Stinson found it. Ain't that something, eh, Tonkin? Makes you wonder why Stinson keeps looking for gold they already found." Krylic eyed Milt over his coffee as he took a drink. "You happen to have any theories on that, Tonkin?"

Milt paused. Kristen's words about his non-disclosure becoming public being a good thing flashed through his mind. He even thought of saying something about it to Krylic and beating Berts to the punch.

"Theories on the gold?" Milt asked. "All I know is they found it. They're not looking for anything anymore. It's all bullshit rumours, Rob."

Krylic smiled. "Thought you might say that." He reached into his back pocket, took out a wrinkled piece of paper, unfolded it, and spread it out on the counter. "Then maybe you want to explain this for me?"

Milt scanned the wrinkled paper. At the top was a scribbled handwritten title that said "Crate Shipment #43." Milt glanced further down to see what looked like jotted-down serial numbers from one to twenty-six. He noticed some of the numbers were crossed out with red lines.

He looked back up at Krylic. "So…what the hell is this? Where did you get this?"

Krylic raised his eyebrows and slowly nodded. "Ah…so now I have your attention. And by the way, twelve of the numbers are crossed out."

He picked up a lunch menu. "You know what? I'm getting a bit hungry. How much is your grilled cheese here?" He put up his hand to get Diane's attention.

"Two ninety-nine, but that includes a side order of fries." Milt pushed down the menu Krylic was holding. "So, what is this list supposed to be, Rob? Why are you showing me this?"

Krylic removed Milt's hand from the menu. "Easy, Tonkin. I do better on a full stomach."

Milt looked up as Diane interrupted the conversation. "Ready to order?" she asked.

"Uh…yeah," Milt said. "Bring Rob here a grilled cheese and bring me… You know what? Bring me a beer, Diane." He turned to Krylic. "You want a beer with your grilled cheese?"

Krylic shook his head. "Nah, no drinking on the job, Tonkin. But I could use a refill on the coffee."

Diane wrote the order down on her flip pad. "A grilled cheese with fries, a coffee refill, and…a beer?" She looked at Milt. "You did say a beer, right?" She glanced at her watch, which read 3:20 pm, and then back to Milt.

"Yes…a beer, Diane…that's exactly what I said…please."

"Okey dokey!" Diane replied.

Krylic turned to Milt as Diane walked away. "I got that list last year when I came across this truck stuck in the ditch near the Yars Lake trail cutoff. Crew cab, and it says 'Black Forest Surveying' on the side. Figure they are either in the bush or gone for help for their truck, so I decide to do them a favour and winch it out for when they get back. But I need it in neutral."

"So, you broke in?" Milt said.

"Breaking in is when you break something, Tonkin. I conveniently let myself in using CAA-approved tools."

Milt shrugged. "Alright."

"Well, when I get in the truck, I see there were hard hats with miner lamps in the back seat, but they had duct tape over the front. I reach back and peel a little bit of the tape and see 'Stinson Mine'."

"Yeah? So, maybe Stinson is thinking about restarting the Davidson Mine and doesn't want anybody to know about it."

"Tonkin, I wasn't fucking finished."

"Alright…I'm listening…"

"I picked up this steel clipboard case I see on the passenger floor and popped it open, and out fell all these maps and shit of the Davidson Mine and Yars Lake."

Milt shrugged. "Makes sense if they were surveying."

"Yeah, it would if that's what they were fucking doing, but they weren't." Krylic pointed to the paper. "That's where I got this list. I copied it from one I found in the case, and guess what date was at the bottom?" Krylic flipped over the piece of paper and pointed at some writing. "Right there, Tonkin. December 22, 1971. Now, why does that sound familiar?"

Milt stared at the date. "Okay, what the hell are you talking about? You making this up as a joke or something, Rob? Why the fuck would Stinson be up there after all these years, looking around for the gold from Rick's crash again? You sure you copied this right?"

Krylic flipped the paper over again and flattened out the wrinkles. He leaned towards Milt and lowered his voice. "Don't worry, it's fucking copied right. And this is my theory, Tonkin, and maybe you can shed a little bit of light on it. I figure the Stinson Mine might have found the gold, alright, like you say, but I'm thinking they didn't find all of it. I'm thinking some of it is still missing. I'm just wondering if it is still up there, or maybe it's right in front of my fucking face right here, tied up in this fancy restaurant. What do you think of that theory?"

Milt leaned towards Krylic. "Well, I would say that is a pretty shitty theory there, Rob," he whispered back. He sat up. "I don't have the fucking gold! Never did! So, I don't know what you are talking about. And if you think otherwise, why don't you go to the cops yourself and tell them your little story, see what they think of your theory?"

Krylic sat back and laughed. "Right…okay…whatever you say, Tonkin. But if that's true, why don't you help me out on this? If there is something there, no use letting Stinson or any other out-of-town shithead find it. You know, I heard the Stinson Mine offers nice rewards for lost gold. I'll even help you out with looking for that phantom DeMello kid if it makes you feel better."

Milt paused as the two men were interrupted by Diane bringing their order. She set a grilled cheese down for Rob and a beer in front of Milt. Then she reached over to the back counter, picked up a coffee pot, and refilled Krylic's cup. She glanced at Milt's worried face as she poured. "You two men doing alright here? Anything further I can get you?"

"No…no, we're good, Diane," Milt replied. "Thanks for this."

"You're welcome," Diane said. "Just holler if you need something."

Krylic pulled the sheet of paper off the counter. "Will do!"

Milt turned back to Krylic. His face was tense. "You sure about this shit, Rob? You sure these guys were from Stinson?"

"Oh, they're from Stinson, alright, because I picked them up down the road hitchhiking when I was returning to town and drove them back to their truck. First thing they did was start bullshitting me on why they were up there."

"What kind of bullshitting? You ask them straight out whether they were working for Stinson?"

"Fuck, no." Krylic replied. "Then they would know I was in their truck. I just asked them what Black Forest Surveying was. They said they were surveying for new hydro lines. As if hydro is going to spend money running power up to a dead mine. And I would fucking know about that, anyway."

Milt took a large drink of his beer. "So, you just dropped them off? Were they from out of town?"

"Yeah, they said they were from Southern Ontario and it was their first time up, but I knew that was more bullshit because I had seen the one guy around before. He was a young, muscular guy, but he had this grey in his hair. Well, not like a ninety-year-old… sort of like…what do you call that when—"

"Salt and pepper." Milt said.

"Yeah, that's it."

"So, what happened when you dropped them off?"

"Nothing. They thanked me and just drove away."

"Black Forest Surveying, eh? I'll have to watch for the truck if it shows up around here this year. Maybe I will even look up this company. Give them a call. Play dumb and ask them if I can get some surveying done."

"Go ahead, look them up, but you won't get very far," Krylic said. "That's why I knew for sure they were lying. I already called the number I saw on the side of their truck. Didn't exactly match. Got some crane company in Southern Ontario called DM Lifts. The guy said he never heard of Black Forest Surveying and he was fucking pissed that they might be confused with his number."

"Wow," Milt said, taking a drink of his beer. "That's one fucked-up story, Rob. You know that, right?"

Krylic stared at Milt. "Fucked up or not, are you going to help me, or what?"

"I don't know…I need to think about this. You said there were twenty-six crates on that shipment list? And you are sure it was dated December 22, 1971."

"That's what I copied down, twenty-six fucking crates," Krylic replied. "Why don't you phone up Stinson yourself if you don't believe me."

"Okay, but why me? Why do you need my help? You know the area better than I do."

"Tonkin, I have done my research. You're the closest one to all this shit that is not dead or gone missing. You have the smarts to know where any gold might have gone. And I thought you might have an interest in it, considering it was your best friend that stole the gold, and aren't you still helping to take care of his mother over at the nursing home? I figure you have a vested interest."

"Yeah…" Milt let out a long breath and rubbed his mouth. "You know what? Let me think about it, Rob. I need to digest this a bit more. I'll call you. How's that?" Milt looked through the order window and caught a glimpse of Kristen coming into the kitchen through the back door.

***

Kristen waved at Jamie as he lifted a hamburger patty onto a bun and placed it on a plate with some fries.

"Afternoon, Jamie! Everything under control?" she asked. She flipped her Abby apron off a hook and put it on. "Milt on cash?"

Jamie placed the hamburger plate onto the ledge of the order window. "He's out there near the cash, if that counts. Talking to a MNR guy."

"MNR guy? Now what?" Kristen was heading for the kitchen door when Diane opened it from the other side and ran into her.

"Sorry, Kristen!" Diane said. "I was just coming in to see if Jamie could help clear some tables while I work the cash for a few minutes."

"No, I got it," Kristen replied. She walked with Diane into the dining area and stopped at the opposite end of the counter from where Milt was talking to Krylic.

"Is that Milt talking to Rob Krylic? And is he drinking a beer?"

"Yes and yes," Diane replied. "They have been talking for a while."

"About?"

"No idea."

"Well, I'm about to find out," Kristen said, marching toward the two men.

"Hey, gentlemen!" she said, startling them. "How has the service been today?" She smiled.

"Oh…hi, hon," Milt replied. "You know Rob Krylic, right? He works for the MNR," Milt said, gently smiling back.

"I sort of figured that, Milt, from the MNR patch on his arm." She turned to Rob. "How are you, Rob? Enjoy your lunch today?"

"Yeah! It's been great, Kristen. I should come in here more often."

"And what about you, Milt? You want another beer?" Kristen raised her eyebrows.

"Uh…no…I'm good, hon. I'm just coming off break now. I'll meet you back in the kitchen." Milt stood and placed a hand on Rob Krylic's shoulder. "Hey, thanks for coming in, Rob. Sounds like we are in good hands with our wildlife enforcement in Tear Falls. Listen, I will be in touch, okay?"

Krylic smiled through a mouthful of grilled cheese. "Looking forward to it. And thanks for the lunch!"

"You bet!" Milt said, giving Krylic a pat on the back.

Milt entered the kitchen to find Kristen leaning against the wash sink with her arms crossed.

"Rob Krylic, Milt? Really?" she said. "You are now getting advice from a deranged MNR guy with a gun?"

Milt walked over to the kitchen dishwasher, opened it, and started taking dishes out. "He was just filling me in on what he knows about searching for some of these missing people. He's up in the Yars Lake area all the time. He had some interesting things to say. And it's not a gun. Well…not a real gun. It's a tranquilizer pistol."

"He's a lunatic, Milt!" Kristen replied.

"He is crazy, Milt." Jamie chimed in while lifting a basket of chicken fingers out of the fryer.

"Did I ask you, Jamie?" Milt said, giving him a hard stare. He turned back to Kristen. "Okay, I admit he is a bit odd. But he was spilling a lot of shit, Kristen, that's got me thinking."

"Spilling shit? Well, that makes sense. Do you know he used to tell us in grade six on the school playground that he would smell his own shit! And in grade nine, he was suspended for twisting the head off Mrs. Prines's stuffed Canada goose…twice!"

"All I did was talk to him, hon. I'm not having him over for poker or to go for a beer."

Kristen turned to Jamie. "What do you think, Jamie? You were a few grades behind him. You know his reputation."

Jamie wiped his hands on a towel. "Hey, I'm staying out of this one. I'm going to go help out front. Let me know if you need help with any orders."

Milt stepped aside as Jamie strode by.

Kristen came over to where Milt was standing. She reached past him to pick up a glass from the dishwasher and then walked back to the sink and filled it with water. "Okay, what is it now, Milt?" she said with her back to him. She turned around. "What has Mr. Crazy told you that can be any more fucked up than what Berts told you the other night?"

Milt's jaw muscles strained as he took a deep breath.

"What? What is it, Milt? Why do you look so strange?"

"I think the Stinson Mine isn't finished lying, Kristen."

Chapter 12

STAR TREK LAWYER UP!

en looked over at Silas and whispered. "I thought you said your parents' lawyer was some run-of-the-mill, common-guy lawyer. These waiting chairs must be a thousand apiece. And we came up nineteen floors of a twenty-floor building. You know what that means. And why is there no secretary here? Where is she, in the back with him?"

Ben leaned on his leather armrest and whispered back. "Will you relax? His message to me was just to walk in and make ourselves comfortable. You were the one that insisted we have a lawyer look things over or you weren't coming, remember? Why do you think he is meeting with us on a Saturday? The guy is in demand." Silas leaned back into the chair. "These are nice chairs, though."

Both men looked up as a large panelled door opened and a man stepped out of an office. They glanced at each other as he approached. He was wearing a black Star Trek t-shirt, denim shorts, and leather sandals. Silas looked at his thin, receding brown hair and estimated him to be in his late fifties.

The man straightened his red-rimmed, round glasses as he put out his hand for a shake. "Now, which one of you is Silas?" he asked, shifting his hand back and forth between the two men.

"That would be me, Mr. Schonberg." Silas and Ben stood, and Silas shook Schonberg's hand. "And this is my friend Ben Lee."

"Pleased to meet you, Ben," Schonberg said, shaking Ben's hand. "C'mon in. Sorry to keep you waiting. I was trying to figure out how to use that phone in there. Enough buttons on it to be an arcade game!"

Silas and Ben followed Schonberg into the office and sat down in silver-studded black leather chairs positioned in front of a large mahogany desk. Silas leaned forward and felt the thickness of the desk and then gazed around the room at the walls filled with paintings and photographs of exotic places.

Both men watched as Schonberg walked over and picked up a worn brown burlap carrying bag from the corner of the room. He brought the bag back and nearly lost his balance as he went to sit down in a spring-supported black netted chair. "Whoa!" he said. "Not used to these high-tech chairs."

Ben looked at Silas and raised his eyebrows. Silas gave him a shrug.

Schonberg pulled papers out of his bag. "So, I've been doing a little reading on this Tear Falls place mentioned in the contract." He passed copies of the contract to Silas and Ben and then leaned on the desk with his arms folded. "Quite the happenings for a little town in the middle of Northern Ontario, wouldn't you say?"

"Yeah, it's had its moments, that's for sure," Silas said, smiling. Ben nodded.

"Oh, I would say more than a few moments. You've got a gold heist from, I think it was, '71, lost treasure, and a cast of interesting characters looking for it, if the newspaper articles I have read are correct. Not to mention some missing people. Have to think there is a book or movie in there somewhere."

Silas laughed. "Well, if all goes right with this trip, I think maybe I could write one."

"Right. What an excellent segue into our discussion today, gentlemen. We're going to talk about that," Schonberg replied.

"About me writing a book?"

"No, about your right to publish one," Schonberg said with a smile. He flipped open his copy of the contract and picked up a pen. "So, first tell me, when is this northern sojourn to take place?"

"Last part of June. In about three weeks," Silas said. "Looks like you have done a fair amount of your own travelling yourself." He pointed to a large picture of some pink flamingoes on the wall.

Schonberg put down his pen and let out a chuckle. "Ah, now I understand the confused looks. I should have clarified with you, Silas. This is not my office. This is a friend of mine, Rene Sife. He is into commercial real estate here in Toronto." Schonberg looked around the room. "Does quite well, by the look of things. He was kind enough to let me use his new office when I told him I had a meeting with a client downtown. He still hasn't got around to putting his name on the door. Too busy, I suppose."

"Oh, okay. Hence the trouble with the phone," Silas said, smiling.

"You got it," Schonberg replied, grinning back.

Ben leaned forward. "So, where do you work out of, then, Mr. Schonberg? What kind of law do you practice?"

"Call me Steve," Schonberg said. "I work out of my home, north of the city. I prefer it that way. No stressful commutes, and coffee line-ups are, at worst, one person deep." He slid open drawers and rummaged through them as he continued. "My area of practice is collectibles."

Schonberg took two pens from a drawer and passed them over to Silas and Ben. "Buying and selling of rare sports merchandise, nostalgic toys, and of course..." he tugged at his t-shirt. "I'm a sucker for movie memorabilia."

"Wow! That's cool!" Ben replied. "Never knew that stuff required a lawyer."

"The high-end stuff does. It can get pretty pricey, and that's where I come in to put people's minds at ease with a deal. But I still do wills and some small business reviews to keep food on the table."

Schonberg tapped the cover page of the contract with his pen. "Okay, how do you want to do this? You want to go through it page by page, or do you just want my opinion and you can ask me questions?"

Silas picked up his copy. "I think we get the gist of it." He looked at Ben, who nodded. "So, I guess your opinion would be a good place to start."

Schonberg clasped his hands in his lap as he leaned back and gently rocked the chair. "Well, I have to admit, it's the first contract I've seen of this nature. But from what I gather, this individual, Marty DeMello, wants to hire you to search for his lost son, and he wants to pay you for it and reward you if you find evidence of his whereabouts or fate, correct?"

"That's the way we understand it," Ben replied.

"I see. Okay, well, a little unusual, but that doesn't mean it's a bad contract." Schonberg sat up and opened the first few pages. "First thing you should know is a great deal of this contract is about disclosure. Who owns the rights to say what to whom and with whose permission, which means Marty DeMello's permission, including publishing a book." He looked at Silas. "And be aware, this contract clearly states Mr. DeMello is not to be held liable for any misfortunes or unforeseen consequences during your trip."

"Yeah, we figured that. He made that perfectly clear when we met with him," Ben said.

"Then there is the question of proof. Basically, without physically turning this individual over to Mr. DeMello, be he alive or dead, confirmed photographs or videos plus DNA evidence as determined by a certified forensic lab are the only acceptable proof."

"DNA evidence?" Silas said. "How the fu—" He stopped himself. "Let me rephrase that. How are we supposed to get that if the guy is still running around, hiding in the bush? What about just a snapshot or maybe a fingerprint from something?"

"Nope, says you need DNA evidence matching familial lines. The contract is quite explicit on that. But I'm sure a picture or video evidence couldn't hurt if you can get it. You might want to talk to him further about any other possible proof."

"Doubt he would budge," Silas said. "I don't—"

"What about the money?" Ben blurted out.

Schonberg turned to him. "Ten thousand to hire you and a hundred thousand for confirmation you have found his son or evidence of his demise. That part is on the last pages, including the method and timing of payment."

Ben nodded. "Yeah, I know, but how do we know he will pay us? The guy has spent time in prison. I'm not sure what we would do if he didn't pay up."

"Prison?" Schonberg said, glancing at Silas. "I didn't exactly come across that in my readings. Is there more to this I should know about?"

"Nah...don't worry about that, Steve," Silas replied. "It really has nothing to do with the trip. Mr. DeMello is harmless. He's just anxious to find his son." He glared at Ben.

"Hhmm...okay. I leave it to you two to judge his character. But to answer your question, the reward money is held in trust with Mr. DeMello's lawyer. There should be no problem with being paid, providing you meet the contract obligations."

Ben picked up his copy of the contract and started to write. "In trust...okay...that's good!" He looked up. "Alright, but do you see any problems with us signing this contract? Are we going to be sued for not finding this guy?"

"No, you are not going to be sued for not finding him," Schonberg replied. "You won't get the reward money, but ten thousand sounds like a fair wage for a week's work, wouldn't you say?"

Silas placed his copy on the table. "So, basically, you see nothing in here that is going to bite us in the ass, and the money is guaranteed as long as we find this guy with acceptable DNA evidence?"

"That about sums it up," Schonberg said, gesturing with open hands. "I have made some highlights on important clauses that you can call me for clarification, but I don't see anything in the contract that alarms me."

"Okay…great, then!" Silas said. He turned to Ben. "Satisfied?" Ben leaned towards Silas. "What about the list?" he whispered. "That's minor."

"But I think we should ask Steve about it. It is strange."

"Alright, if it puts your mind at ease." Silas turned back to Schonberg. "There is one more thing that is not in the contract. In all the paperwork Mr. DeMello gave us, there was a list of things it looks like he might want us to buy."

"Supplies for the trip?" Schonberg asked.

"Well, not exactly. It was…I don't know…just sort of random stuff. But he wanted eighteen of everything he listed."

"Alright, what kind of things? Should I write this down for future reference?" Schonberg picked up his pen.

Ben leaned forward and pulled a piece of paper out of his back pocket. Silas looked at him with surprise as he began to read. "Has here things like eighteen purple jawbreakers, eighteen bazooka army men, kneeling stance, eighteen twenty-ounce jars, seventy-five feet of snare wire…" Ben looked up. "Just a lot of crazy crap like that. Oh and eighteen Nazareth, and at the end of our last meeting, he said get to know Nazareth. I'm thinking that is something religious-related."

"Mind if I take a look at that?" Schonberg asked, reaching across the desk.

Ben handed him the paper, and Schonberg reviewed the list. "Interesting but looks harmless enough." He handed the paper back to Ben. "I guess the best course of action is to ask him. The Nazareth thing could be a biblical reference of some kind. If you remember your religious studies from high school, it's a place located in the Middle East with lots of history."

"So, should we be worried about a list like this?" Ben asked.

Schonberg leaned back. "Like I say, best way is to ask him about it. There is no reference to it in the contract."

"Okay, that's good enough for me," Silas said. "Guess we'll ask Mr. DeMello, then. I don't think I have any other questions." Silas looked at Ben. "You?"

Ben sat up. "No…no. I'm good. Sounds like we can call you if we do?"

"Absolutely," Schonberg replied.

"Well, thanks for meeting with us, Steve," Silas said. "My parents have always spoken very highly of you. How do we pay you for this?"

Schonberg placed his paperwork back in his bag. "No charge, Silas. I have known your parents for years and know the challenges your father is going through right now. I hope you find this person and collect that reward. I'm sure it could go a long way to helping them out." He smiled at the men.

"That's very generous of you," Silas replied as both he and Ben rose from their chairs.

"Very," Ben added. "Thank you."

"You're very welcome," Schonberg replied, and he stood and shook the men's hands. Then he picked up his burlap bag and draped it over his shoulder. "Well, I'm off to the Comic-Con downtown. Hoping to scout for more collectibles and listen to a live interview with William Shatner. Hence the t-shirt." He smiled at Silas.

"Ah…I get it. Nice!" Silas said, grinning back.

The three men walked out of the office, and Schonberg turned to lock the door. "You two go ahead. I'm going to use this reception phone to make a call. Looks a little less intimidating."

"Sure thing," Silas said, and he and Ben waved goodbye. "Thanks again."

"Stay safe, gentlemen, and enjoy your trip," Schonberg called out as he held up the phone receiver. "Everyone from Toronto should travel and enjoy the hospitality of a small town like Tear Falls."

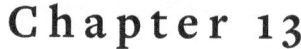

Chapter 13

VANCOUVER SIGHTS

"Fuck Tear Falls!" Conrad Reese said as he picked up a crystal decanter of whiskey and poured himself a drink. "Bunch of fucking Northern Ontario hicks with nothing better to do but stick their noses in everyone's business. Couldn't wait to get the fuck out of that town." He took a large drink, walked over, and looked out the tall glass windows of the Lino Gold Corporation boardroom overlooking Vancouver Harbour. He turned back to Ron Fykes, sitting in a chair at the end of the table. "And you. Fuck. You come in here in a tight t-shirt and jeans. And what's that on your damn head? The Al Pacino look with a splash of fucking Jay Leno? How about wearing a fucking tie here once in a while to at least make my secretary think you have some legitimate business to discuss?"

"Easy, Reese!" Fykes said, leaning forward to sip his coffee. "I actually think I may have a date with her. She might like a thirty-year-old hanging around after staring at your fat fucking belly all day."

"That's funny," Reese replied. "Real fucking funny." He walked over to Fykes, set his drink down, and leaned on the table. "This is it. You know that, right? The final sale goes to the board at the end of September. Everything needs to be done now. The gold needs to be found fucking now."

Fykes took a cigarette from a case in his pocket. "I can smoke in here, right?"

"Shithead!" Reese replied.

"Thought so." Fykes lit his cigarette and took a long drag. "We'll find it this time. Only a few more spots to check."

"And what about Krylic?"

"Krylic? Still circling around up there like a fucking mosquito. Feed him a few 'yes sir, no sirs' when he stops us, and we're good. Just a fucking annoyance." Fykes took another drag on his cigarette. "But I would say you got bigger problems than Krylic."

"Bigger? We?" Reese raised his eyebrows. "I think you fucking mean you. What kind of problems do *you* fucking have?"

Fykes laughed. "Typical." He rocked back in his chair. "I have been talking to Dom Santtini about renting his trailer again out at Saphora Lake. He tells me Tear Falls has a new sergeant in town who is looking into a lot of shit, including the crash and the missing people. Thought that may be of interest to you before I go."

Reese walked back to the window with his drink. He pointed to the ships out in the harbour. "What would you do if one of those cargo ships out there hit a rock and cracked open and spilled diesel or oil all over our beautiful harbour? What do you think you could do about it?"

"What the fuck does that have to do with anything? What the fuck can I do about it?"

Reese turned back to Fykes. "Exactly, asshole!" He walked over to a map laid out on the table and tapped it hard with his finger. "This is what interests me. What the fuck am I to do about some brown-nose sergeant running around Tear Falls trying to be a community hero again? All of them are gone before the next report comes out saying the same horseshit, anyway. They never find anything. Stop wasting time on shithead sergeants trying to make a name for themselves." Reese shook his head as he sat at the other end of the table. "So, let's talk about something fucking important. What's your plan?"

"Just bringing one person this year," Fykes replied. "I met him at my dive club from the Cayman Islands. His name is Klaus

Tritzman. Solid guy, rock climber, hunter. He knows his way around the outdoors. He usually heads to the Yukon in the summer for a whitewater tour-guide gig, but I convinced him this side trip to Tear Falls could be a lot more lucrative. Besides, he'll fit right in up there. Tall, skinny fuck with a raggedy old brown beard. Man of few words. Just to your liking, Reese." Fykes laughed.

Reese finished his drink and slid the empty glass across the table. "My liking is you find those fucking crates! My liking is I never have to see your fucking face in here again and listen to your bullshit about how my money has been spent on you coming up with jack shit."

Fykes smiled and slowly nodded. "Jack shit…really? That's what you think?" He jumped up from his chair, walked over to a silver tray in the middle of the boardroom table, and put his cigarette out on it. "Well, you know what I don't understand about all this jack shit? Why the fuck do you keep paying me to look for it?" He hit the top of a chair several times with his fist. "And you know what, Reeesy boy? I've been thinking a lot about this shit over the winter. And something doesn't make sense. Something doesn't smell right. Starting to think I should be asking for a raise. What d'ya say? You worried about something more if someone else finds those crates? Something more than a little accounting problem?"

Reese laughed. "You are so full of shit, Fykes. What the fuck are you talking about? You get more money for a month of searching than you get for six of tanning your ass with tourists at some shithole dive resort. Makes too much sense, if you ask me." He rose, walked to the back table, and poured himself another drink. "You know, you are an ungrateful fuck!" He downed the whiskey. "But I guess that's what I get for doing my brother-in-law a favour and giving my shit-for-brains nephew a job!"

"Thought you would say something like that," Fykes replied. He sat in a chair and rolled it back on its wheels to stretch his legs, his hands clasped in his lap. "So, why don't you just write the gold off, then?"

"What?" Reese replied, looking over.

"I said, why don't you or Stinson just write the fucking gold off? Seems pretty simple to me. Why all this fuss to find gold crates from twenty years ago? Can't see why that would hold up a sale. Why the fuck would anybody buying Stinson give a shit about your fucking loss?"

"Because, asshole, it makes Stinson look bad. It makes me look bad, and it's fucking money! Something I've wasted enough on you already."

Fykes shook his head. "Bullshit!" He stood up. "There's more to it than that. You're a lying bastard, Reese! I haven't quite figured it out yet, but when I do, I think that extra money is coming my way." He headed for the door. "I leave in two weeks. Make sure your jack-shit money is in my account before I go."

"Find those fucking crates!" Reese yelled. "And take that camera case by the door with you. I want fucking proof of when and where you find it. This is your last fucking chance!"

Fykes picked up the leather camera bag from a table by the door and looked it over. "Last fucking chance…." he said under his breath. He held up the bag as he left through the door. "I'd say I'm your only fucking chance!"

Chapter 14

SUN RAY BEACH

oddy Simone took out four beers from his basement bar fridge and brought them over to the table. "Here you go, boys. Compliments of the Tear Falls NearNorth. It pays to own a bar in town."

Oakey looked at the label. "You allowed to do that, Roddy? Take beer from your own bar and take it home?"

Roddy reached over and grabbed a deck of cards off the bar counter and placed them on the table. "Why, you gonna tell?" he said with a smile. "A guy from Crescent Lake reserve squealing on a big black guy in town who owns a bar. Now that's handing the cops a fucking wet dream!"

Oakey laughed. "Yeah, well, maybe you better meet her first." He took a drink of his beer.

"Meet who?" Roddy replied, dealing the cards.

"The new sergeant." Oakey said. "It's a she, and I thought she would have come into your bar to bust up a few fights by now. According to Milt, here, she is a good-looking older version of Wonder Woman who can kick ass!"

Roddy grinned as he glanced over at Milt. "That true, Milt? Making good with the new local sergeant again? Maybe you can introduce me, and Wonder Woman won't come in asking me if I'm a retired football or basketball player like some of the others."

Roddy waited for a quick comeback, but Milt seemed not to hear and continued to stare across the room. "Earth to Milt!"

Milt turned his attention back to the table and picked up his cards. "Yeah, yeah. I'll put in a good word for you." He turned to Stu Fields, seated next to him. "Hey, Stu, what do you know about Rob Krylic over at the MNR? You ever run into him with your marine business?"

"Once." Stu threw two dollars to the centre of the table. Then he turned to face Milt. "But he don't like outsiders there, Mr. Tonkin. He only likes local folk. Local folk like you!" Stu smiled as Oakey and Roddy burst out laughing.

Milt smiled back. "What the fuck are you talking about? What's he got against you?"

"Stu's whiter than him," Oakey said with a smirk as he threw two dollars on the table.

Stu smiled. "Nope, nothing to do with that. He doesn't consider me a local, Milt, because I have only been here for five years. Guess that doesn't meet his criteria of being a real Tear Fallsian. He brought in an old ten-horse Evinrude this year to be fixed. We talked a bit. Everything was fine up until I told him I bought the place off of Ken Jarson last year. I told him Ken still worked on weekends and would take a look at it. Fuck, the next thing I know, he is teeing off on Ken on the phone about selling his business to a fucking out-of-town foreigner and why he didn't come to him first. He came in the next day, picked up his motor, and walked out."

"Really?" Milt said. "That's a bit bizarre."

"What's bizarre about it, Milt?" Roddy said. "The guy has always been a bit strange. And he has been known to have a temper when things don't go his way."

"Yeah, I'm starting to gather that, but how do you know? You have some run-ins with him?" Milt met Stu's two-dollar bet. "You're up, Oakes."

"I'm in!" Oakey said, placing his money in the pile.

Roddy picked up the deck of cards for the draws. "No run-ins. He just came into the NearNorth a few years back on a Saturday at ten at night. I'm behind the bar, serving, and he makes a bee-line towards me, and I see the guy is still wearing his fucking uniform. I'm thinking, what is this? A MNR bust! He starts yelling over the music if Puppy Powers is around."

"Puppy Powers?" Oakey said. "And I'll take three, Rod. Now, there is one fucked-up dude!"

"What do you expect from a guy whose first name is Puppy?" Stu said, laughing. "Give me two cards."

"Three and two," Roddy said, dealing out the cards. "Milt?"

"Ah, I'll take three," Milt replied. "Yeah, then what?" He pulled his cards towards him.

Roddy took three cards and placed the deck aside. "I point Powers out to him at the end of the bar. He goes over to him, where Tracy is serving, and then she comes back and tells me I better go over there because she thinks there is going to be a fucking fight."

Milt stared at Roddy. "A fight? Fucking Krylic can't be more than five-eight. Powers would kill him. Isn't he close to your height? Six-four or so, and what…220, 240?"

"He's got to be in that area," Roddy replied. "But when I get over there, I hear Krylic yelling something about Powers closing the sluice gates at the hydro dam. He shuts up as soon as he sees me, but I can see his face is beet red. He then slides me a few bucks and tells me to buy Powers a beer and takes off."

"Powers is just on maintenance over there at hydro," Oakey said, throwing a five-dollar bill in the pot. "He can't make any decision to close any sluice gates."

"Fucked if I know," Roddy replied. "I brought him a beer and asked him about it, and he just said Krylic was freaking out about water levels upstream."

"Why are you so hung up on Krylic anyway, Milt?" Stu said. He tossed his cards over to Roddy. "I fold."

"No reason, really," Milt said. He matched Oakey's raise. "He just came into the Abby the other day, and we started talking about some of the shit that's happened up at Yars Lake with the people going missing and the campsite robberies."

Roddy threw his cards down. "I'm out!" He crossed his arms and leaned on the table. "I know this hits close to home, Milt, but are you on the missing DeMello kick again with talking to Krylic? Did he tell you anything interesting that wasn't beyond his usual bullshit?"

"Yeah…well…" Milt delayed his answer. "You know what? Give me one card." Milt passed a card from his hand to Roddy.

Roddy exchanged the card for one from the top of the deck and continued to stare at Milt. "And…well…what'd he say?" Roddy asked.

Oakey glanced over at Milt and could see his discomfort. He decided to bail him out. "Hey, give me one card, Rod!" he said, flipping a card in his direction. "And I raise…" He reached into the chest pocket of his shirt and pulled a bill out. "Twenty!"

"Yowsa!" Stu yelled out. "We got the Cincinnati Kid here!"

Milt nodded at Oakey. He knew Oakey was bluffing, but he also knew that wasn't the point. He looked at Roddy. "Nah…he didn't say anything, Rod. You're right, just his usual bullshit." He took out his wallet and snapped a twenty between his fingers. "And I call, you lying bastard!" He laid his cards down. "Three of a kind."

Oakey picked up his final card. "Shit!" he said, throwing his hand down. "Nothing. Was going for a flush."

"I'm not surprised," Roddy said, collecting the cards.

"What, that Krylic was bullshitting?" Stu asked.

"No, that Steve McQueen over there had nothing," Roddy said, nodding and laughing in Oakey's direction. "Hey, who wants another beer?"

Oakey threw up his hand while looking at Milt. "I could do with one!"

***

Oakey and Milt said goodbye to Stu and Roddy and hopped into Oakey's pickup.

Oakey sat back and looked over at Milt. "You know, Roddy's beer wasn't meant to go."

"He doesn't give a shit," Milt said, taking a drink and smiling. "And don't even start."

"I'm not going to. You are," Oakey said. He leaned forward and started the truck. "What the fuck was that? You bring up Rob Krylic like you are doing some sort of fucking psychological profile, and then your face contorts like Houdini when Roddy asks you what he said. Fuck, I thought you were going to say he admitted to killing someone."

Milt laughed. "You got any hog legs in the back?"

"Right beside the gun in the locker box...why?"

"Why don't you drive down to Sun Ray Beach, and we'll drink a few."

Oakey looked over his shoulder as he backed the truck out of Roddy's driveway. "Fuck, this better be good, or I'm going to be in trouble."

"Hey, I take full responsibility for my own actions." Milt said with a grin.

"Yeah...well, at two am, I'm sure Kristen will hold me fully responsible for mine." Oakey placed the truck in drive and headed for Sun Ray Beach.

Oakey turned off the highway and headed down a small hill of an oil-paved road to the deserted beach. He drove slowly along the strip of pavement bordering the water and stared out of the windshield. "Actually, not a bad night." he said. "Fuck, look at those stars!"

Milt looked out his side of the truck as Oakey cruised slowly by a few pavilions and a small playground set on the beach. He laughed.

"What?" Oakey said, smiling.

"I remember coming here at one in the morning with Rick after an afternoon shift from Rennet Mine over twenty years ago. We had a few of the summer students who were done for the summer, and Brian Pallsiner was here with that stupid fucking Scooby-Doo van he used to drive." Milt took a drink of his beer and then choked as he continued to laugh.

"Yeah…so?" Oakey said, laughing, too. "What's so fucking funny about that?"

Milt threw the empty beer bottle on the passenger floor and wiped his mouth. "There was this one student, Cindy Criles. Fuck, she had a body. So, Pallsiner looks at Rick and says, do you wanna fuck her? Because I have a bed in the back of my van. You can fuck her, you know! And Rick says…" Milt leaned his head back and laughed again.

"What! What did he say!" Oakey said, trying to contain his own laughter. He pulled the truck in front of a small logged fence bordering the beach area and parked. "Fuck, stop laughing, Tonkin, and fucking tell me!"

Milt looked over at Oakey, shaking his head with a big grin. "He says no…I'm still using hockey tape on my dick the doctor gave me after I got it caught in the cone crusher at work!" Milt opened the door in a fit of laughter and stumbled toward a picnic table on the beach.

Oakey stepped out his door, opened his lockbox in the back, and pulled out two half-liter bottles of beer. He could still hear bursts of laughter from Milt. "It wasn't that funny, Tonkin!" he yelled.

Oakey came up to Milt and handed him his beer. He sat on top of the picnic table and joined Milt in watching small waves of water lap the beach under the moonlight.

"Whatever happened to Pallsiner, anyway?" Oakey asked.

"Ah…he rolled that fucking van coming back from a Jets game in Winnipeg the next winter and was killed. Never was meant for winter driving." Milt took a drink of his beer. "Shit, these bottles are big." He looked at the label.

"He was older than us, though, right? What…forty?"

"Thirty-nine. And the reason I remember that is Rick said he told him he would never live past forty." He turned to Oakey. "Fucking ironic, isn't it? The guy tells Rick, of all people, he won't live past forty."

"That fucking gold ended up being a curse, Milt. More shit than Rick could ever have imagined." Oakey set his beer down and looked up at the star-filled sky. "So, what had you so bent out of shape tonight with Krylic?"

Milt jumped off the picnic table and walked a few steps to the beach edge. "The gold," he said, looking down at the small waves of water struggling to reach his shoe.

Oakey sat up. "The gold? Oh, fuck, now what? What the fuck are you talking about? Don't tell me Krylic is buying into that bullshit, too. You set him straight, right? Told him Stinson found it long ago?"

Milt turned and stared at Oakey. "Yeah, I set him straight with Stinson, alright. But that's not exactly what happened. Stinson got their gold, but I was the one who actually found it."

Oakey laughed. "Now I know why you wanted me to come here and drink. Start making sense, Mr. Tonkin, or I'm not taking you home."

Milt walked back to the table and hopped up beside Oakey. He took a drink of his beer while staring at the dark lake. "I am making sense, Oakes. I was the one who fucking found it. I just told the Stinson Mine where to look. Negotiated a reasonable finder's fee with the help of a smart lawyer from down south, and that was it. Or so I fucking thought."

Oakey drew his head back as he turned to face Milt. "You're shitting me, right? My Indian tingly sense is saying you are yanking my chain. You just doing this so you can test me on my drinking memory tomorrow?"

"Nope…no yanks here, buddy…and probably not enough drinking for what I'm going to tell you." Milt finished his beer and placed the bottle aside. He turned back to Oakey. "Remember that sketch I had that was in Rick's gun when Galverson gave it to me from the crash? The one I showed the DeMello twins before David took a potshot at me for all that shit that went down at Galverson's cabin nine years ago?"

"Yeah, I would think I would remember that!"

"Well, that sketch was for real. I used that to find the gold two years after Rick's crash."

Oakey stepped off the picnic table and turned back to face Milt. "You're fucking kidding me, right? And if you're not, you are a fucking bastard. Are you fucking serious?"

"I am serious," Milt said. He lifted his hands in defense. "So, I guess I'm a fucking bastard."

"You lucky piece of shit." Oakey said. "How much did you get? When was this?"

Milt shrugged. "Told you. I found it in the spring of '73, but I didn't know what to fucking do. The cops were still up my ass, thinking I had helped Rick steal it, so I got a hold of Abigail Strebe. You know, the lawyer who was the daughter of the original owner of the Abby. She put a deal together for me to get the reward money, but I had to sign a non-disclosure agreement with Stinson. Actually, with that asshole manager Conrad Reese, who signed for them. Couldn't legally say a thing. Still can't."

"You found the fucking gold? Twenty years ago? Really? And you are just telling me now? What the fuck! What kind of fucking friend are you?"

"A good one because I just fucking told you. I shouldn't even be telling you now. They will sue my ass off if they find out. I didn't even tell Kristen until a few years ago. Why don't you go get some more beers, because that's not what is bugging me about Krylic."

"Fuck off! Get 'em yourself!" Oakey said.

Milt laughed as he hopped off the table and headed back to the truck.

Oakey walked a few steps and let out a breath as he looked down the deserted beach. "Fucking guy." he said under his breath.

"Got something better!" Milt yelled as he came trotting back.

Oakey turned to see Milt place two plastic red cups on the picnic table and fill them with Canadian Club.

"Hey, take it easy. I don't want to have to sleep here." Oakey said, walking back to the table.

Milt handed him a cup. "Cheers!"

"Cheers, you lucky bastard," Oakey replied. "Do I need to sit down for this?"

"Nah, just me."

Milt sat on the table and leaned forward, resting his arms on his thighs and holding his cup. "I couldn't tell you, Oakes. Like I said, Stinson and my lawyer said I would really be fucked over big time if I breathed a word. And believe me, it's haunted me ever since. But Krylic screwed me up even more with what he told me the other day when he came into the Abby."

"Yeah, and how is that? He told you where to find Chad DeMello?"

"No way. He thinks Chad DeMello is long gone. And he's probably right on that one. Nope, he thinks those people got lost looking for the gold in the Davidson mine tunnels. Basically, he thinks the cops are fucked and looking everywhere but in the shaft tunnels."

"So, what's the big fucking deal, then? It wasn't Chad DeMello, and you're fucking rich."

"I said I got a deal for finding the gold. I didn't get rich fucking cashing it in. So, Krylic—"

"Stop!" Oakey said, putting up his hand. "I'll be the judge of that. You going to tell me how much first?"

"Jesus Christ!" Milt said, setting his cup down. "Fifty grand! There, you happy? And before you start thinking I'm fucking Bill

Gates, it was paid out over ten years. And guess who has been helping to pay for some of Rick's mom's care in the home? Or Trent Campbell's son's wheelchair? Or maybe your discount on that truck you bought a few years later at fucking Wonnikie's? You ever think about why he gave an Indian such a great deal? Fuck, you want me to write it all out for you!"

Oakey raised his eyebrows. "Come to think of it, that was a great deal on that truck. And Wonnikie did include the tape deck with a Billy Squire tape in it. Shit…that was you?"

"Fucking forget it." Milt said, waving off Oakey with his hand. "Least I could do for someone who saved my life."

"Hey…fuck…" Oakey took a long drink. "Okay…forget what I said about the money. Tell me, then, what the hell this has got to do with Krylic. Is he looking for the gold now, or is he pissed that he found out you beat him to it?"

"Not quite. I told him I didn't have the gold, but I wasn't going to say anything about getting the reward money for pointing the Stinson Mine in the right direction. I can think of better people to tell than Krylic. But he is convinced Stinson is still up there, looking for it. And…I don't know…shit, now I'm thinking he might be right."

"Now you are fucking yanking my chain. You just told me you found it, and now Stinson is looking for it? Get your story straight, for fuck's sake!"

"Thought I did have it straight, but if I'm to believe Krylic, it could be both."

"Alright, this is too much. I am going to sit down for this." Oakey took a seat on the bench below Milt. "Continue the report, Peter Mansbridge."

"Well, he told me he was helping pull a truck out of the ditch up near the Yars Lake trail cut-off last year. Broke into it because nobody was around to put it in neutral to winch it out."

"Broke into it." Oakey said, nodding. "Nice."

"Yeah...well...he gets into the cab and sees Stinson miner hats and flips through some files they had in a clipboard case on the floor. Finds paperwork on Rick's 1971 plane crash and the shipment of gold. He says it listed twenty-six crates with serial numbers. Some of the numbers were crossed out."

"Okay, so Krylic found some old paperwork from the crash in their truck. Could be they are just checking something out. Last I heard, that's not illegal."

"Oakey, Krylic said they had tape over the Stinson name on their mine hard hats and the truck they were driving had some fucking surveying company logo on it that he said doesn't even exist. They didn't want anyone knowing it was Stinson that was up there."

Oakey shook his head and took a drink. "I don't know, Milty. Stinson sneaking around up there is a long way from there being more lost gold. You really think you should believe anything Krylic fucking says?"

"Give me your glass."

"What?"

"I said give me your fucking glass!"

Oakey held out his glass, and Milt filled it with the Canadian Club and then refilled his.

"Now, pay attention," Milt said. "When I found that gold, Abigail negotiated me a ten percent cut. She said they wouldn't go for it, but Reese signed, though he swore his fucking head off."

Oakey shrugged. "So, you fucked them over. So what?"

"I found only twelve crates, Oakey. I was so nervous I counted them ten times and memorized the serial numbers. To this day, I know them like the back of my hand. They were on Krylic's list."

Oakey knit his brow. "Jesus Christ! You just said Krylic told you about a list of twenty-six? What the fuck is up with that? Are you saying there is more out there? Fourteen more fucking crates from the crash?"

Milt nodded. "That's what the math says, if Krylic is right about the shit he is telling me. And he has no reason to make up some random number like twenty-six. He has no idea I only found twelve."

"Holy fuck!" Oakey said, shaking his head. "So, if Krylic is right, where is the rest of it? Did Galverson stash more somewhere else? Maybe the DeMello twins did get to him, and they were just looking for the crates you found."

"I have no fucking idea. All sorts of crap are flying through my head on this," Milt replied. "But here is what is even more fucked up. I have looked up some things on the Cessna Rick stole. If there were twenty-six crates on that plane, it means it was overloaded. That's another eight hundred pounds plus the fuel Rick put in that night to steal the plane. Easily over a thousand pounds of extra weight. No wonder he was having problems flying the fucking thing."

"How the hell did it get off the ground, then?"

"Probably with great difficulty, but I bet Rick must have known something was wrong. Maybe he noticed the extra crates when he was up in the air. Maybe the plane was out of balance. I think he knew he was going to crash somewhere and decided Yars Lake was his best option."

"Shit, this is crazy!" Oakey said, letting out a long breath. "So, Stinson never told you about these extra crates? And why is Krylic telling all of this to you? What's he getting out of it?"

"Krylic wants me to help him find it. Thinks I'm the best one to know where it might be. I even get the gut feeling he thinks I have already found it. And Stinson? Never said anything about extra crates to me. In fact, I remember to this day, when I signed, Reese slammed the file shut, thanked me, and said fucking case closed. He was happier than a clam."

"Alright, but I still don't get something. Stinson would have nothing to gain by overloading a plane. Why not do two trips? And why all secrecy now? Fucking announce some crates are still missing and offer another reward. Might fucking piss off Krylic, but I bet you would get another stampede up there and someone would find it."

Milt stared at Oakey. "People have tried, Oakey, and to date, at least two have gone missing, along with a few robberies."

Oakey blinked several times. "Okay, just fuck off. Just fuck right off with that. Don't tell me you think Stinson had something to do with the people going missing and all these campsite robberies. That's worse than your crazy DeMello theory!"

"Like I say, I don't know what to think anymore, but something is really fucked up with this, and it ain't just Krylic." Milt finished his drink and then threw his cup into a trash can beside the table. "And Christ, I have no idea why Stinson would want to overload that plane Rick stole, but if they did and Rick died because of it, they're in a heap of fucking trouble." He shook his head. "Do you know, last month, I got a call from that asshole Berts from Hamilton?"

Oakey sighed. "C'mon, Milty. That guy is not worth the paper he writes on. Don't get him mixed up in this shit. He loves to try and make money writing about other people's crap."

"Yeah, well, it turns out he may already be mixed up in it. He called me in the middle of the night and told me someone wants the information he found out about Rick and his family and the Stinson gold shipments from the research he did writing his book on the crash."

"Why would that asshole call you and tell you that? I wouldn't trust that prick. You know what he is like. He could have just made that story up to try and get more out of you."

"Yeah, I know." Milt brushed some sand from his shoes. "I was thinking the same thing. Then he said this someone faxed him the last page of my non-disclosure agreement with my signature on it and negotiated a trade for any information he might have."

Oakey let out a whistle. "Holy shit. You're just full of fucking good news tonight, aren't ya? You have any idea who this person is?"

"Can't say I do. Just another fucking mystery to add to my list. But it's now crossed my mind it might be someone from Stinson."

"You've told Kristen about all of this, I hope."

"Unfortunately, yes. And as you can imagine, she is none too pleased. In fact, she has hinted about us selling the Abby and just getting the fuck out of Tear Falls. She has had enough of all this shit."

"Well, I don't know if I blame her," Oakey replied. "So, what are you going to do, talk to someone at Stinson? Your lawyer? And what are you going to do about Krylic?"

Milt rubbed his face with his hands. "Christ, that rye is strong!"

"Yeah, half the bottle in a cup can do that," Oakey said. "Stop avoiding the question."

"I guess I have no choice on what to do. I'm going to pay another visit to our friendly new sergeant," Milt said. "First one since Singh who seems to give a shit about Tear Falls—and, I guess, our fucking nursing home."

"Another theory from the crazy Tear Falls man. I'm sure that will go over well," Oakey said. "You better be careful, buddy. Mead might place your name permanently in that crazy-man file they have over at the station."

"Ah…I figure she will listen. I imagine she doesn't want anyone else to go missing on her watch." Milt jumped off the picnic table and grabbed the rye bottle. "And you, my friend, are going to help me with Krylic." He headed to the truck.

"Oh, no, don't you get me mixed up with that psycho!" Oakey yelled. "This ain't no Batman and Robin show!"

"It's not!" Milt yelled back over his shoulder. "It's Wayne and Shuster! Home, James!"

Chapter 15

SEVENTIES REDUX

S ilas turned to Ben. "Now, let me do all the talking, alright? We make it short and sweet. We hand him the signed copy and tell him we leave next weekend and that we will keep him posted on any developments. Good?"

Ben glanced over as he drove. "What about the money?"

"He's going to give us the money. That's part of the deal. Were you not listening to Schonberg?"

"How?"

"I don't know. Jars of loonies. Why does it matter, as long as he gives us five grand up front? It's in the contract."

"Speaking of jars, you going to ask him about the list, and what about the money in the envelope?"

"Shit, you're a piece of work. Okay, you can ask him, alright? Just time it properly. Don't piss him off. And don't forget the religious part about Nazareth. Want to make sure we are not walking into some crazy cult thing."

Ben smiled.

"What?" Silas asked.

"I don't know. For someone who says he has this all figured out, you sure seem to be stressed out about it." Ben drove past a Port Larch highway sign. "Where did he say to meet again?"

"Jake's Pizzeria." Silas looked down at a map. "Second set of lights and then take a left on Rhine Street." Silas surveyed the town through the front windshield. "And I'm not stressed. Just... fuck, I just want it to all work out." He looked at Ben. "And I know this might be like trying to win the lottery, but holy shit, that money would come in handy for my parents. No more bullshit letters of house payments overdue, worrying about the cost of medications for my dad, or my mom crying in the middle of the night. Just my half of the ten thousand will help with some of the crap they are going through."

Ben moved into the left turning lane and stopped at the red light. "Okay, let's both just take it easy. We're going to make this work. Like you say, we have a signed contract with this guy… this…convicted felon, and he is going to give us our fucking down payment. But I'm going to tell you something. I'm not going all the way up to this shit-dick town of Tear Falls in the middle of nowhere to collect ten grand. We're going to find this fucking guy or the gold or both. And we ain't fucking leaving until we do." Ben lifted the lid on the truck's centre console. "Now, what do you want to hear as we do our *Apocalypse Now* approach to the pizza place?"

"How about Spandau Ballet?" Silas replied, leaning his head back with a smile.

"Spandau Ballet? I always knew you were a sick man," Ben said. "AC/DC will do the trick!"

Ben drove back and forth in the parking lot of the strip mall. "Jake's Pizzeria? Where is it, Magellan? I don't see any sign."

Silas opened the map book. "He said 440 Rhine Street West, and this is it. It's got to be here somewhere. Pull into that space by that vacant store."

Ben parked in front of a large, three-panelled, tinted window storefront. He looked at a side door with peeling green paint. "I don't know, Silas. You may have to call him."

Silas scanned the parking lot. "Shit, we're twenty minutes late." He turned back to the store window. "Hold on! There!" He pointed at a small sign tucked in the corner of the window. "It says Jake's Pizzeria. This has to be it. And you know, I think I see people moving around inside."

Ben stared at the sign, shaking his head. "You know, this is right out of *Goodfellas*. I thought you said this guy couldn't get around without that scooter? Now we're meeting him at an abandoned pizza place a half-hour from the retirement home?"

"I said he couldn't walk, not drive." Silas opened the truck door. "Don't worry about it. It's a strip mall. Places go out of business and disappear all the time."

"Yeah, and so do people!" Ben yelled as he opened his door.

Silas pushed the restaurant door open and stopped. He looked back at Ben. "Care to step inside?" He held the door open for Ben.

Ben stepped by Silas and gazed around the restaurant. It was bustling with workers and customers. Red, green, and white checkered table cloths were draped over fully occupied tables and booths stretching to the back of the building.

"What were you saying?" Silas said with a smile.

"Hey, could be all a front." Ben replied.

A waitress approached the two men. "Two?" she asked.

Actually, we were meeting a person here. Older gentleman. Little shorter, grey beard," Silas replied.

"Oh, Mr. DeMello. Sure, c'mon back."

The waitress led Silas and Ben to the back of the restaurant. She pointed to the right, to a secluded raised booth by the kitchen.

"There he is. He likes to sit there and watch how fast the orders are coming out."

Silas and Ben walked over and sat in the booth.

"Gentlemen!" Marty DeMello said, putting out his cigarette. "How are my fearless fucking explorers today? Any problems finding the place? You're a little late."

"No, not at all," Silas replied. "Perfect directions. Just a little late getting out of Toronto." He glanced at Ben.

"Yeah, no problems," Ben said, nodding.

Marty folded his arms and leaned on the table. "Come here, gentlemen."

Silas and Ben leaned forward.

Marty stared at both men. "Now, let's get something straight right from the fucking start. If I can't trust you to give me a straight answer on something like finding this place, how the fuck am I to trust you way up in Tear Falls with my money? There is no fucking sign because I own this place! Reputation is what makes money, something you will fucking learn sooner or later."

"We didn't—"

"Forget about it!" Marty said, cutting Silas off. He leaned back. "Now, did you bring me some fucking signatures, or are you going to bullshit me on that, too?"

"No, we got that," Silas said, reaching into a large manila envelope. He took out the contract, flipped to the signature page, and passed it across the table. "No bullshit. We're ready to go."

Marty nodded as he looked it over. "Good, but who the hell is Blessing Lee? Am I fucking missing something here?"

"Blessing Lee?" Silas said. "Can I take a look at that, Mr. DeMello?"

Marty handed the paper back to Silas. "She related to you, boy?" He looked at Ben.

"Yeah, actually, she is my sister," Ben said. He gave Silas a nervous glance.

Silas handed the contract back to DeMello while giving Ben a hard stare. "Yeah, apparently, she decided to sign on. Hope that is okay?"

"You can sign on your whole fucking family," DeMello replied as he set the contract aside. "Like I said, I'm not getting mixed up on how you split any fucking money." He pointed at Silas. "Just remember, son, you are the one upholding everything I've said in this contract. That's what your signature means, understand?"

"Fully understood," Silas replied.

"Good!" Marty said. "You two ready to go over the details? You need to know where the fuck you are going, wouldn't you say? Don't want you getting lost on me." Marty lit up a cigarette. "All I need is for you to wind up fucking dead in a den with a black bear playing the xylophone on your bones!" He laughed as he exhaled a cloud of smoke above the two men's heads. "Agreed?"

"Agreed," Ben and Silas said in unison.

Ben signalled to Silas to hand him the large envelope he was carrying. Ben took out the paper with the long list of items and the envelope of money. "We do have a question about this list, Mr. DeMello. We are not sure what to do with it or the money. Do you want these things bought for someone up there?"

Marty signalled to a passing waitress, who stepped over to the booth. "Hey, Marty," she said. "What's up?"

"Rosa, can you bring me an SC with orange juice and bring these two tired travellers...what...a beer?"

"Sure." Silas said.

"A light beer for me," Ben added.

Marty looked at Silas. "You got the fucking map in that envelope? Take it out. We're going over it again, and then I will tell you why you have that fucking list."

Silas flipped through the papers, pulled out a folded map, and handed it to DeMello.

DeMello spread out the map of the Yars Lake area and turned it around to face Silas and Ben. "You see this red dotted line and how it splits? That's the trail from the Bitman logging road to the Davidson Mine and a cabin at Yars Lake. About an hour hike in. You can stay in the fucking cabin if you like. Used to be owned by Pat Galverson, the guy who went missing I told you about. Little run down, but far as I know, it still has a working roof to keep the rain from pissing on your head." DeMello put one finger on the Davidson Mine and one on the location of the cabin. "Now, it's about half a mile from the cabin to the mine, and this is where the shit on that list comes in." He reached over and picked up a jar on the seat beside him and slid it to the centre of the table. "There's your fucking answer to the list!"

Silas and Ben stared at the jar. Inside were items from the list: a multi-colour pen, a toy soldier on bended knee, holding a bazooka, a purple jawbreaker, a piece of paper with a picture, a needle, and a cassette.

"I don't get it, Mr. DeMello," Silas said, looking closer at the jar. "This have something to do with a scavenger hunt for Tear Falls? What are we supposed to do with this stuff?"

DeMello sat up and repositioned himself to rest his shoulders against the back of the booth. "You shits didn't look up Nazareth, did you?"

Ben cut in. "Well, actually, we did. We know it has historic and religious significance—"

"Fuck that religious shit, boy! It's a fucking band from the '70s, for fuck's sake! Look closer at the tape in the jar!"

Ben picked up the jar and rotated it to see the cassette. He read the label. "Razamanaz, Nazareth."

"That's fucking right! My kid's favourite band! Chip off the old block!" DeMello shouted. "Christ, you young fucks!"

"Here you go, gentlemen," Rosa said, interrupting. She placed a tall glass of Southern Comfort and orange juice in front of Marty and two beers on the table for Silas and Ben.

"Fucking forget about it. Doesn't matter anyway if you don't know who they are." As DeMello took a long drink. Silas and Ben looked at each other. After a second, they did the same with their beers.

DeMello picked up the jar. "All these things are from my kid's fucking childhood. Things I used to buy him when we went to the store or for a treat. The picture is of him and me, and at the bottom is a place to sign where it says 'blood brothers.' When he was a kid, I did that for fun when he asked me to sign a note asking me to be his dad forever. Used a little drop of blood from my finger. He kept that fucking note right up until he went missing when he was eighteen."

"So, the jars are mementos to give to other people up in Tear Falls you know? Friends, family?" Ben asked. "I'm not sure I understand."

"No! You're bringing them with you to fucking Yars Lake. I have seventeen more of them in two boxes up front, along with the snare wire."

"I don't get—"

"Then shut the fuck up and listen!" DeMello said. He pointed at the map. "You are going to take the jars and hang them with snare wire on tree branches along the path from the old Galverson cabin to the Davidson Mine. Every hundred feet or so, just like a fucking trap line, only this time, it's to find my son. Let him know I'm still alive. Let him know I'm still thinking about him. He'll realize what these things mean and know it only could have come from me." DeMello leaned back. "He may even decide to sign the picture in blood with that needle to let me know he's alive. That way, you get your DNA evidence for your fucking reward even if you never find him. Understand!"

"Yeah…sure…I…" Silas stumbled on his words as he peered at the jar. He looked up. "We got this," he finally said, and he looked at Ben for support.

"Yeah, yeah…absolutely. We'll take care of it, Mr. DeMello," Ben added.

"You better," DeMello said. He finished his drink. "Now, a word of advice about this fucking town of Tear Falls. It's a place where everyone knows everyone and everyone is into everyone else's shit whether they admit it or not. They are going to know you are from out of town." DeMello pointed at Ben. "Especially you, Confucius! So, do yourselves a fucking favour and buy some fishing gear or something. Make it look like you are tourists. I don't even give a shit if you say you are looking for the gold. But if word gets around that you are looking for my son, the deal is fucking off."

"We won't breathe a word," Silas said. "Thanks for the advice."

"I know you won't," DeMello replied with a grin. "Anything else?"

Silas reached into his pocket and brought out the envelope of cash. "There is this. Not sure if it was a mistake, but there is quite a bit of money in here."

DeMello laughed. "Keep it! Use it for your travel expenses, including some fucking fishing rods. Consider it incentive pay." He moved to the end of the booth and stood. "Let's go to the front, and I will give you the rest of the jars."

Ben looked at Silas and bit his lip. "The down payment?" he whispered.

"Oh yeah. Mr. DeMello, we were just wondering about the upfront money. How do we get paid before we go?"

DeMello took a step back towards the booth and pulled out a wad of cash from his pocket. "I have it right here," he said, fingering some bills. He stopped and broke out in a big smile as Ben and Silas stared at the money. "Fuck, you two shits are green," he said, laughing. He put the money back in his pocket. "Get your lawyer to call mine. They will work it out. Let's go!"

***

Ben glanced at the box of jars on Silas's lap as he drove the truck back to Toronto. "I don't care what you say; that is really fucked up! We are supposed to string these jars in the middle of the woods like human bait? You don't think that is weird?"

Silas looked at the jars and then back at Ben. "Maybe…but I will tell you what's fucked up. It's you not telling me your sister put her name on the contract! When were you going to tell me that one?"

"Don't get all excited. She told me you asked her before me, anyway. You have a problem with her coming now?"

"I don't have a problem with her coming—"

"I didn't think so," Ben interjected.

"Funny," Silas said. "It's about logistics. Now we're going to need extra gear and supplies. Changes a whole bunch of shit. And I thought she had a wedding to plan for, anyway."

Ben leaned over and turned on the radio. "Well…not too sure about that now. Mark has now extended his thesis until next spring. Blessing is not very happy. She is starting to think the wedding is becoming more of a hassle to him than anything else. But I'm staying out of it."

"That ain't good. I can see your sister being pissed about that."

"Pissed enough to want to go on this lunatic trip. And by the way, don't panic about the money with her coming. You still get your half. I will split mine with my sister."

"Don't worry about that. We can work it out," Silas replied

Ben nodded at the box on Silas's lap. "Hey, open one of those jars and take out the Nazareth tape." He signalled and merged into the fast lane of the highway. "Knowing fucking DeMello, it might come in handy to recognize that music someday."

Chapter 16

TONKIN TALK

"Fykes! How the fuck are you?" Dom Santtini said as he stepped out the trailer door and down the steps. He stuck out his hand for a shake. "Welcome back to the best accommodations in all of Tear Falls." He flashed Fykes a toothless smile.

Fykes ignored Santtini's hand and walked by him with his duffel bag. "The power fucking working this year, Santtini? Why don't you take some of that grease off those coveralls you are wearing and use it on the fucking generator, you useless fuck!" He leapt up the steps and disappeared into the trailer.

"A nice fucking day to you, too!" Santtini hollered after him.

"Hi, I'm Klaus Tritzman." a man said as he stepped up to Santtini. Tritzman placed his bags down and extended his hand. "You must be Dom Santtini."

"Fucking right, I am!" Santtini said, vigorously shaking Tritzman's hand. "Ah, a fresh partner. You're a tall fuck, too. Not sure if the bed in there will be to your liking."

Tritzman picked up his bags. "Floor is good enough for me. Better for the back," He walked by Santtini and into the trailer.

Once Fykes and Tritzman were settled, Santtini made two bacon sandwiches and brought them to the trailer booth table. He placed them in front of the two men. "Your boss here doesn't drink nothing but soda water, so what can I get you, Mr. Big and Tall? Beer, rye? Well-stocked bush trailer fridge at your disposal."

"Better take it while you can, Tritz, or this fuck will be back in the middle of the night to steal it," Fykes said, laughing.

"Yeah, sure…give me a beer," Tritzman said. "Thanks."

"Good enough," Santtini said. "I may just fucking join you on that one." He walked over to the small fridge and took out two beers and a can of club soda. He turned and threw two cans toward the table. "Catch!" he said, grinning.

Tritzman caught his beer with his left hand and threw out his right to catch the can of soda in front of Fyke's face.

"Holy fuck!" Santtini returned to the table with his beer and sat down. "You play baseball or something? He's got quick hands there, Fykes. I like that!"

Fykes took a big bite of his sandwich and chewed as he stared at Santtini. "You got anything useful to say, or are you going to sit there and talk useless shit all day?"

"Maybe both," Santtini said with a laugh. He leaned back and tapped the top of his open beer with his finger. "My boy was up at Yars Lake in the spring. He was taking a look around with his friends."

"Yeah…big fucking deal. They find anything interesting?"

"Nope." Santtini took a drink. "But their campsite got robbed." He peered at Fykes over his beer.

Fykes stopped eating and stared at Santtini. "Yeah…well, it's a dangerous fucking place up there, isn't it? Something you want me to fucking do about it?"

"Nah, but like I told you over the phone, I think our new sergeant does. Even heard that asshole Tonkin was in to see her a few weeks ago."

Fykes placed his sandwich down. "Tonkin? You told me she was talking to fucking Krylic. What would she be talking to fucking Tonkin about? Thought he would have had enough police shit."

"Couldn't tell ya," Santtini said, smiling.

Fykes sat back and placed his hands at his side. "What do I pay you for? Maybe you can fucking tell me something about that?"

"You pay me—"

"To fucking find this shit out!" Fykes yelled. He jumped up and stabbed the table with a large hunting knife.

Santtini bolted up in his seat, knocking his beer off the table. "Fuck, take it easy, Fykes!" He stared at the knife. "I'm gonna talk to some people and fucking find out. Christ, you're a crazy bastard!"

Fykes laughed as he leaned on the table and then turned to Tritzman. "I didn't scare ya, did I, Tritz?"

Tritzman raised his eyebrows as he stared at the knife. "It is a pretty big knife."

Fykes pulled the knife out and checked the blade. "Fuck, no… standard-issue diving knife." He pointed the tip toward Santtini. "You might want to buy yourself one, asshole. Works good at slitting things open…like some nice pickerel."

Santtini stepped out of the booth and wiped himself off. "You know, you are a crazy fuck, Fykes. Fucking makes me wonder why this guy came with you."

Fykes placed the knife back in his hip sheath. "Wonder? Now there's a fucking start." Fykes sat down. "Get the fuck out of here, Santtini. I'm renting this place now."

"Gladly," Santtini replied. He walked to the door and turned around. "Hey, I'll get it fucking done. I'll find out."

"Do that. I will be waiting right fucking here when you do," Fykes said.

Santtini opened the door and took a step out.

"And hey, Santtini!" Fykes yelled after him.

Santtini turned and stared at Fykes. "Yeah?"

"You did fix that generator, right?" Fykes asked, smiling

"Yeah, it's fucking fixed."

"Good, because it would be a shame if there was a short on our last day here and it burned this shithole to the ground!"

***

Milt stepped into the NearNorth restaurant and looked around. He didn't see his meeting guest, so he made his way over to the bar and sat down to order a coffee.

"Hey," Tracy Rellis said as she stepped out from the kitchen. "What brings our competition to the NearNorth at three in the afternoon on a Sunday? You're not here to steal Roddy's business secrets, are you, Milt."

"Not a chance," Milt said, smiling. "He gave those up to me long ago in poker. Wouldn't mind a coffee, though."

"Sure thing," Tracy said, and she walked over to the coffee machine. She took down a cup and poured as she spoke. "Roddy is not in, Milt. Was he expecting you? He usually takes Sunday afternoons off." She walked back and slid the coffee over to him. "Cream, sugar?"

"No, I'm trying to cut back," Milt said, taking a drink.

"Okay, then…" Tracy said, nodding. She spread her hands out on the bar and leaned forward. "You're not here to meet Roddy. The place is nearly empty… I guess you leave me with no choice. Kristen fired you at the Abby, right?"

Milt laughed. "Oh, if it could be that easy, Tracy." He looked behind him. "No, actually, I was supposed to meet someone here around three. Our new sergeant, to be exact."

"Oh…the good-looking one." Tracy said with a smile.

"Why does everyone say that to me?"

"Maybe because she is…I don't know…good looking. You're married, Milt, not dead! What's up? Or should I ask?"

"You just did." Milt said, folding his arms on the padded bar ledge. "She has been the first sergeant since Singh, Tracy, that actually seems to be taking an interest in Tear Falls. Just want to see if I can focus her mind on our inability to find missing bodies and Chad DeMello. You know, little hobby of mine, trying to find people who tried to kill me."

"I see," Tracy replied. "But why did you want to meet her here?"

"I didn't. Her idea. Part of her getting-to-know-Tear-Falls program, as she has described it to me. Did you know she bought the old Halgren place on the lake?"

"Really? Lots of work there. Didn't you tell me that was originally built by Rick's dad?"

"Yeah. Has an elevator and everything in it. Sad thing is, his dad never had the money to finish it. I imagine she has no idea on that part of its history."

Milt looked at his watch, which read 3:15. "Well, seems I may have been stood up. I'm going to have to go back to the Abby." He placed a five-dollar bill on the bar. "If she comes in, let her know I was here."

"What's she look like, again?" Tracy asked. "Brunette, shapely, right?"

"Yes, Tracy, but I don't think she will be too hard to spot in her police uniform."

Tracy leaned forward and whispered, "Well, I think she is here…minus the uniform."

Milt turned to see a woman standing at the restaurant entrance. He looked twice to make sure it was Sergeant Mead. Her brunette hair was down, and she was wearing a loose-fitting red t-shirt. A thin black belt with a silver buckle was wrapped around the waist of her black jeans, and she wore red cotton walking shoes.

"Yup, that's her, alright," Milt said, nodding.

"Well, are you going to be a good host and go over and greet her, or are you going to leave it to the underpaid hired help?"

"Yeah, right," Milt said, sliding off his stool and picking up his coffee. "Guess I should know better."

He gave Mead a wave and walked over. "Hello, Sergeant," he said. He extended his hand for a shake. "No uniform?"

"Technically, it's my day off. Police do have a civilian life, Milt," Mead replied as she shook his hand. "And please, Jocelyn will do just fine."

"You got it," Milt said. "Care for a coffee?"

"Would love one."

Milt directed her towards a booth, and the two walked over and sat down.

Mead reached into the front pocket of her jeans. "And you know…" She pulled out a business card. "This was left at the station for me by the owner of this restaurant, with a note on the back for a free coffee." She read the card. "A one Roddy—"

"Simone," Milt finished. "Figures."

"Oh, you know him?"

"Yeah, you could say that," Milt said. "You haven't met him yet?"

"Not yet, but I was hoping to thank him today. Generous of him." She looked around the restaurant.

"Well, he's not in today, but don't worry. I will be sure to thank him for you when I see him," Milt said. He waved at Tracy, pointed at his cup, and put up a finger for one more. Then he turned back to Mead. "So, thanks for agreeing to meet with me again."

"Not a problem, Milt. We seem to be on the same team in wanting to get to the bottom of a lot of things in Tear Falls. So, what do you have for me?"

Milt paused for a moment. He was unsure how to begin the conversation and kept thinking of Oakey's warning about a crazy-man file at the police station with his name on it. He was glad when Tracy interrupted.

"Here's your coffee," she said, placing a cup in front of Mead. "Sugar is at the end of the table, and I have cream here if you would like."

"Thank you," Mead replied, holding up her cup to the small container in Tracy's left hand. "Just a small amount of the cream, thanks."

"Sure thing." Tracy said, pouring the cream and placing the silver container on the table. She folded her arms. "You're our new sergeant, right?"

"That's right. Well, I've been here for a few months now, but I'm really starting to appreciate small-town life. You can tell that people look out for one another in Tear Falls. I can live with that. And by the way, I love your red hair."

"Thanks! Takes a while to do the long braid in the morning, but it's great for working. And it's great to hear you like Tear Falls." Tracy replied. "We do tend to stick together." She turned to Milt, who was blankly staring at his coffee. "Refill, Milt?" She patiently waited for his response as she glanced at Mead with a nervous smile. "Milt…?"

He looked up. "Uh…yeah. When you have time, Tracy." He raised his cup to Mead. "Second-best coffee in all of Tear Falls," he said with a grin.

Tracy raised her eyebrows. "I'll be back with a refill later," she said and then turned and walked back to the bar.

"So, where were we?" Milt asked, picking up the silver container and pouring cream into his coffee.

"Well, I think you said over the phone you had some news for me, something the police should look into."

"Yeah, that's right. Can you pass me the sugar jar there?" Milt said, pointing to the end of the table on Mead's side.

"Of course," Mead said, reaching for the jar and passing it to Milt.

"Well…" Milt poured a long stream of sugar into his coffee.

Mead watched. "You know that's not good for you."

"Yeah, so I've been told." Milt placed the container down. "I was talking to Rob Krylic from the MNR the other day. You know him, right?"

"Actually, I bumped into Mr. Krylic a few weeks ago downtown. I would say he is one interesting individual."

"That's probably an understatement. Anyway, he is up around Yars Lake a lot. Guess he feels it's a hotbed of poaching or something. So, I asked him straight out about his opinion on the missing people. He didn't buy into my Chad DeMello theory. He said—"

"The people went missing in the shaft tunnels."

Milt leaned back. "That's right. He mentioned you had asked him about it."

"I didn't ask him anything." Mead took a sip of her coffee. "I simply asked him what I should expect for tourists this summer, and he went off on a tangent about the whole Yars Lake thing. Lectured me on how the police searches were useless and we would never find anyone lost in those tunnels. Then he started to grill me on my own plans for looking into the matter. There is an itch there somewhere that needs to be scratched."

"Well, Sergeant…"

Mead furrowed her forehead.

"Sorry, Jocelyn… I think, Jocelyn, it's a little bit more than an itch. He had a story for me the other day when he came into the Abby for lunch. An interesting story about the gold from my friend Rick's crash. He thinks it's still up there. And he seems to think he has pretty good proof that Stinson has had people over the past few summers looking for it at the Davidson Mine." Milt gazed over his coffee to gauge Mead's reaction.

She stared at him as she gently rubbed her hands together. Milt sat back, interpreting her silence as confirmation that his reputation with the Tear Falls police was now sealed.

"Okay…" he said with a sigh. "I know—"

"Milt, why are you getting involved with this?" she said, cutting him off.

"What do you mean, getting involved with this? I'm just telling you what I've heard."

"No. I mean the entire thing. The DeMello kid, the missing people, and now the gold again. Don't you think you would get more out of spending the time running your business? Maybe quality time with your family? Or Rick's mother? I imagine Rick would appreciate that a lot more than you chasing around, looking for some sort of closure on the DeMello boy. Don't you think his mother deserves that from you? Deserves more from family than time alone in a nursing home?"

Milt rested his elbows on the table and clasped his hands together as he stared back at Mead. "You know, maybe you have a point there, Sergeant. It's interesting that you say that about Rick's mom. But I thought I was meeting with the police today and not my psychiatrist. I just thought helping out Tear Falls was a pretty good use of my time."

Mead responded with a small smile. "Right...okay, Milt. I'm sorry, and point taken. But let me tell you something about our Tear Falls MNR officer before you start believing anything he says. I mentioned to Constable Devon my conversation with Krylic, and he was quick to fill me in that he has had numerous complaints filed against him by out-of-town tourists and the Stinson Mine for what could be construed as harassment. Devon even cautioned him personally about it. Probably has a gripe against Stinson for buying the Davidson Mine and warning him about trespassing. I gather he feels unappreciated in this town. So, I wouldn't be surprised if he would want to have a rumour stirred up about Stinson and the gold again. And who better to start with than the best friend of the person killed in the crash of a Stinson plane?"

"Wait, did you say Stinson now owns the Davidson Mine? They bought that old property?"

"That's what all my reports say. They bought it five years ago. I guess they felt there was a liability issue or at least bad PR with people wandering around looking for their gold. And apparently, if Krylic has his way about spreading rumours of people disappearing in Davidson Mine tunnels, they have a point."

"Shit, I never knew that," Milt said. "And harassment…? Of Stinson workers…really…Krylic?"

"Yes. Probably the very people he has talked to you about. As I understand it, Stinson has been sending people up to the mine for years to check out the site. Fix damaged fencing, check out the old buildings. Reports say they have had a few run-ins with Krylic over jurisdiction and mine-surveyed property lines. In fact, he was accused of pointing his tranquilizer pistol at one of them. They didn't press charges, but I'm still looking into the matter."

Milt let out a breath. "Wow! I knew he could be a hothead, but I knew nothing about Stinson owning the Davidson Mine and the complaints about Krylic."

"I imagine Mr. Krylic is not going to volunteer that information. But why don't you tell me what he did say about more lost gold, and I will have Constable Devon look into it?"

"Yeah…more lost gold. That is worth looking into." Milt stared at his coffee and then looked up. "You know what, Sergeant… sorry, Jocelyn? Come to think of it, you are right. Krylic had no proof other than the story he told me. I'm sorry…I get all caught up and ahead of myself on this crap. And you are not too far off on me needing to spend more time on other things. I'm sorry to keep wasting your time on my stupid theories. Just don't make a crazy-man file on me down at the station, okay?"

Mead laughed. "I think we have better use for our files, Milt. Not to worry. And I enjoy our conversations. I learn more of how things operate from your end each time we speak."

"Happy to be of assistance," Milt replied. "Well, I'll let you get back to your afternoon."

"Hey, I needed the coffee," Mead said with a smile. She slid to the end of the booth and stood. "Keep in touch, Milt. The police rely on engaged citizens like you to help keep the community safe."

Milt rose and shook Mead's hand. "Wouldn't be my first time I have been engaged with the community," he said, smiling. "Have a great Sunday, Jocelyn."

"Thanks, Milt." Mead turned and headed for the front door. She waved at Tracy as she exited the restaurant.

Tracy waited for a moment and then walked over to Milt and stood beside him with a coffee pot in her hand. They both watched through the restaurant bay window as Mead drove away.

"That was short. No new information?" she said, still gazing out the window.

"Actually, more than I ever anticipated" Milt replied. He turned to face her. "Makes me want to place a call to Southern Ontario."

Chapter 17

TRANS CANADA

"Hey! Back it up!" Silas yelled as Ben and Blessing pulled up to the curb in front of his home. "Everything is in the garage."

Ben drove his pickup truck forward and then reversed up Silas's driveway. He and Blessing jumped out, and Silas directed them into the garage.

"It's all here," Silas said, pointing to three duffel bags on the floor. "Our basic hiking supplies, food, and a tent over by the door. You guys just throw in your personals, and we're ready to go."

"Where are the fishing rods?" Ben asked, looking over the gear. "Thought DeMello said we needed to look legit."

"We'll buy that stuff up there," Silas replied. "Stores down here don't know what they are talking about. I asked for fishing rods in one store, and the guy pointed to a plastic toy bin."

Blessing stepped up beside the two men. "Hey, I thought we were using packs?" she asked, pointing to the green bags. "These look like they are from the army."

"Probably are," Silas replied. "Picked them up at the surplus store down the street. But they have straps and harnesses, so they will do the trick. C'mon, open up the back cap on the truck, and let's load. Want to be north of Toronto by eight am."

***

Silas looked at his watch as Ben drove past the sign for the city of Barrie on Highway 401. "Not bad," he said. "Quarter to nine. Should make the campsite near Sault St. Marie by dinner."

"Any tickets, and you're paying." Ben said, glancing past Blessing at Silas.

"Not to worry, my friend. I'm a salesman, remember? I can sell anything," Silas replied.

Blessing rolled her eyes as she reached down to her bag on the floor and took out a flip pad and map. "Okay, I have been doing some reading on Tear Falls and this crazy story, and I have some ideas for our search."

"Uh-oh. Here we go," Silas said with a smile. Blessing glared at him, and he quickly added, "Sorry…please continue."

"Thank you," she said. "Now, from what I have read on all of this, if this Chad DeMello is still alive or met his demise, he would still be right around the Davidson Mine and Yars Lake."

"I think we gathered that much," Ben said.

"Or…" Blessing glanced at Ben. "He could be long gone to Mexico."

"Mexico?" Ben said. "How do you figure that?"

"I don't," Blessing replied. "But as good a place as any, right? According to the book Silas gave me, that is where the guy who stole the gold was heading. I'm just saying it may be why he has never been found. He slipped away and left the area years ago, even if it wasn't Mexico."

"I don't buy that," Silas said.

"Alright, then let's go with my first theory." Blessing opened her map book. "We know this Yars Lake is about fifteen minutes from the mine where a lot of people think the lost gold is hidden. And that is why Chad DeMello was up there with his dad and uncle in the first place. So, I'm thinking he didn't stray too far from there after he ran off into the bush. It also might be a good reason why they have never found him, even a dead body."

"And why is that, because he found the gold and flew first class to Mexico." Ben said with a smile.

"No, wise-ass." Blessing replied. "Because the mine shafts offer the perfect cover for someone who wants to hide out. They are treacherous, to begin with, and they weave all over the place with dead ends. Would have even hidden him from the helicopter searches and the infrared cameras the police use."

"Yeah, but you can't live in there. Have to come out eventually for food or water."

"Sure, but everything written about the guy said he was a professional survivalist. Even people interviewed who knew him thought he could stay out there a long time."

Silas looked over. "Hey, I guess that's the whole reason we're on this trip, right?"

"I guess," Ben said. "His dad certainly believes it."

"Which brings me to another matter of my research," Blessing added. "If the mine is a good enough place to hide a person, it's a good enough place to hide the gold, right?"

"Ergo, our headlamps," Ben said.

"Yes, but here's the thing," Blessing replied. "Those crates that were in the plane, the bars of gold? They weigh around eighty pounds apiece. I looked it up. You're not going to be hauling that kind of weight very far down a shaft tunnel, even if you're Hulk Hogan. Too difficult."

"So, what's your point with all this research?" Silas asked. "How does this get us any closer to the DeMello kid or the gold?"

"Because," Blessing said, staring at Silas, "we don't have to go very far into any of these shaft tunnels to cross them off the list. Maybe a hundred feet tops. We're better off checking off as many open shafts and tunnels as we can for any evidence rather than wasting time or risking our lives going too far in. Capisce?"

"Alright," Silas said, nodding in agreement. "Makes sense. Now, how about the jars?"

"Jars?" Blessing asked with surprise.

Silas leaned forward and gazed over at Ben. "You didn't tell her about the jars, did you?"

Ben looked over his shoulder as he merged into the fast lane. "How far is Sault St. Marie again?"

***

Silas lifted himself slightly off the log and poked the campfire. He watched a plume of crackling embers rise and flame out. "Well, so much for your brother's late-night campfire stories." He sat back down. "It's 9:30, and he is out like a light."

Blessing was sitting on an old stump. She looked back at Ben's shadowy figure as he slept in the tent. "Yeah...don't think he realized how far this was." She turned back, leaned forward, and folded her arms. "Thanks for the sweatshirt, by the way, and I didn't know you were a Toronto Argonauts football fan."

"Hey, no problem," Silas said. "Shampoo bottles come open. And at least most of your clothes will be dry and clean in the morning."

Blessing stared at the fire. "What is it about fires that keep you so mesmerized, anyway?"

"Probably our primitive caveman roots," Silas said. He placed a log on the fire. "I would think nighttime in a forest was a pretty scary place back then without lanterns or flashlights."

"Yeah, I imagine so," Blessing said with a smile. "Thank God for the lighter."

"Or getting to know how to use a flint, as my dad would say," Silas said with a laugh.

Blessing grinned. She sat up, took a deep breath, and looked at Silas across the fire. "You really think we are going to find this guy? Find any piece of him way the hell up there in the middle of the Northern Ontario bush? Even with all those crazy jars you guys brought along?"

Silas turned over a log with his wooden poker. "To tell you the truth, I think we have a better chance of running into the Irish Rovers than finding that guy."

"Irish Rovers?"

Silas smiled. "Yeah! They sang that song 'Wasn't That a Party.' I would always hear it around St. Patrick's Day and ask, who are these guys? Then I listened to some of their music and thought they weren't half bad."

"Only you, Silas," Blessing said, laughing and shaking her head.

Silas picked up the plastic cup resting beside him on the log and took a drink of his beer. "To be honest, I really don't know what we will find. It's all pretty screwed up. I keep listening to that Nazareth tape from the jars over and over, thinking there might be some hidden message in the lyrics."

"That is weird," Blessing said as she looked back down at the fire. "It's even weirder that I agreed to come on this trip."

Silas nodded. "Yeah, now that is fucked up." He looked over at Blessing and grinned.

"Thanks for the moral support," she replied.

Silas stuck his poker into the ground. "Okay, why did you decide to come on this trip? I thought wedding plans took up all your spare time?"

"They do. When there is one to plan."

"What? When did this happen? What's going on?"

Blessing stood and stretched. "Not a conversation I want to have tonight, Silas. This trip is my reprieve from cancelling wedding hall menus and expensive flower orders."

Silas let out a breath. "Whoa, okay. Not going to argue." He reached behind him, pulled a beer out of a small cooler, and held it up to Blessing. "Sleep aid?"

She laughed. "Nope. The ride up here was enough for me. I'm done." She headed for the tent. "Put the fire out before you turn in. Don't need three people from Toronto blamed for burning a provincial park down."

***

Ben looked at his watch, which read 7 am, and poked his head into the tent. "Rise and shine, Raiders of the Lost Ark! Time for the Bennet toast breakfast special, and then let's hit the road."

Silas rose from his sleeping bag, rubbing his eyes. "Shit, I forgot what he was like amped up on coffee. He must drive the people at his work crazy."

With her eyes still closed, Blessing said, "All the people at the city planning department are amped up on coffee." She opened them and looked at Silas. "Why do you think our roads are so crooked?" She threw off her sleeping bag and stretched. "C'mon, let's get going. He will be pissed if we let his breakfast get cold."

***

Ben called out to Silas as he fueled the truck. "What the fuck is with these gas prices? We are going to be in the hole before we even reach Tear Falls. Hey, you even listening to me?"

Silas turned and came over to Ben. He crossed his arms and leaned on the truck. "You never told me the wedding was off. You just said that Mark guy was staying longer in England."

Ben finished filling the truck and placed the pump handle back. "Indefinite wedding delay, and was I supposed to?" Ben said. "Move, please."

Silas stepped aside, and Ben picked up the window squeegee. He followed Ben to the front of the truck as Ben started cleaning the windshield.

"Yeah, I think it would have been the friend thing to do, shithead." Silas said.

"Sorry, buddy. That is on a need-to-know basis."

"Oh, really?" Silas replied as he followed Ben around the front of the truck. "And what basis would that be?"

Ben stopped and faced him. "The basis of my survival." He walked a few more steps and started cleaning the passenger side of the windshield. "Hey, look. It's her business, alright? I'm not going to be the one going around blabbing about her called-off or delayed wedding. I knew she would tell you when she was ready." Ben looked closer at the windshield. "I swear to God they should use whatever is in bugs for glue."

"So, that's it, then?" Silas said. "You're going to leave me hanging on why?"

Ben pointed over Silas's shoulder with the squeegee as he watched Blessing leave the store. "There's your answer walking this way. Ask her." He placed the truck keys in Silas's hand. "And by the way, you're up for the first shift."

Silas shook his head as Blessing approached. "Let's go," she said, holding up a bag. "Survival food for the road."

Silas took his eyes off the highway for a moment to look over at Ben as he juggled the store paper bag in his hands. "Can you save some for the rest of us? Shit, it's only ten o'clock, and you have already had two bags of chips, two Mars bars, and three pixie sticks, and you've chewed through five Double Bubbles!"

Ben looked back at Silas while chewing on a big wad of gum. "Hey, I like the Bazooka Joe comics."

Blessing laughed as she opened the glove compartment and took out her flip pad. She placed it on her lap, and after glancing over her notes, she looked up. "Did you know at least four people have gone missing over the years up at this Yars Lake since the crash?"

"That supposed to make us feel better?" Silas replied.

"No, but one of them was the guy who found the plane that crashed with the gold. A guy named Pat Galverson. Described as sort of a hermit living up there. He had a cabin on Yars Lake. Rumours were he took the gold from the plane."

"Yup," Silas said. "Marty DeMello mentioned him a number of times. Would be a good man to talk to if we could find him."

"Uh…he's been missing since 1973, so I don't think that will exactly work out. But there is a name that keeps coming up in a lot of the articles about Galverson. In fact, he was a good friend of this Rick Torrison, who stole the gold and died in the crash."

"Yeah…and who would that be?" Ben asked.

"It's this guy Milt Tonkin, and I think he still lives in Tear Falls, if what I found in my search of phone numbers is correct."

Silas sat up and gripped the steering wheel. "Hey, I know that name. Marty DeMello mentioned him, too, when he was telling me the story about his brother being shot."

"Yep, that's the guy, alright," Blessing said. "So, maybe we should give him a call when we get to Tear Falls. He seems to be a common link with a lot of people in this story, missing or otherwise."

"That's a bad idea, sister," Ben said. "We have explicit instructions, in fact, contractual obligations not to breathe a word of why we are in Tear Falls, or we forfeit the money."

"Not to breathe a word about looking for Chad DeMello," Blessing replied, "but we could ask him his advice on the gold. And who knows, he could slip something in there about Chad DeMello. You never know."

"I'm sure that would go over well." Silas said. "We go knock on this guy's door and ask him for directions to the gold, and by the way, you have any comment on the whereabouts of Chad DeMello? Probably get a punch in the face."

"We don't have to go to his place," Blessing replied. She reached under some pages of her notepad and pulled out a small photocopied newspaper clipping. "That's him and his wife with some politician. They are proud new owners of a local Tear Falls restaurant called the Abby Corner café. I'm sure, if you spend some money ordering a meal, he may throw in a side order of a gold story."

Chapter 18

UNDER ADVISEMENT

"Rujoy! How are you?" Milt said loudly into the phone as he paced the back yard of his home. "How is the weather in the banana belt of Ontario?"

"I'm not going to complain, Milt. June is the best month here in Waterloo for me. Warm but not too hot," Rujoy replied. "The ice off the lake up there yet?" he asked with a laugh.

"The only ice here is now going into our drinks after some fine fishing," Milt snapped back.

"Ah, I miss that, Milt. Fresh pickerel lightly battered in seasoned flour and sautéed in an old skillet with a good helping of butter. Nobody understands that existential culinary experience down here. I need to make a trip up there soon. Is this an invite call?"

"Hey, you are welcome anytime. That goes without saying." Milt picked up his coffee and took a drink. "But I'm phoning about another matter."

"Yes...not sure if I like the sound of that, but go ahead."

"Well, we got this new sergeant up here named Jocelyn Mead, and—"

"And you have already hit her up about your Chad DeMello theory, right?"

"Of course," Milt said, "but actually, she has been a little different, Rujoy. She didn't roll her eyes at me. In fact, she read up on all the missing people and did a lot of research into Rick's story. She even mentioned some of your reports."

"Really? My reports."

"Yep, but there is something else."

"I knew there would be a punchline."

"Always is. I was talking to this guy, Rob Krylic. You remember him, right?"

"The peculiar guy who works for the MNR."

"That's the guy. The other day, he came into the Abby and started spouting off that Stinson is still searching for gold up at Yars Lake from Rick's crash. He shows me this piece of paper with crate numbers on it and says they have people sneaking around up there and looking and don't want anyone to know about it."

"Ah shit, Milt. That could be anything. Not sure I would go to the bank with what Krylic says."

"I didn't. I went to Mead."

"Wow! You have courage, Mr. Tonkin. And how did that go over with the new sergeant?"

"Well, after I told her what Krylic said, she asked why I would believe Stinson would be looking for more lost gold." Milt stopped walking and took a long drink of his coffee. Then he set the mug back on the deck. "Now, why would she say something like that, Rujoy? About more lost gold? It's almost like she knew someone found some gold, even though you told me nine years ago the police said not one bar had been recovered."

"Look, Milt. I didn't—"

"You didn't what, Rujoy? What exactly did she read in your reports? What did you write about me and the fucking gold after David DeMello nearly killed me over it?"

Rujoy took a deep breath. "Milt, I had a job to do. It was no concern of yours. It was a matter between the police and the Stinson Mine. You do remember what you said to me after all that shit, right? You gave me a lead, and I followed it."

Milt briefly looked skyward. "Fuck!" he said as he started pacing again. "Well, guess what, Rujoy? That information has been leaked to that bastard reporter Chris Berts from Hamilton.

He knows all about me having found the gold and my non-disclosure, and it's already coming back to bite my family and me in the ass. Thanks for letting me know, buddy!"

"Milt, stop being an asshole! I know nothing about any leak of your Stinson agreement to Chris Berts. I haven't been in Tear Falls for nine years, and I have been retired for three!"

"Leaked or not, why didn't you tell me you knew of my non-disclosure? Why didn't you tell me you knew I found the gold? And who cares about police policy or fucking rules? It would have been the nice-friend thing to do."

"Funny you should say that because I was wondering the same thing about a friend way back then. But I guess it was against their rules to tell me as well, right?"

Milt shook his head as he walked up his porch steps and sat down at the top. "It still hurts, Rujoy. I feel like I have been played, and it ain't a good feeling."

"Would it really have made a difference if I did tell you? You probably would have been more worried than you are right now. It was irrelevant to the police that you found the gold. What was important is it was found and it closed the fucking case and all the bullshit that went with it from the Stinson Mine."

Milt let out a long breath. "Okay, then tell me what you know about Krylic saying there is more lost gold from Rick's crash up at Yars Lake. Any police truth to that, or is Mead going to play me on that, too?"

"What part of retired didn't you get? I have no damn idea about any more gold, and I have no idea what Mead is thinking. What I do know is she is a sworn officer, Milt. She will have her reasons for conducting any investigation in a way she thinks will be in the best interest of solving a case and protecting the public. And that may or may not include you, whether you like it or not. Mead is not there to solve your personal problems or your DeMello vendettas. Get used to it!"

"Thanks for the update, counsellor. Lecture over?"

Rujoy breathed heavily into the phone. "Lecture over."

"Good. You know, she chewed me out about how I take care of Rick's mother."

"Well, somebody should. You're a shitty family man. Everyone knows that."

"No, really. She has a real problem with it. She went on and on about nursing homes and how Rick's mother doesn't belong there and Rick would have never agreed with it. That's all I need, the local Sergeant looking over my shoulder about how I care for Rick's mother."

"Shit, who cares, Milt? I could think of worse things the police could harass you for. All sergeants come with their quirks. You know that by now."

"Finally, we agree on something," Milt said, cracking a smile. He sat back. "So, give me your best sergeant and friend advice. How do I get to the bottom of all this shit? Do I confront her?"

"Well, with Mead, there is not much you can do. It's her prerogative on what to disclose about any ongoing investigations or police matters. But if it was my call and there were some unanswered questions about the crash or the gold, I would think you would be a good person to bring on my side."

"And Krylic and the story Stinson is still looking for some gold?"

"With Krylic, I would say you are on your own. He just gave you a piece of paper and a story. Short of finding it, you need more proof that the gold actually exists for Mead to take any interest. And I imagine, whatever Stinson is doing up at Yars Lake, they are not going to be knocking on your door to tell you about it. Sorry I can't be of more help on that one."

"But you're convinced my non-disclosure leak wouldn't have come from the police, from your report."

"Look, Milt. I don't want to burst your bubble, and I know it's important to you, but you're not exactly a Hollywood celebrity, and I'm thinking your non-disclosure is not a matter of national security. Why would someone with the Tear Falls police feel a need to be talking to a reporter about it? Makes no sense. What makes more sense is for you to go back to the source. Talk to Berts. In fact, use the Krylic story as bait if you have to. Even if it is bullshit about some other gold, it might be enough for him to be willing to investigate a bit further. Big payoff to him for another book if it's true, right?"

"Yeah, you are at least right on that one."

"Hey, I'm not a miracle worker. But if I know you, the digging won't stop until you hit something."

"Only my wife and true friends know that. I will take your recommendations under advisement."

"Do that. And you know what? Let me look into Mead. I will talk to some of my connections and see if I can get an idea of the type of sergeant you got running that town. Might get me back in the good books of one hell of a good Tear Falls fishing guide."

"It's a deal," Milt said with a laugh. "And keep lots of rope handy for search and rescue. Who knows how deep I can dig this fucking hole!"

***

Ron Fykes and Klaus Tritzman walked into the Tear Falls Legion Hall and looked around. "Nice little place," Fykes said with a smile. He looked at the portrait of the queen. "Makes me feel all patriotic." He spotted Dom Santtini sitting at a table at the back of the hall. "Watch this," he said. "He's got his head down, playing those fucking casino cards they sell here."

The two men made their way over to Santtini's table.

"Hey!" Fykes yelled as he brought his fist down hard on the table. Santtini jumped, and Fykes laughed. "Stop fucking gambling!"

"Jesus Christ!" Santtini said, looking up. "Don't fucking do that to me! I nearly spilled my fucking beer!"

Fykes and Tritzman sat down. "You shouldn't be fucking drinking at three in the afternoon, anyway," Fykes said. "Give your fucking liver a rest, will ya?" He gazed around the room. "So, what's up, asshole? Why the meeting? You're taking away from our searching time."

Santtini put his lottery cards in the chest pocket of his green work shirt and tilted his hat up. "I checked into a few things, and we have a problem."

"Not the first time I've heard that. Tell me what our fucking problem is."

"Krylic has been shooting his mouth off around town, spreading the rumour that Stinson has people back up at Yars Lake looking for something."

"Big fucking deal. Nobody believes anything that fucking guy says."

"Nobody except Milt Tonkin," Santtini said. He sat back and took a drink of his beer. "Krylic told him about the crates. Seems he thinks you are looking for twenty-six of them. That right?"

Fykes turned to Tritzman. "Tritzy, why don't you go get us some drinks and get our grease monkey investigative reporter here another beer?"

"Sure thing," Tritzman said. He pushed his chair back and headed for the bar.

Fykes turned back to Santtini. "What the fuck did you just say? How the fuck does Krylic know about the crates, and who is fucking telling you this?"

"My ex is friends with one of the waitresses at the Abby restaurant. Tonkin just bought that place last year. She overheard Krylic talking to Tonkin over coffee about Stinson up at Yars Lake still looking for gold. She even saw Krylic take out a piece of paper and start telling Tonkin about there being twenty-six missing crates. She saw the paper with the number circled."

"That bastard must have broken into our truck last year," Fykes said, shaking his head. "Fucking cunt."

Santtini leaned forward and rested his crossed arms on the table. "You should know something else."

"Yeah, like what?" Fykes reached into his pocket and took out his silver cigarette case. He tapped the case on the table. "Hurry up. I need a fucking smoke break."

Santtini stared over Fyke's shoulder, watching Tritzman as he talked to the waitress at the bar. Fykes turned and looked in the same direction and then turned back. "Don't worry. He will be there for a while. C'mon. Fucking talk!"

"After I heard what Krylic said, I went and talked to my friend Kenny Strites over at the Tear Falls nursing home. He was the supervisor that night when they were loading the plane in '71 that was stolen with the lost gold you are looking for. He is in a wheelchair now with those fucking oxygen tubes stuck up his nose. Guy drags one foot out of the fucking grave each day he wakes up."

"This some sort of fucking sob story?" Fykes replied. "Why do I fucking care?"

"Oh, you'll fucking care. When I told him I knew there were extra crates on that fucking plane he was loading that night, the guy starts gasping. Fucking nurse had to come over and make sure he was alright. I wheeled him back to his room and gave him a few shots of whiskey to calm his nerves, and he started to talk."

"About…? Get to the fucking point."

Santtini leaned back. "Your boss there is a fucking crook, Fykes. He had extra crates put on that plane with serial numbers that didn't match the bars in them. Those extra crates were supposed to come back to Stinson empty and be recorded like they never went out. Problem is, because of the crash, they didn't come back. He's been trying to hide the extra gold in the books for years, but that ain't going to work when they sell the company. If someone finds that gold, it ain't going to add up. That's why his nuts are in a knot about you finding it. The numbers stamped on those bars are going to lead right back to Stinson and Reese.

I imagine the people buying are going to be none too fucking pleased with that little fucking part of the deal." Santtini smirked as he took a drink. "You asked me what you fucking paid me for. I guess you just got your fucking money's worth!"

Fykes stared at Santtini as he took out a cigarette and then placed the case back in his pocket. "And what the fuck did this guy want for telling you this?"

"Nothin'," Santtini replied. "He was just scared shitless I was going to sell him out and accuse him of cooperating with Reese. The guy wants to die in peace, not in a fucking jail cell. Reese gave him a hefty bonus to keep his mouth shut."

Fykes leaned forward. "So, let me get this straight. This fucking guy is saying Reese placed extra crates on that plane that were stolen from his own mine? How many extra crates? How the fuck could Reese get away with that?"

Santtini shook his head. "I don't fucking know the pacifics."

"Specifics, numbnuts."

"Fucking whatever. All I know is Strites is telling the truth, because I fucking tested him."

"How? You got a fucking portable lie detector test?"

"I told him to write down on a piece of paper the number of crates on that plane and I would do the same. If they matched, we would know we were both telling the truth, and it fucking matched. Smart, ain't I?"

"Yeah, you're a regular fucking Einstein." Fykes said. He turned and yelled at Tritzman at the bar, "Hey, where are our drinks?" Tritzman looked back with a smile and put up his middle finger. Fykes grinned as he turned back to the table. "Fucking guy. Like to see him bring her back to your fine fucking trailer accommodations out in the bush," he said with a laugh.

Santtini smiled and took a drink. "So, what are you going to do about what I just told you? Maybe we can get us some extra money from that fucking weasel boss of yours. I could use a new generator."

"We?" Fykes said, raising his eyebrows. He leaned forward. "There is no fucking we in this shit, you lazy bastard. Never was. You just did the job I already pay you for. And I'm not worried about that asshole Krylic. I'll have a little word with him with the tip of my diving knife about his B and E into our truck. He'll shut the fuck up."

Santtini sat up. "Fuck, it ain't Krylic you should be worried about. He couldn't put a two-piece puzzle together. But Tonkin fucking can. He's like a dog with a fucking bone with his Tear Falls hero bullshit. Right from the fucking start when his best friend died in that crash. He's already dragging Mead into it, and it won't be long before he drags me, you, and Reese into the same shithole. If you want to take care of something, take care of his skinny fucking ass!"

Fykes sat back and shook his head with a smile. "Okay, asshole, what do you fucking propose?"

Santtini shrugged. "Make him worry about something else."

"Like what?"

"Like that fucking restaurant he bought last year, the Abby. Maybe it could suffer a little fire mishap that will keep his mind elsewhere."

"You volunteering?"

"I think—"

"Volunteering for what?" Tritzman asked, interrupting the conversation. He set the men's drinks on the table.

"Nothing," Fykes said as he stood. "You get your date?"

"Maybe," Tritzman said with a smile.

"Good, because we're fucking going." Fykes walked towards the door.

"Hey!" Tritzman yelled after him. "What about our drinks!"

"Give them to Mr. Capone over there. I have to make a call. Let's fucking go!"

Chapter 19

BENACIS AND BERTS

Ben looked at the map as Silas negotiated another curve on Highway 205. "Man, can they not straighten this highway out?" Silas said. "And I swear the lanes are getting narrower." He glanced at Ben. "Update, please? Who knows when we will come across another gas station."

Ben ran his finger down the map. "Well, we left the junction of the Trans-Canada about an hour ago, so according to this map, about another hour."

"Another hour? We'll be at the Arctic Circle by then!"

"Hey, take a heart pill and enjoy the scenery," Ben said. He looked out the window. "Besides, have you ever seen so many lakes and trees? I may actually have to try some fishing up here." He turned to Blessing, who was staring out the passenger window. "What'd you say, B? Ready to be on the Bob Izumi show?"

Ben's comment was met with silence, so Silas leaned forward to glance at Blessing. "Hey, Ms. Blessing! This northern air lull you to sleep?"

Blessing turned back to Ben and Silas. "GAAP," she said.

"What?" Silas replied.

"Don't worry," Ben said to him. "She had too much root beer at the A&W back there."

"I think you did when you bought those A&W mugs!" Silas replied. He looked over at Blessing. "What are you talking about, B? What gap?"

Blessing undid her seat belt, reached into the back seat, and grabbed back her briefcase.

"Oh, shit! Here we go!" Ben said, dipping his head to avoid the swinging case.

Blessing unsnapped the case on her lap and took out some papers. "GAAP stands for generally accepted accounting principles. It's what publicly traded companies like Stinson must follow when issuing their financial statements."

"MBA helicopter inbound!" Ben said, laughing.

"Will you let her finish." Silas said. "So, what about it, B? What's that got to do with anything?"

Blessing held up some papers. "I was able to get the Stinson public financial statements from 1971 to 1991 faxed to me from the Tear Falls library. And here is what is interesting. Stinson said they recovered the gold after the crash in 1971, but if you look at their financial statements from that year, you see a special capital loss charge of hundreds of thousands of dollars. That means they didn't find anything."

"So, what that Berts guy wrote in his book was right, then," Silas replied. "Shit, no wonder people have still been searching for the gold."

"Well, maybe not," Blessing said.

"Okay, sis, are you purposely trying to confuse us?" Ben asked, raising his eyebrows.

"Nope, just listen." Blessing flipped to another piece of paper. "This is their financials for 1973, and guess what shows up?"

"Picture of Chad DeMello? Shit, I don't know," Silas said. "What?"

"A special capital gain of three hundred thousand dollars, but it's about half of the original loss from '71." She placed both pieces of paper on the dash. "So, they must have found something." She turned to the two men. "Just not all of it."

"Okay, but how do you know that was the gold?" Ben asked. "Maybe it was some expensive piece of mining machinery that fell down a shaft."

"And then they found it again two years later?" Blessing said. "No way! These types of entries could only be from the lost gold, and these statements are proof a good chunk is still out there."

"Fucking MBAs are worth all the money," Silas said.

"That's not what—"

"That's exactly what I have always said," Silas said, cutting Ben off. He sat up in his seat and looked in the rear-view mirror. "Jesus!"

"What?" Ben asked, leaning forward and looking in the passenger-side mirror.

"Cops!"

Blessing snapped her briefcase shut and threw it in the back seat. "Get rid of these, too!" Ben said, grabbing the papers on the dash and stuffing them in the glove compartment. "Okay, just relax and pull over somewhere. Remember, this is my truck. Don't want it impounded."

Silas spotted a gravel parking area by a small lake and signalled out the window to the flashing truck behind. He drove another five hundred feet and pulled over.

"Were you speeding?" Blessing asked as they waited in the truck.

"Don't think so," Silas replied, shutting off the truck.

A moment later, he was startled by a tap on his window.

"Can you roll down your window, please?" the officer asked.

Silas turned the key halfway and pushed the button to bring the window down. "Was I speeding?" he asked. He looked more closely at the officer's uniform.

"I'm not here for speeding," Rob Krylic said. He pulled out a card and handed it to Silas. "I'm with the Ministry of Natural Resources. Vehicle conservation spot check. Want to make sure no hunting or fishing laws are being broken. Where you coming from?" He peered at Ben and Blessing.

"All the way from Toronto," Silas said. "Up to experience the Great White North and try our luck at fishing," he added with a smile.

"Uh-huh," Krylic replied. He looked over the truck. "Extended cab. Nice!" He turned back to Silas. "You all have your fishing licenses?"

Silas glanced at Ben and Blessing. "Uh...well...not yet. We were going to get them up here."

"Mind stepping out of the truck?"

Silas opened his door as Blessing and Ben did the same.

"Why don't you three just take a seat on that log over there while I take a look at the truck."

Blessing raised her eyebrows as she walked with Ben and Silas to the log. The three sat down, and Ben whispered, "Does he have the authority to do that?"

"Not sure," Silas replied, stretching his legs out. "But keep an eye on him."

Krylic walked around to the passenger side of the truck. He opened the passenger door and looked inside. After scanning the back seat, he popped the glove compartment and rummaged through the contents.

"Sir?"

Krylic was surprised as Blessing came up behind him. He turned around. "Ma'am, I asked you to stay over there."

"I know, but I figure I can help speed this up if you tell us what you are looking for."

"Well, I'm looking for any signs of overfishing, illegal hunting. Even banned produce."

"Banned produce...? Really? Isn't that a border thing?"

"Can be," Krylic replied with a shrug. "If you just open up the back tailgate for me, you can be on your way."

Blessing glanced at Ben and waved him over. She pointed to the rear of the truck, and he met Krylic there. "Just our packs," he said as he unlocked the cap and lowered the tailgate. "No dead moose." He joked, but Krylic ignored him.

Krylic stepped forward and examined their gear. "Those helmets?"

"Yeah," Silas replied as he joined the group. "Specialized for rock climbing."

"Rock climbing…in Tear Falls?" Krylic said. "Can't say I have a lot of people come here for that."

"Ah…you don't need Mount Everest to enjoy a good climb," Silas replied. "I think there are a number of rock faces along some of the lakes around here that will do the trick. Think we'll combine it with the great fishing."

"To each his own." Krylic pulled forward a box containing the tops of the canning jars. "You plan on making a lot of jam while you're here as well?" He was reaching out to pick up a jar when Blessing lurched forward and placed a hand on his arm. "Please don't touch those, sir!"

"And why is that?" he replied, eyeing her hand.

"Well, I bought those jars for my aunt to can her Italian benacis. The jars have been specially sterilized. She says even fingerprints can contaminate them." She gave Krylic a big smile.

Krylic removed his hand. "Well, certainly don't want your aunt to be tracking me down for that," he said with a laugh. He pushed the box back in. "Okay, close it up. Just a routine check. You are free to go."

"Thanks, officer," Silas said.

He walked back to the front of the truck and jumped in, followed by Blessing and Ben. They waited until Krylic drove away.

"Italian aunt?" Silas said, looking over at Blessing. He started the truck. "And what the fuck is a benaci?"

"I don't know," Blessing said with a smile. "But it sounds pretty Italian to me!"

Silas turned the truck around and pulled back onto the highway. "I'll quote you the next time I order a meal at an Italian restaurant."

***

Roddy swung his white bar towel over his green plaid bush shirt and sat in the booth. He stared at Milt. "So, why is it you use my establishment for your clandestine meetings and not your own restaurant?"

"Because you have a well stocked bar to calm my nerves," Milt quipped back. "Coffee just doesn't cut it for meetings like these." He looked up as Tracy placed a bottle of Labatt Blue in front of him on the table.

"Thanks, Tracy," he said.

"Anytime, Milt," Tracy replied. "Wave for refills."

"Always do." Milt turned back to Roddy. "And it ain't exactly clandestine, if you care to look around."

Roddy nodded as he watched people standing at the bar for takeout orders and the lunch crowd filling the tables. "Yeah, I guess you're right," he said with a smile. He leaned back and brushed the seat of the booth. "You know, it was this very booth that I sat in when I talked to Rick over twenty years ago about how to try and help his mother. All that hospital bed and wheelchair shit." Roddy ran his hand across the top of his head. "The only difference then was I didn't have some of this grey hair."

"Shit, at least you still have all yours," Milt said, laughing. "Kristen reminds me every day I should use that crap they advertise on TV. You remember how long my hair used to be, Rod? Rick would be laughing his fucking head off if he could see this pathetic turf I got going now."

"That he would, Milt," Roddy said with a grin. He leaned forward, and his grin disappeared. "Milt, it's probably none of my fucking business—"

"But you are going to make it your fucking business," Milt interrupted.

"Yeah…I guess you're right."

"Fire away."

"Well, you really knocked my socks off when you told me you found the gold and all this other shit now coming from Krylic, but do you really think this is the right way to go? To be meeting with this guy? You could be making it a lot worse. I mean, you have a reputation and a business to run."

Milt crossed his arms and leaned on the table. "That's exactly the point, Rod. I wanted you and Oakey and my closest friends to hear things from me first. Berts is going to come out with it sooner or later anyway. Think it might be in my best interest to try and do it on my terms. You know how rumours fly around this fucking town. By the time it's finished, I will be lumped in with the DeMellos."

"And Mead told you to fuck off about Krylic? She doesn't believe you about his story?"

"Basically. She told me some Constable Devon might look into Krylic, but I've got a gut feeling she doesn't believe me about a lot of fucking things, including how I take care of Rick's mother. No other reason she would have held back on telling me she knew about my non-disclosure. Nope, as Rujoy said, I need more than Krylic's stories. I need someone to give me some real proof Stinson has gold out there. Or Mead won't budge."

"And you think this Berts guy can get you this? The proof?"

Milt looked over Roddy's shoulder and pointed in the direction of the bar. "Soon find out. That's him over there, ordering a drink. Short, bald guy with the jean jacket."

Roddy looked in the direction of the bar. "Hefty fella, ain't he! Maybe he should back off on the drinks." Roddy stood and gave the table a quick wipe. "Good luck, my friend. I'm in the kitchen if you need me to throw him out," he said with a smile. He walked away as Chris Berts approached.

"Milt, my good man!" Berts said as he placed a beer in front of Milt and a glass of whiskey on the other side of the table and sat down. He reached across the table and shook Milt's hand. "Always a pleasure!"

"Wish I could say the same," Milt said, reaching out for a quick shake. "But I guess it says something that you made the trip up all the way from Hamilton. You sneak the plane ticket in on the *Hamilton Watch* newspaper's dime?"

"That paper doesn't have a dime, so there is no sneaking to be had," Berts said. He took a drink of his whiskey and then held the glass up for an examination. "Ah, Forty Creek! Nice to see the NearNorth has good taste." He set the glass down and crossed his arms across his thick stomach. "Nope, this is my doing, my money, Milt. Lucky if I can get that paper to pay for my fucking pen, let alone a flight. Speaking of which, why the fuck does it cost so much to fly on that Twin Otter into Tear Falls and lose your hearing at the same time? Does that seem reasonable to you?"

"Fucked if I know." Milt replied, taking a drink of his beer. "Probably because people like you from Southern Ontario don't understand two-way traffic."

Berts laughed. "Not bad! Mind if I quote that in my next book?"

"I imagine you will anyway," Milt replied.

"Probably," Berts said, taking another sip. He placed his glass down and then gave the table a light tap with his knuckle. "So, who is going to go first? You said you have a proposal for me and probably my next book. I'm open to both if things are right."

Milt sat up. "Well, you're going to publish a story about my non-disclosure agreement with Stinson, right? That's what you are going to do whether I like it or not?"

"I don't think I have a choice, Milt. It's pretty big news." Berts took out a piece of paper from the chest pocket of his jacket and threw it on the table. "This confirms everything I was thinking from the get-go. Stinson was lying that they found the gold in '71. Shit, the fucking police were lying. All I want is your side of the story, and I promise I will be fair."

"You're going to be fucking fair? Now, there's a fucking stretch!" Milt said with a smile, and he sat back. "Like when you wrote about my friend Rick? You made him out to be an arch criminal. Out for nothing but money. Not a word about him trying to help his dying mother."

Berts shook his head. "Christ, Milt. C'mon, I thought we left all the hostilities on the phone. Is this what this meeting is all about? I flew all the way up here so you can sit there and beat up on me on what I wrote about your friend?"

Milt smirked. "Maybe." He paused and took a deep breath. "Okay, then who is it, Berts? You must have some fucking thoughts on the matter. Stinson? The police?"

"Milt, you're raising a flag up the wrong pole. Like I told you on the phone, I have no idea who this person is. All they sign is the letter B, whatever that means. Could all be a ruse, for all I fucking know." Berts picked up the piece of paper. "What I do know is this is a big fucking deal! This amounts to a cover-up, maybe police collusion, and it would be nice to know fucking why." Berts threw the paper back on the table. "So, are you going to help me, or am I going to tape that to the Stinson Mine gate tomorrow morning and wait for them to call?"

Milt glanced at the paper and then back at Berts. "You know, you are a fucking bastard. Go ahead, do what you want, but it won't get you the fucking story. I'll deny it, say it was some kind of fucking forgery. You think Stinson is really going to cooperate with you? Nah, you need me, Berts, and maybe…and I'm having some second thoughts right about now…I might need you."

Berts lifted his glass and swallowed hard as he finished his drink. He set the glass down and stared at Milt. "You conduct all your business dealings this way?"

Milt shrugged. "I dish out what I receive. Seems fair to me."

Berts slowly nodded. "Okay…alright…I get it. Fuck what I just said. You tell me what you want me to do. Tell me your offer for your side of the story, and I will try and do it—within the confines of the law, if you please."

Milt reached forward and gripped his beer. "I want you to tell Rick's story…the right way. And I want you to investigate this Conrad Reese guy and expose the Stinson Mine for the lying piece of shit they are. I want all those cocksucking people involved in this crap to go to jail. They're worse than the fucking DeMellos."

"Is that all? Maybe you want to elaborate, because I see a big jump from you signing a NDA, which I assume was to your benefit, and there being proof to throw someone from Stinson in jail."

"Are you fucking agreeing to tell Rick's story or not? All the details of him trying to save his dying mother? If that's the deal, then I will tell you enough to make your next book put fucking John Grisham to shame."

"Never liked John Grisham, but I'm definitely intrigued. And if what you tell me about your friend Rick is true, I will write every word. Promise." Berts stretched his arm across the table and watched as Milt studied his open hand. "Best I can do, Milt. I don't have any other agreements in my pocket."

Milt reached out and shook Bert's hand.

Over at the bar, Roddy snuck up on Tracy from behind and said, "What's your assessment?" as he peered in the direction of Milt's booth.

She set the glass she was wiping on the counter. "Well, I just saw them shaking hands, so it can't be all that bad. Who is that guy, anyway?" she asked, looking over her shoulder at Roddy.

"Chris Berts from Hamilton. The guy who wrote *The Torrison Treasure* on Rick's crash. Kind of an asshole, but apparently, Milt feels he could use his help on a matter. Just hope it works out."

"Ah...I see. Chad DeMello?"

"Probably somewhere in the conversation if I know Milt, but I think it has more to do with Rick and the gold. I will let Milt explain it to you." Roddy pulled out a bottle of Forty Creek from under the bar. "In the meantime, it looks like our guest might be running a little dry." He poured a shot of whiskey into a glass and headed for the booth. "I'll take care of this one."

Roddy placed the drink on the table and watched Berts scribble on a notepad with his head down. "Hope I'm not interrupting anything!" he bellowed.

Berts looked up, startled, as Roddy pointed at the glass of whiskey on the table. "On the house!" he said with a smile.

Berts nodded and pulled the glass closer. "Well...I've never considered Forty Creek an interruption."

"You're Chris Berts, right?" Roddy said as he put out his hand. "I'm Roddy Simone, the owner of this place. You wrote The *Torrison Treasure*. It was a good book!"

"Yeah, that's right," Berts replied, gripping Roddy's hand. "And thanks for the read. Happy you enjoyed it."

"Hey, anybody from Southern Ontario that thinks Tear Falls is worth writing about can't be all that bad."

Berts laughed. "Glad I made the cut!"

"Well, don't let me interfere in a good conversation. Just wanted to bring you over a refill." Roddy turned to Milt. "You good, Mr. Tonkin?"

Milt looked up and smiled. "Yes...yes, I am, Mr. Simone. Thanks for asking."

"Good. Just holler for anything more." Roddy picked up Berts's empty glass and winked at Milt as he headed back to the bar.

Berts closed up his notepad, returned his pen to his chest pocket, and sat back. "I think I have enough, Milt. And you're right. This would make one hell of a book." He leaned forward. "But I'm afraid I need more to go on if we're to make a deal."

"More to go on?" Milt said with a rising voice.

"Easy," Berts replied, putting his hands up. "Unless you want the entire bar in on this."

Milt glanced around and then repositioned himself with his arms crossed on the table. "I thought more to go on was your fucking job. Why did I tell you all this?"

"Look, Milt, don't take it personally, but all I got from you is a story you heard from this Krylic guy, someone whose name you said is the very definition of bullshit. Where's the proof this extra gold exists?" Berts picked up the piece of paper. "But this, Milt, is our bird in the hand. We can still get Stinson on a lot of crap with just this agreement."

Milt grabbed the paper out of Bert's hand. "Fuck the agreement! It means nothing! Stinson will weasel their way out of this paper and probably drag me with it. They'll blame Sergeant McIntyre, who is now dead. They'll blame the fucking pilots, the people that loaded the plane. Who the fuck knows? They'll even blame fucking Rick for not counting the crates." Milt threw the paper back. "This is a crime that killed my friend. Use your reporter magic, for Christ's sake!"

Berts studied the wrinkled paper and then looked up. "What did you say?"

Milt finished his beer and pushed the bottle to the end of the table. "Fucking forget it. Do what you have to do. I'll figure it out." Milt moved to the end of the booth.

"No, wait, Milt! Don't go!"

"What?"

"You said the people that loaded the plane. What people? You know these people?"

"I know the guy who was the supervisor for the loading that night. His name is Kenny Trites. He is in a room down from Rick's mom at the nursing home. Why?"

"Because he might talk, Milt. He would know if something was unusual in the shipment that night. Too many crates!"

"Yeah? And why would he have not said something by now, Sherlock?"

Berts laughed. "People have all sorts of motivations for doing or not doing things, Milt. That's at least one thing I have learned in this business. Let me speak to him and anyone else I can find. Maybe I can work my reporter magic, and we can reach a deal... for Christ's sake!"

Milt nodded with a smile. "The reporter magic...I guess it's worth a try. And that's all I'm fucking asking." He stood. "You can call me at the Abby if you come up with anything."

Berts took out his pad of paper and wrote down a number. He ripped off the sheet and handed it to Milt. "That's my cell number. I'm staying at the Vicster bed and breakfast off of Old Silver Pines Road. Retired teacher who bought—"

"Yeah, I know who she is," Milt said, looking at the number. "You forgot what town you are in, Berts." Milt took the paper and ripped off a piece. "Give me your pen." He wrote down a number and handed it back to Berts. "That's my cell number. Call if your magic comes up with anything. Maybe I will do the same if I feel it's worth it."

"Fair enough," Berts replied.

Milt took out his wallet and threw some bills on the table. "Oh, and by the way, you might want to match that tip," he said, pointing at the money.

"Oh, and why is that?" Berts asked, chuckling.

Milt leaned on the table. "Well, if you are ever in here at night and a fight breaks out, Mr. Simone over there can be selective about who he decides to save."

Milt broke out in a big smile. He then turned, waved at Roddy, and left the restaurant.

Chapter 20

TEAR FALLS

Ben stared straight out the front windshield as Silas drove slowly down the main highway through Tear Falls. "Seems like an okay place. At least we know they produce green energy with that hydro dam we crossed. Quaint."

Silas glanced at Ben. "How can it not be quaint? Did you see that sign back there? Population eleven hundred. What happens when there is a wedding? Half the town shows up?"

Blessing, who had been looking out the passenger window, turned to face Silas. "At least someone is having a wedding."

Ben forced a smile. Silas returned the expression but remained silent.

Blessing rolled down her window and rested her arm on the door ledge. "But hey, at least no traffic jams, and you gotta love these small-town store names." She pointed out the window. "Cassandra's Arts and Crafts, Becker Pharmacy, Riley Hardware…"

"Oh…hold on!" Silas pumped the brakes and steered the truck hard off the highway and into a gravel parking lot. A cloud of dust floated over the cab as the truck came to a stop in front of a store.

Blessing coughed and covered her mouth. "Silas, what the hell are you doing?"

Silas pointed up at the building sign. "A and T Outdoor Supplies!" He turned to Blessing and Ben. "DeMello said we should look like we belong. Then let's do it and get our pro fishing gear." He jumped out of the truck before Ben or Blessing could respond.

Inside the store, Silas picked up a fishing pole from a display in the store and examined it. "Where is Blessing?" he asked as Ben walked up.

"She's over at the souvenir clothes racks." Ben stretched his head above the display and looked over Silas's shoulder. "Don't look now, but here comes the sales pitch." he whispered.

Silas turned to see a man approaching, wearing a short-sleeved yellow cotton shirt, brown dress shorts, and strapped black leather sandals. The man placed his hands on his hips and flashed them a big smile. "Just in time, gentlemen! We just started our cast-into-summer sale." He stared at the fishing pole Silas was holding as Silas stared back at the man's shirt logo of a crossed fishing rod and gun, bordered on either side by a jumping fish and moose.

"All of these are on sale?" Silas asked, turning his attention back to the display rack.

The man stepped forward and took out a pole. "Every last one," he said, flexing the fishing rod. He placed it back in the rack and then looked at Silas. "Every one except the Titan X47. That expensive fishing rod is usually snapped up by professionals or guides looking to impress. And by the way, my name is Adam." He reached out and shook Silas's hand. "You boys have anything in mind?"

Ben came from around the display to join Silas. "Do you have any...like...starter kits?"

The salesman tried to contain a smile. "I don't know if you would call them starter kits, but we do have some rod and reel and tackle sets all ready to go. Why don't you fellas make your way over to the front sales counter, and I will bring some out from the back?"

Ben and Silas nodded and followed the salesman's directions to the front of the store. Silas rested his hands on the glass counter and said as he gazed at items in the display case, "See, I told you they know what they are talking about up here. This guy will get us all set up." He moved sideways a few steps and stared closer. "Uh-oh."

Ben looked over. "What?"

Silas tapped his finger on the glass. "Sony Handycam. But that can't be right. Says 350. Those go for twice that in Toronto."

Ben came up beside Silas. "Maybe it was frozen in the snow."

"Almost," Adam said as he came around the other side of the display, holding some fishing rods and a small tackle box. He placed the items on the counter. "That, my friends, was brought in by a man from out of town who said it was a gift for his outdoor hikes up here. Said it was useless and traded it in for bug spray, two pairs of rubber boots, and a long fishing knife."

"Shit, I would take that trade," Silas said. He looked up. "Can I take a look at it?"

Ben creased his brow. "Silas, can we stick with the fishing rods? We're going to spend more than we make if you keep this up."

Adam took out the camera and placed it on the counter. "It's got the low-light mode too. In case you want to record a Sasquatch walking by your tent or something," he said with a grin.

Blessing came up behind the two men and placed an armful of sweatshirts and t-shirts on the counter. "Hey, what's that? You guys buying a camera?"

Ben turned and eyed the stack of clothes. "Jesus! We're going to go bankrupt on the first day!"

Adam interjected. "Look, why don't I give you a package deal for all this and a written, seven-day money-back guarantee. If you are not happy with the camera or anything else, even after you use it for a week, bring it back. You know where to find me."

Silas looked at Ben and then returned his gaze to the video camera.

"Hey, don't look in my direction," Ben said, raising his hands. "My small instant camera is good enough for me. Not sure what use lugging that thing around is going to be."

Silas reached past Ben and slid Blessing's clothes pile closer. He reached into his back pocket, pulled out his wallet, and took out his credit card. "You guys go out to the truck. I'll take care of this. We'll split everything up later." He turned to Adam. "Now, let's make a deal."

***

Fykes sat in his truck in the NearNorth parking lot and lit up a cigarette. He looked at his watch, which said that it was just after 10 am. He flipped his cell phone open, hit redial, and placed it to his ear.

"Conrad Reese."

"Hey, did I drag your sorry ass out of bed, Mr. Reese?" Fykes said, laughing.

"Yeah, my sorry ass is on the thirty-second floor, enjoying a nice coffee in my housecoat and a view of the blue ocean. You got something for me, or do you just like hearing yourself fucking talk?"

"Right...well...you may want to grab something stronger there, because some things have come to light here that change this whole fucking game. Actually, your fucking game. You ever heard of a guy named Kenny Trites?"

Reese stood and went out onto the balcony and he sat in a chair. "How do you know fucking Kenny Trites? He come to fucking see you or something?"

"Thought so."

"You thought what?"

"That you fucking knew him." Fykes took another drag of his cigarette. "I want more money, Reese. A lot more fucking money for finding the gold."

"You think—"

"Shut the fuck up! I don't want to hear your shit anymore! I want fifty grand deposited into my account tomorrow! And that's just the fucking start!" Fykes sat up in his seat. "Do you know what is going to happen to you if that gold is traced back to you? If Trites now decides to talk to the cops? Santtini just mentioned he knew about the missing crates, and he nearly shit his pants. No fucking way is he going to keep quiet. You better hope we find it before someone else does!"

"You want fifty grand, you steroid-shooting fucking junkie? Fuck You! Fucking find it first. And Trites is a fucking piece-of-shit liar whose brain rotted out long ago. Fuck him! Let him say whatever he fucking wants!"

"Whatever you say, Reese. Whatever you say…but I'm parking my truck and my ass until I see something come through in numbers. No more bullshit!"

Reese stood and walked to the edge of the balcony. "That's right. Whatever I say. You want to play games with someone like fucking Trites? See where it fucking gets you. Thinking maybe I'll cut your pay so you can spend a fucking winter freezing in Canada for once instead of tanning your ass off at that bullshit thing you call a job down south. Get it fucking done!"

Reese clicked off his phone. He leaned on the railing and stared out at the harbour. "Fucking prick." He walked back into his condominium and headed for his office. There he sat down at his desk, poured himself a drink from a bottle in the side drawer, and then dialed a number.

"Where are you?" Reese asked when a man answered.

"Oh, Mr. Reese, how are you? I'm at work," the man answered. "Shitty Saturday paperwork catch-up."

"Really. Well, I'm going to make it even shittier for you. Kenny Trites has talked."

"To who?"

"To some fucking guy named Santtini who passed the information onto my nephew. Now my nephew is using Trites as a fucking way to try and extort more money out of me for the gold."

"Shit!"

"You got to go see my nephew and do something about this."

"Like what, Mr. Reese? Is he still staying out at the trailer on Saphora Lake?"

"Like something to keep him preoccupied. Cite him for some bullshit wildlife thing. Pull the plug on the fucking trailer. I don't fucking know. Just do something to keep him busy until I talk to Trites."

"Mr. Reese. I'm not sure—"

"Listen... Bobby. Or does that name rub you the wrong fucking way. Do you know what we are dealing with here? You come up with a plan or your payments to the DeMellos stop tomorrow. You stall my nephew from searching for the gold until I straightened Trites out!"

"I...I do have a plan, Mr. Reese. I have a good lead on the gold. I'm going up to Yars Lake tomorrow to check it out. Fuck your nephew, and fuck Trites. I'll get this done."

Reese sat and finished his drink. "You better have a plan. Otherwise, I hand your nuts over to the DeMellos to swing from a fucking pine tree up there. You understand, Mr. MNR officer?"

"Understood." Krylic replied as he heard the phone go dead. He set the receiver down and stared at the paperwork.

"Fuck!" he yelled as he swung his arm across the desk, sweeping the papers to the floor. He stood and walked over to a steel office cabinet. Then he opened the door, took out a tranquilizer rifle, and grabbed a leather pouch filled with darts. He walked back to his desk, threw the pouch on his chair, and checked the rifle's sight. "Twenty-four hours! That's all I'm fucking giving them!"

Chapter 21

LIQUID MOON

"Here you go, Oakes!" Milt said, sliding a beer over to Oakey on the other side of the long table. He placed a small plastic glass of white wine in front of Kristen and sat beside her on a laminated wooden chair. "Fuck, can the Legion not bring out better chairs for these socials? You need an ass of steel to sit on these things!"

"They should invest in better air conditioning," Stu Fields said. "Fucking hot in here."

Stu's wife, Melissa, frowned at him from across the table. "How about taking off the leather jacket, cool guy. It is June, you know."

Stu smiled and took a drink of his beer, raising his eyebrows at Milt.

Milt laughed as he leaned on the table. He turned to Kristen. "Who's this shindig for, again? Who's getting married?"

"Myles Lefevre and Carolynne Rula," Kristen replied. "Look at your ticket. And don't start complaining about the loud music. We're here for a fundraiser. People did the same for us in our younger years."

"I won't complain about the music," Milt said. "It's Sound Explosion playing the tunes. Calvin Erst has been doing these things forever, even if his playlist is ten years out of date."

He looked over at the door. "And look at this... Here come the out-of-towners." He took out a five-dollar bill. "Can I borrow your pen, Stu?"

"Me first!" Stu replied. He wrote a number on a five-dollar bill, placed it in a plastic cup in the centre of the table, and then handed the pen to Milt.

"Yeah…and how do you know these people are out-of-towners?" he asked, looking in the same direction.

"C'mon, Stu," Oakey said. "You think those two young guys and that girl buying tickets at the drink table are from around here?"

"Why," Kristen asked, "because two of them look Asian?" She turned in her seat and glared at Oakey.

"Nope," Oakey replied, "because all of them have on those stupid souvenir t-shirts Adam Stems sells at his store."

***

"Well, this is one way to get an idea of the local culture," Blessing said as she scanned the room.

Silas came up beside her and placed some drink tickets in her hand. "You really think you're going to blend in just because you have that Tear Falls t-shirt on? The black designer jeans give you away, Ms. Toronto."

"Hey, you're not doing much better. Cargo shorts, new hiking boots, and your t-shirt?"

"Yeah, but I have a story. I just came back from the Himalayas," Silas replied, smiling. He spotted some open chairs. "Let's grab those. Halfway between the music and the bar can't be all that bad." He waved at Ben at the drink ticket table to follow them.

***

Oakey rolled up his own signed five-dollar bill and placed it in the plastic cup. "So, how did that meeting go with you know who?" he asked, looking over at Milt.

"It went," Milt said, taking a drink of his beer. "Met him at the NearNorth. He's going to use his supposed reporter skills to look into things. Says Krylic could be fucking bullshitting. Starting to think the same if I don't come up with something soon to say otherwise."

"You still want me to talk to him with ya? Make sure he is telling the truth? We could tranquilize him with his own fucking gun and beat it out of him," Oakey said with a laugh.

"Ah, don't think it makes much difference with Krylic. Doped up or not, he would still bullshit. And no use trying to go back to Mead or confront Stinson unless I can get more proof."

Stu leaned in. "So, basically, you're fucked," he said with a smile. "Finding Chad DeMello doesn't seem all that bad now, does it?"

"Thanks for the fucking support, Stu. Why did I even tell you?"

"Because I do give you support. Beer support," Stu replied, raising his beer.

Kristen interrupted by grabbing Milt's hand. "Greg Khin Band, 'The Breakup Song'! Let's dance!"

Milt threw some drink tickets over to Oakey as Kristen pulled him up. "More beers, Oakes! It's going to be a long night!"

***

Ben slumped down in his chair and looked at his watch, which read 12:45 am. He reached into his pocket and handed Blessing the truck keys. "All yours."

Blessing took the keys and shook her head. "Thought so." She looked over at Silas, who was leaning heavily on the side of the table with his forearm as he glanced around the room. He faced Ben and Blessing. "You know, these people really know how to party...and fight!"

"And drink," Blessing said. "Glad you two did your best to keep up."

Silas raised his bottle. "Hey, last taste of civilization before we go out into the wild gold yonder." He tilted it high and finished his beer. "Well, I got to take a piss," he said, setting the bottle down.

"Thanks for the update!" Blessing yelled as Silas rose and headed for the washroom.

***

Milt took the five-dollar bills out of the plastic jar. "Let's see. Oakey had 11:35. Stu, you were the early bird at 10:45. I had 11:15, and yup, looks like Melissa, you are the winner at 12:10 because I do believe the fight started at about 12:05." Milt pushed the money over to her. "Congratulations!"

"You shouldn't indulge them in their childish games, Melissa," Kristen said. She turned to Milt. "Ready to go there, Mr. I Didn't Want to Come Here in the First Place?"

"Yup," Milt replied. "Bathroom break first."

He walked into the bathroom, and as he stepped over to the urinal, he gazed at the man beside him and read his t-shirt out loud: "Tear Falls. We got the power." He laughed. "Good one!"

Silas smiled back. "Yeah, a souvenir from a store here in town. I'll see if people from Toronto can figure it out."

"Toronto, eh? And what brings you to our neck of the woods?"

Both men walked to the sinks to wash their hands. "Just some R and R camping," Silas said. He punched out some soap from the dispenser. "Going up to a place called Yars Lake. Supposed to be a good spot to catch some fish. Got my Titan X47 all set up and ready to go."

Milt took a moment to look down at Silas's new hiking boots. Then, as he stepped over to the towel dispenser, he said over his shoulder, "Titan X47...all strung up to catch some little ol pickerel. You must have been at Adam Stem's store." He turned back and pushed his paper towel through the swinging lid of a garbage can.

"Yeah, well—"

Silas was cut off as the bathroom door swung open with a loud bang and a voice boomed out. "Holy fuck!" A man stumbled in. He came up to the garbage can and slapped Milt's hand in a cupped shake. "Milt fucking Tonkin! What the fuck are you doing here? I thought new owners of restaurants never came out on the weekends."

"Hey, Matt," Milt replied, manufacturing a smile. "We sneak out when we can. Where are you these days?" He grabbed a few more paper towels and handed them to Silas.

Matt slouched and leaned his back against a sink. "Ah, fuck, Milt. Still at the fucking town dump. But hey, it's a fucking job, and I'm learning to speak black bear!" He laughed as he pushed off the sink and headed for the urinal. "But don't let me interrupt, gentlemen. Nature calls!"

Milt raised his eyebrows at Silas as the two men left the bathroom. As he turned to leave for his table, Silas said, "You're Milt Tonkin, the owner of the Abby Cafe?"

Milt stopped. "Yeah, that's right. Shit, I must be doing something right if people from Toronto have heard of the Abby."

Silas turned to see Ben and Blessing staring at him. He turned back to Milt. "Mr. Tonkin, can you come over and meet my two friends from Toronto? They have heard lots about the Abby."

***

Kristen watched Milt take an abrupt right and follow Silas over to his table. She shook her head. "Okay, now what is he up to? Who is he with?"

Stu stood and took his leather jacket from the back of his chair. "Who knows, Kristen? Maybe he is going to give out coupons for the Abby at their table for a free morning breakfast. But sorry, I can't stick around to find out. Marina opens at seven tomorrow."

Melissa rose and pushed a drink ticket over to Kristen. "Still a few minutes till last call." She smiled.

"Thanks," Kristen replied. "I may use it to bribe my husband to leave."

Melissa laughed as she and Stu waved goodbye to Kristen and Oakey and left for the door. Oakey pulled a chair in front of Kristen and turned his head in Milt's direction. "What the hell is he talking to them about? You want me to break it up?"

Kristen slid her drink ticket over to Oakey without breaking her gaze on Milt. "No. I'm sure Calvin is about to play 'Stairway to Heaven' for the final song. In the meantime, why don't you go over and use this for last call, Oakey? No harm in being prepared."

***

Milt sat back in his chair and smiled. "Well, I appreciate the fan club, guys, and I figured you three were not exactly up here for the fishing, but as much as some people may give another story, there is no proof any missing gold is up there." He leaned forward. "But hey, it's not bad for tourism, wouldn't you say?" He grinned, slapped the table, and stood. "Enjoy your stay in Tear Falls."

"But we do have proof!" Blessing blurted out.

Ben flashed a surprised look at her. "Uh…I don't know if you should bring that up," he said.

"Why? It's public knowledge. Anybody can find it if they know what they are looking for."

Milt cast a confused gaze at Blessing and Ben. "Find what?" he asked, supporting himself on the back of the chair. "And what exactly is public knowledge?"

Ben let out a long breath. "Go for it, B."

Silas looked up at Milt. "Sit down, Mr. Tonkin. You might want to take some notes."

Milt sat, and Silas pushed a beer over to him. "Haven't touched it."

***

"Oh…there it is! 'Stairway to Heaven'!" Oakey said, laughing. "Calvin never misses a beat."

"Yeah, you would think he could have at least changed that song from twenty years ago," Kristen replied. She looked in Milt's direction. "Damn it!"

"What?" Oakey asked, turning in his chair. "He's not moving?"

"The young lady just left, and Milt just sat down again." She shook her head and sat back. "What am I going to do with this guy, Oakey?" She glanced up at the hall clock, which read 1 am.

"Now that, I don't know, but I think we are being hailed."

Kristen looked back to see Milt waving frantically and signalling for them to come over.

She stood and picked up her wine. "I knew this would come in handy." She finished the glass. "Let's go, Oakey. Can't wait to see what this is all about."

As Kristen and Oakey approached, Milt pointed to some chairs with his beer. "Have a seat. I'd like you to meet Silas and Ben from Toronto. And their friend, Blessing, has gone out to their truck to get some papers."

Kristen sat down beside Milt and smiled at Ben and Silas across the table. "I'm Kristen," she said, "Milt's wife." She looked at Milt. "At least for now."

Oakey walked to the other side of the table and sat down beside Silas. "And I'm Oakey." He reached out and shook Silas's and Ben's hands. Then he said to Milt, "So, what have we got going here? A debate over when the Leafs are going to win the cup again?"

"We can get to that, but maybe something more important," Milt replied with a nod.

"Okay, Milt," Kristen said. "Calvin is playing 'Stairway to Heaven,' and you know what that means. So, can we wrap this little friendly tourist meeting up? We don't need to be involved in any more schemes or ideas."

Blessing returned. She sat down and pushed two pieces of paper to the center of the table. "Got this faxed from your local library. This is what proves there is gold missing. Oh, and by the way, my name is Blessing." She glanced at Kristen and Oakey.

Milt stared at the papers and, without looking up, said, "Blessing…meet Kristen and Oakey."

Kristen forced a smile, and Oakey gave Blessing a wide grin.

Milt looked up. "How does this tell you there is missing gold up at Yars Lake? It's just a bunch of lines and numbers."

"Tell them, B," Silas said. "Give them the condensed MBA."

"Well, it doesn't specifically say Yars Lake and the gold," Blessing said, "but nowhere else in their yearly statements do you see special entries for hundreds of thousands of dollars. Only in 1971 and 1973. Sort of coincidental it would be when the crash happened. And in 1973, well, I figured they must have recovered something that year."

"Nineteen seventy-three…" Oakey said. "Will you look at that, eh, Milt? Something in 1973." He glanced at Milt over his beer as he took a drink.

Kristen grabbed the papers from Milt's hands. "Are you saying this proves there is still gold out there from our friend Rick's crash?"

"Hey, I thought—"

"Hush!" Kristen said to Milt. She looked back at Blessing. "Well?"

"Strong possibility," Blessing replied.

"It's why we are up here," Silas added. He glared at Ben for support.

"Yeah! Exactly!" Ben said, receiving an elbow from Silas. "But we're still going to try some fishing, too."

Kristen held up the papers. "Can we get a copy of these? Where are you kids staying?"

"Can't see why not," Silas replied. He looked up as the hall lights came on and the music stopped.

Kristen called out, "C'mon, Calvin! One more!"

"I can't play one—"

"Just do it, Calvin!"

"Yeah!" Oakey added over his shoulder. "And make it fucking Def Leppard or something!" He looked back at Silas. "Sorry." He gestured towards Kristen. "Please, continue."

"Yeah...right...well." Silas turned back to Kristen. "We're staying at the NearNorth tonight but headed up to Yars Lake by the afternoon for a week of camping."

"Okay, stop by our restaurant, the Abby, on your way out tomorrow, and we will make a copy there while you have a free lunch on us. We'll even throw in some sandwiches to go. How is that for a deal?"

"Sounds good to me," Ben said, looking at Silas and Blessing. They nodded in agreement.

Milt looked up as a man placed an empty case on their table. The man started collecting beer bottles and placing them in the box. "Sorry, Milt. Time to shut 'er down."

"Yeah, no problem, Shaney." Milt said, standing and stepping to the end of the table. He was joined by Kristen. "But give these friendly Torontonians here a few minutes to finish their drinks. It's what keeps our economy going." He winked at Tom Shaney and then shook hands with Blessing, Ben, and Silas. "Thanks for the talk and the information."

"You're welcome," Blessing replied.

Milt looked at Oakey. "You coming, Oakes, or you going to dance to Def Leppard? We'll meet you out in the truck."

"Yeah, yeah...I'm coming!" Oakey said, bobbing his head. "This is a good song, though, 'Photograph'!"

Oakey stood and yelled at Calvin Erst. "Good fucking choice, C! You're the fucking man!" He turned and leaned on the end of the table. "You folks have a great camping trip up at Yars Lake, okay?" He glanced at Milt and Kristen as they left the building and then turned back to the table. "And if you really want to make

Mr. Tonkin happy by finding something up there, put a person named Chad DeMello on your list."

***

"Hey, that wasn't such a bad motel," Silas said as he loaded up the truck. He looked back at the sign. "NearNorth Motel & Bar. I'll have to remember that for when I write my book on this trip."

"You?" Blessing said as she placed her gear on the back tailgate. "How about we?" She turned and stared at Silas. "And don't you have to clear everything with that Star Wars lawyer of yours first?"

"He's into Star Trek, Ms. Sagan," Silas replied. "There's a difference."

Ben cut in between Silas and Blessing and threw his pack into the truck. "You both don't know the difference. Too busy watching *Friends*!" He closed up the gate and walked around the driver's side of the truck. "C'mon, let's go and collect our free meal."

As Ben drove back onto the main highway through Tear Falls, Blessing looked at the map. "Should be about ten minutes up on the right-hand side." She glanced at her watch. "And it's 10:20. Guess that means a free brunch."

"I hate that term, 'brunch,'" Ben said. "It's like you were too lazy to drag your sorry ass out for breakfast and then can't hold out for lunch."

"It's just a term," Blessing said.

"Yeah, then how come you never hear anyone saying they are going for linner?" Ben replied. "See, now that would be a cool term. It would mean you were too busy for lunch and need to be working through dinner."

"Go ahead, then. Start using it," Blessing said, smiling. "I'm sure it will make it into the Webster's Dictionary in no time."

Ben gazed over at Silas, who was staring blankly out the front windshield. "Hey, man, you going to help me out on this one? We could come up with a new word for Scrabble."

Silas turned to face Blessing and Ben. "I think we should tell him."

"Tell him? Who...and what?" Ben asked.

"Mr. Tonkin," Silas replied. He popped open the glove compartment and took out the Stinson financial statements. "Tell me, why is it he so interested in these papers Blessing has? Something is up."

"Didn't he say something about holding the Stinson mine accountable?" Ben said.

"Oh, c'mon! There is more to it than that," Silas said. "Maybe he is looking for the gold, too. Maybe he is going to blackmail someone. We don't even know this guy. He's not giving us the full story."

"And we are?" Blessing replied as she took the papers from Silas's hand. "What exactly do you propose we tell him?"

"I say we tell him we have been talking to Marty DeMello."

"Are you fucking crazy?" Ben said, leaning forward to stare at Silas. "Are you not the guy that has been lecturing us all trip that we could lose the money if we blab a word?"

"I don't say we tell him we are working for him, just that we bumped into him," Silas said. "Where we got the idea to come up here to look for the gold in the first place. Might jog his memory on a few things."

"No fucking way!" Ben replied. "He'll see right through that. I didn't come all the way up to Tear fucking Falls to have this Tonkin guy steal our thunder...and money!"

"Okay, calm down, Ben," Blessing said, raising her hand. "Why are you saying that now, Silas?"

"Because you heard what he said to us last night. The guy has lived here all his life. He probably knows the Yars Lake area like the back of his hand. He may be able to give us a lead. And you did mention he was the last one to see Chad DeMello alive."

"Well, I vote no," Ben said. He spotted a hanging Coca-Cola sign with the Abby Cafe printed underneath and signaled to turn off the highway. He brought the truck to a stop underneath a large picture window of the restaurant. "You're the deciding vote, Blessing."

"Well…I say we just play it by ear," she said. "We can see where the conversation takes us. He may bring it up himself."

"And if not?" Silas asked.

Blessing reached across his lap and opened the passenger door. "And if not, at least I have a few pieces of paper to get us a free brunch," she replied with a smile.

Once they were inside and waiting to be seated, Ben turned to Silas and Blessing. "Welcome to *Happy Days*!" he said with a grin.

"I actually think it looks pretty cool," Blessing replied, gazing around the restaurant.

A waitress walked over. "Booth or table?" she asked.

"Booth, please," Blessing said.

"Sure," the waitress replied. "This way, please." She looked over her shoulder. "Have you ever been here before?"

"No, first time," Silas said as they sat down. "In fact, first time in Tear Falls."

"Well, welcome," the waitress replied.

She turned as Milt stepped up next to her. "I can take this order, Diane," he said.

"All yours," Diane replied, and she handed Milt three menus.

Milt sat down, took out his order pad, and passed out the menus. "If I can make a recommendation of the blueberry pancakes topped with whipped cream and side orders of seasoned breakfast sausage and a bowl of mixed fruit."

"Hhmm…that sounds good." Ben said. "I'll go for that with an orange juice."

"I think I will have the Abby burger with fries and a Coke," Silas said. "It is brunch time, right?"

"You can order whatever is on that menu," Milt replied, smiling.

"What are you going to have, B?" Silas asked, turning to Blessing.

"I'm going to have the tuna melt with coleslaw and water, please."

"The tuna melt…" Milt repeated while staring at Blessing.

"Yeah…is that okay…Mr. Tonkin? I can order—"

"No…no…" Milt said, cutting her off and writing things down. "All excellent choices." He quickly gathered up the menus. "I'll get these orders to the kitchen and be right back."

Silas glanced at Blessing and Ben. "Well, that was weird."

"Maybe it's hard to catch tuna up here," Ben said with a grin. "But hey, no complaining. Remember, this is a freebie. Better get those papers out, Blessing."

***

Milt walked into the kitchen and handed Jamie the order. He walked over to Kristen as she was preparing sandwiches on a large cutting board and leaned his back against the counter beside her. "Our trio is here," he said.

"Good," Kristen replied without looking up. "I will have these sandwiches done in no time."

"Yeah…" Milt watched her work.

Kristen looked up. "Is there a reason you are supervising my sandwich-making?"

"No…no. I was just wondering if Berts has come up with anything yet."

Kristen placed the finished sandwiches in foam containers. "Well, I'm sure, if he has, he is certainly one to call you." She handed Milt the containers. "Here, put these in the refrigerator out front and go get copies of those papers. We're not throwing away free food for nothing, right?"

"I hope not," Milt replied.

***

Silas rotated his glass of Coke. "Now, this is a cool glass! Look at the way it's shaped. Bet Elvis drank out of glasses like these."

"They are pretty cool," Ben said, examining his orange juice.

"You don't see glasses like that down in Toronto, do you?" Milt said, coming back to the booth. He sat down and tapped the side of Silas's glass with his finger. "And they last a lifetime." He sat up and placed his hands on the table. "So, the Stinson information. You brought it with you?"

Blessing reached into her small side purse and took out the papers. "Here they are. I brought the ones from '71 to '75 just to give you an idea. You can get the rest from the Tear Falls library if you like. And these are yours to keep. The owner at the NearNorth made the copies for me."

"Oh, he did, did he?" Milt replied as he shuffled through the pages. "One hell of a nice guy, that owner of the NearNorth." He looked up. "Well, I want to thank you for getting this information to me, and it will go a long way to getting some answers from a mine that has been less than truthful over the years. Good luck with any searches up at Yars Lake, but keep your wits about you."

Milt stood, but then Silas said, "Mr. Tonkin...there is one thing. Can we ask you a question?"

Milt sat down again. "Sure, but trust me, you're better off bringing Bugs Bunny up there to find any gold than asking me. I'm really not that good at it."

"Well...no..." Silas looked nervously at Ben and Blessing. "What I really wanted to ask about is... you know this missing kid Chad DeMello?"

Milt slid slowly back into the booth. "You could say I'm familiar with the name. Why? What's he got to do with any of this?"

"Well, we know most of the story from newspaper articles about what happened with you and things way back then," Silas replied, "but why do you think they have they never found him... or his body? Do you think he could still be out there?"

Milt straightened his glasses. "Good question." He took a deep breath and cast a smile around the table. "Do you people know what a liquid moon is?" He shook his head, not waiting for a response. "Of course you don't. You grew up in Southern Ontario."

He leaned against the table. "So, let me explain. Up here, our lakes can get as still as glass. They reflect everything. Your face, a paddle in the water, a fishing rod, and if it rises at the right time, the moon. When we were little kids, we would chase and try and scoop the moon right up out of the water, but of course, it always disappeared. But we would keep trying anyway, even though our parents explained to us it wasn't real." He gazed at Silas. "So, yeah, to answer your question, I've thought about him still being alive up there. But the more time goes on, the more I feel Chad DeMello is my liquid moon. I could be chasing him forever and never come up with anything. I keep trying to find reasons why that guy might be alive, and everyone else keeps telling me the reasons he's not. And after all these years, I'm starting to believe they have to be right."

"Wow." Silas said. "So you do think it's possible."

Milt tapped the table. "For my own sanity, I have to say no." He leaned back. "You have to know it's a dangerous place. It's unrealistic to think he is alive after all this time. One misstep, and you could be in real trouble wandering around up there."

"Yeah, like listening to Nazareth too loud on a Walkman and stepping into a hundred-foot mine shaft," Ben chimed in.

Milt raised his eyebrows. "Yeah...listening to that music could definitely do that, alright." He rubbed his hand across the table.

"Okay…but why all these questions about this kid Chad DeMello? I thought finding the gold was your quest."

Silas shrugged. "Just part of the mystery of the whole area, I guess." He glanced at Ben and Blessing, who remained silent.

Milt laughed and stood. "Yeah, well, Tear Falls has more than its fair share of that." He folded the Stinson papers and placed them in his back pocket. "Have a good time camping, and gold or not, remember to cast your line into Yars Lake. It's one hell of a fishing hole." He glanced at the kitchen. "Your food should be out shortly, and don't forget your sandwiches to go."

"Thanks, Mr. Tonkin," Blessing said. "Very generous of you."

"You're welcome," Milt replied. He leaned on the table. "Just remember to include the Abby name when you have your press conference up at Yars Lake."

***

Silas turned the truck onto the Bitman logging road. He hit the eject button on the tape player. "Enough of that Nazareth shit! I don't care if we play it backwards. It's just fucking music. There is no hidden message in the lyrics."

"It was worth a try," Ben said.

Silas shook his head.

"What?" Blessing said as she leaned forward and stared at Silas. "What's that look for?"

"He's pissed because we didn't speak up back there," Ben said.

"Yeah, well, it would have been nice," Silas replied. "We had him going. Did you not see the look on his face when he told us that liquid moon story? The guy believes Chad DeMello is still alive."

Ben turned to Silas. "And what, exactly, were we supposed to say? It wasn't a *60 Minutes* interview! And did you not hear what he said about his own sanity? He said no. Not exactly a nice lead-in to an in-depth conversation."

"Bullshit!" Silas replied. "He was holding back. He still thinks there is a chance."

Blessing let out a long breath. "Okay...does it really matter at this point? Look, we got a nice meal out of it, and short of him telling us he saw Chad DeMello yesterday, I'm not sure what more he could have told us that was going to help. And you know what? I think he now owes us one for the Stinson papers. Who knows? Maybe that will come in handy down the road sometime."

"Down the road?" Ben repeated. "Maybe even down this fucking road, eh, Silas!" He laughed.

"Funny," Silas replied. He pressed on the gas. "Speaking of road, I'm going to guess there are no cops or conservation spot checks on this one. We need to make up some time."

Chapter 22

JARRED

Silas pulled off into a side clearing of the logging road and parked. As he stepped out of the truck, he caught sight of a weathered piece of grey wood in the shape of an arrow tacked to a tree. The words "Yars Lake" were carved into the surface.

"Gotta love the welcoming sign," he said. He walked to the back of the truck, opened the back cap window, and lowered the gate. "No rest for the weary!" he shouted. "Everyone make room for six jars in their packs."

Blessing and Ben joined him, and Silas handed them their packs. "It's close to one now. I figure we will be at that cabin Marty DeMello told us about by two. That gives us plenty of daylight to string up the jars and maybe poke around a bit."

"Last one there has to eat the jawbreakers!" Blessing called out. "Let's trek!"

***

An hour later, Ben spotted the cabin. "Hey! Over here!"

Blessing and Silas came up through the thick bush and stood beside him. "Could do with a paint job," Silas said, "but it looks sturdy enough. Let's check it out."

Blessing walked up a half-broken step onto a moss-covered porch as Silas and Ben walked the perimeter of the cabin. She walked over to a window next to the door and peered in. "Looks empty!" she yelled to the men. Then she stepped over and pressed a rusted latch on the front door and let it swing open. She stepped back, as she was immediately met with the musty smell of damp wood. "Wow!" she said. "This place needs some airing out!"

"Don't worry," Silas said, as he stepped up next to her and then walked in. "We'll prop a few windows open and get the air circulating." He walked past an old table to a wood stove at the back of the room. "Holy smokes. Look at this relic!"

Ben walked in. "Hey, the lake is right down in front, down a path. Dock is rotted out, but we could still cast off some old logs."

Silas turned around. "See, Mr. DeMello was right. Beautiful accommodations. We have a table, two old chairs, a rocking chair, and a wood stove just waiting for some fresh fish. Couldn't ask for more."

"We could ask that it stays dry if it rains," Blessing said. She threw her pack on the table and took out her jars. "C'mon, let's get these set up and see what we can catch on the first day."

***

"Shit, this is thick bush," Silas said as he stepped up onto a fallen log. "Give me another jar and some wire."

Ben handed him a jar and a piece of snare wire. He slapped a mosquito as he watched Silas wire the jar to a tree limb. Silas jumped off the log and looked up at the hanging glass container. "You know, this has got to be one of the strangest things I have ever done on one of my explorer trips."

"And you just had to drag me into it, didn't you?" Ben replied, shaking his head.

Blessing joined the two men. "Hey! The bush breaks into a clearing just up there. I can see some of the mined-out shafts in the side of the rock."

"Good," Silas said. "I think I have two jars left."

"Here, hand one over," Blessing said, stretching her arm out. "I'll see where I can place the last one."

Minutes later, Ben and Silas hiked up to Blessing as she hung the final jar. "There," she said. "Chad DeMello line complete." They took a moment to stare at the five-hundred-foot-long rock face across the clearing. Hollowed-out, darkened shafts stared back.

"Door number one, door number two, or door number twenty-seven?" Silas said. "This could take forever."

"Wow, and half of them are caved in," Blessing added. "I'm starting to understand why nobody has found any gold."

"Or any bodies," Silas said.

"Well, what do you guys want to do?" Ben asked.

Silas looked at his watch. "It's getting close to six. I say we go back and come up with a game plan and return with our gear in the morning." He turned to look at the last hanging jar. "At least we have a marked path."

***

"Christ!" Milt yelled out as he bolted up in bed.

"What! What is it, Milt?" Kristen exclaimed, jumping up beside him. "Did you have a nightmare? You okay, babe?"

Milt wiped sweat from his forehead. "No...no nightmare." He climbed out of bed and pulled his jeans on. "What time is it?"

"Milt, it's 6 am on a Sunday. It's your day off, remember? What's going on?"

"I gotta phone Berts!" He sat on the side of the bed and yanked open the drawer to the night table. "Where the fuck did I put his cell number?"

Kristen stood on her side of the bed. "Okay, Milt, what the hell is going on? Can we not take at least one day off?"

"Kristen, what name did those guys call the girl that was with them at the social Friday night?"

She shrugged. "Blessing, as I recall. Did you happen to hear something different?"

Milt stood and faced her. "No, one time they called her B. And they did the same thing at the restaurant yesterday."

"Oh, c'mon, Milt. You don't think it's the same B from the faxes Berts has been telling you about?"

Milt walked over to his armoire and opened the top drawer. "Well, what do you think?" He shuffled through the drawer's contents. "Little coincidental, wouldn't you say?"

"That's all I would say," Kristen replied. She picked her housecoat up from a chair, swung it over her shoulders, and tied it. "I've told you, Milt. You way overthink these things. There can't be any connection."

He pushed the drawer closed. "I overthink things, Kristen? Well, how about this? When I was talking to them over their free lunch at the Abby yesterday, the one kid mentioned Chad DeMello might have disappeared because he fell down a mineshaft while listening to Nazareth on a Walkman. The rock band Nazareth, Kristen. Now, where did he come up with the notion that Chad DeMello liked to listen to Nazareth? Can't say the newspaper articles on his disappearance would have ever mentioned that. And the only reason we know about it is because John went to school with him and he used to say Chad DeMello was obsessed with that band."

Milt opened another drawer and took out a pair of socks. He sat on a chair and pulled them on. "Fuck, I think I left Berts's number at the Abby. I'm going to have to stop by there on the way out."

Kristen sat on the edge of the bed. "Milt, are you telling me it's these kids…well, they are not kids, but these young adults all the way from Toronto are the ones who found out about your non-disclosure? That they're the ones who have been looking into Rick's and his father's deaths and faxing Berts?"

Milt stood up. "Worse, Kristen! If they were able to find out something as detailed as Chad DeMello liking a particular rock band, who knows what else they know? Maybe they actually have a lead on this missing gold, and if the DeMello's find out or fucking Stinson, they could be in big trouble!"

Kristen stood and stared at Milt. "Shit! You're going up there, aren't you? You're going up to Yars Lake to look for them. You just don't know when to quit being the hero, do you, Milt."

Milt walked out into the hallway, and Kristen followed. He stopped at the top of the basement stairs. "It's not about being a hero." He ran down the stairs. "It's about getting answers!"

Kristen shook her head as she walked into the kitchen. She reached into the fridge, took out a paper bag and a bottle of water, and sat at the table and rubbed her face.

Milt came rushing in, carrying his jacket, a small hunting pack, and his rifle. He grabbed the truck keys off a ring. "Don't worry, hon. it's not the DeMellos up there this time. It really is just for protection against any bears."

Kristen looked back at him with red eyes. "You want me to call Oakcy?" She pushed the lunch bag and bottle of water towards him.

"No need. I can take care of this one myself." Milt stopped as he grabbed the bag and water off the table. "It's going to be alright, hon." He stroked her face, and she grabbed his hand.

"Please be careful, Milt. You're not the only one who wants answers!"

***

Rob Krylic parked his MNR truck in front of the gas pumps of the White Moose and got out. He rested his folded arms on the back box of the truck and waited. A moment later, the bell rang on the front door, and a smiling Harry Tartiak headed his way.

"Hey, Rob!" Harry said as he came around to the pump and unhooked the handle. He looked at his watch. "Early enforcement?" he asked. He glanced at the rifle propped up in the passenger seat. "Or you doing your own early hunting today?"

"No hunting. That's a dart rifle," Krylic said with a nod. "The sun has been up for an hour, and the out-of-towners have probably been fishing for two. Have to let them know we're watching."

"Yeah...you are probably right on that. Fill it up?"

"Just put in fifteen dollars," Krylic replied.

"No problem," Harry said. He looked over his shoulder as he pumped the gas. "Hey, did you hear about that trailer fire out at Saphora Lake last night? Been all over the news this morning. Few cops came through here earlier talking about it."

Krylic stepped from around the far side of the truck and approached Harry. "Fire? What are you talking about, a fire."

Harry topped up the tank and re-hooked the pump handle. "Yeah," he said. He turned to face Krylic. "Apparently the trailer burned to the ground. Cops said something about a generator short. Might have been some fatalities."

Krylic brushed his mouth as he stared at Harry.

"You okay there, Rob?" Harry asked.

"Yeah, yeah... I'm okay," Krylic responded. He looked around. "Hey, you know what, I need to get going. You still have that MNR tab here?"

"Sure do," Harry replied. "Little dusty, but I imagine the MNR is still good for it." Harry smiled, but Krylic ignored him and headed for the front door.

"Could it kill you to smile once in a while, yah cheap bastard?" Harry muttered as Krylic entered the store.

Krylic placed a pair of rubber gloves on the counter as Harry came in and stepped around to the cash register. "Taking those, too?" Harry asked as he rang up the gas.

"Yup," Krylic replied. "Confiscating fish can be a slippery business."

"Well, you're the expert, Rob. Where you headed?" Harry asked. He took out a pad from beneath the counter, pulled a pen from his shirt pocket, and handed them to Krylic.

"Yars Lake," Krylic replied. He scribbled his signature on the pad and pushed it back to Harry. He looked up. "You sure the cops said a generator short for that fire?"

"Pretty sure," Harry replied as he carefully ripped off a carbon copy of the receipt. "But who the hell knows, Rob. These things always seem to take Tear Falls fucking months to figure out." He handed the receipt to Krylic and smiled. "Thanks for the business!"

"Yeah... no problem," Krylic replied. He quickly stuffed the receipt in his wallet and turned for the exit.

"Keep that pad handy for more fill-ups!" he yelled over his shoulder. "Like to support local business!"

"Hey, glad to oblige!" Harry called out as he watched Krylic throw open the door and hurry to his truck.

***

Milt rushed in the back entrance of the Abby and headed for his office.

"You're here early!" Jamie called over from the grill. "Thought you were off today!"

Milt sat at his desk and opened some drawers. "I am!" he shouted back through the door. "Have to run a small errand this morning." He stood. "Hey, Jamie, how early do they get up at bed and breakfasts? Think a 6:45 call is too early on a Sunday?"

"If you are talking about the Vicster, it's a b and b, is it not? Think they are supposed to answer in the morning."

Milt sat down. "Yeah, guess you're right." He picked up the phone and looked up the number from his Rolodex. "You're a smart man there, Jamie!" he called out as he punched in the number.

"Vicster Bed and Breakfast," a woman answered.

"Hi. It's Milt Tonkin from the Abby. Can you put me in touch with a guest you have there named Chris Berts?"

"I believe he has gone out for a morning walk before breakfast, but can I leave him a message."

Milt looked at his watch. "Uh…yeah…sure. Can you please tell him to call me as soon as possible? He has my number."

"My pleasure. And Mr. Tonkin, while I have you on the phone, do you still have our brochures on display at the front of your restaurant? The ones I brought you last year?"

Milt glanced over at his office bookcase and the brochures stacked on a shelf. "Yeah…some of them are out there," he replied. "I will call you if I need more. Please tell him I called."

"I will make sure he gets the message," the woman replied.

Milt quickly hung up. "Christ, that lady is worse than me," he said to himself.

"You say something, Milt?" Jamie said, leaning back from the grill to make eye contact.

"No…no," Milt said. "That woman from the Vicster… Ah, forget it! Just hope she remembers to give my friend a message over there." He stood and came out of the office. "Sorry for the rush, but I'll be in bright and early tomorrow. Thanks for holding the fort, Jamie."

"No problem, Milt. You have yourself a relaxing Sunday."

Chapter 23

MISDIRECTED

Silas stepped out onto the cabin porch and stretched. He took a deep breath. "Northern air!" he yelled back into the open doorway. "Should bottle this stuff and bring it back to Toronto!"

Blessing came out to join him and handed him a mug of coffee. "Nice, but not sure if you would be so relaxed if it were seven in the morning on a forty-below winter day up here."

"Hey, I would just borrow one of your designer jackets," Silas said with a smile.

Blessing responded with a frown. She walked down the porch steps and strolled over to the first hanging jar on the trail.

Silas called out to her, "How long before a squirrel figures out how to break those things open and steal the jawbreakers?"

Blessing walked up to the jar and took a closer look. She circled the jar and then turned back to Silas. "I don't know!" she yelled back, "but I suggest you come here, Silas!"

Silas hurried down the stairs, spilling his coffee. "Shit!" he said, trying to wipe away the coffee stain on his shirt. He strode towards Blessing. "What? What's wrong?" He came up beside her and stared at the jar. "Jesus Christ! What is that?"

"Get Ben!" Blessing said. "Don't touch the jar!"

Silas dumped out his coffee and ran back to the cabin door. "Ben! Come out here! Hurry up!"

Ben raced to the door. "What? What's wrong! There a forest fire? I'm trying to finish cooking breakfast on that antique stove!"

"Forget breakfast. You better come and take a look at this," Silas said, trying to control his breathing.

Ben gazed out at Blessing, who was waving him over. "Bring your camera!" she yelled.

Minutes later, as Ben was taking a picture of the jar, Silas came running back from up the trail. "I checked two others, and same thing. Everything is gone except the photo. And the jars go off the trail and into the bush toward the far side of the lake."

Ben lowered his camera. "Did we say this was fucked up? Because it is now just getting downright fucking creepy!"

Silas took a deep breath. "Let's just bring it back to the cabin."

Inside, Ben sat down, unscrewed the top of the jar, and took out the picture of Chad and Marty DeMello. He flipped it over and studied the crude arrow smeared in red.

Blessing peered over his shoulder. "You think it's blood?"

"Oh, it's blood, alright!" Ben said as he examined the marking closer. "Can't imagine someone has a paint-by-numbers set out here."

Silas took the picture out of his hand. "How do you know? This could be just some sort of practical joke, or maybe someone is trying to scare us. It could be red marker."

Ben looked up at Silas. "Either way, we now know somebody else is up here with us."

Silas set the picture down, walked over to one of the windows near the door, and looked out. "Well, this is what we wanted." He turned around. "Right? Chad DeMello or not, I think we have to check out the rest of the jars. Blessing, I think you should stay here."

"Oh, no!" she said, heading to her pack and pulling out a light jacket and a small stringed carrying bag. "I earned my keep on this trip. I want to find out what this is all about."

Silas said to Ben, "Flip a coin? I just think someone should stay here. We can't lock that door, and I don't want to come back to no supplies."

Ben shrugged. "I'll do it. Breakfast was a bust, so I'll make sure I have a good lunch waiting. You want to take my camera?"

"Nope," Silas replied. He walked over to his gear, pulled out his video camera, and placed it in his small hiking pack. "I'm going full documentary on this one!"

***

Milt turned off Highway 205 onto the Bitman logging road, and glanced at the truck's clock, which read 7:03 am. He was hoping to catch the three hikers still eating breakfast, but he now knew he would not arrive at the cabin until after 8:30. He was reaching to turn on the radio when his cell phone rang. He snatched it off the dash and flipped it open.

"Yeah...hello?"

"Milt...it's Chris Berts. I got the message you called. And perfect timing, because I've got some news for you."

"Yeah...well, I figure I don't need you or your fucking news anymore, Berts."

"Whoa...I see we have some early-morning attitude. I like it! Give it to me, Magnum. Whatta ya got?"

"I've got the paperwork I need to prove there is more lost gold out there and that Stinson has been trying to cover it up. No telling where or who this is going to lead to now."

"Not bad! Let's meet up. Where are you now? Your phone is breaking up."

"It gets even better, Berts. I've also figured out who has been contacting you, who the mystery B person is that found out about my non-disclosure."

"Christ, Milt, You're giving me competition. That's pretty fucking good, but are you sure you have the right mystery person? Because—"

"Damn right, I have the right person! The B person is this group of young people from Toronto that have researched Rick's story. One of them is named Blessing. They're the ones who came up with the paperwork on the lost gold. They're up at Yars Lake as we speak. I'm heading up there now to do my own little reporter interview."

"Toronto? What? No, Milt, you have that part wrong."

Milt laughed. "Fucking bugs you that I beat you to it, doesn't it? No finder's fee on this one, Berts! Sorry!"

"It's not them, Milt. I'm pretty sure the person that has been contacting me about you is Krylic."

"Krylic? Why the fuck would he be contacting you?"

"You're breaking up, Milt. Pull over before I lose you completely."

Milt stopped his pickup on the shoulder of the logging road. "This better be good. I'm already worried about these kids and what they might be getting into."

Once Milt had shut off the truck's engine, Berts said, "You should be." He took a deep breath. "Listen to me, Milt. I worked my reporter magic like you asked, and Krylic has good reason to be interested in you and the gold. He is in hock to the DeMellos big time for some fucking land he bought off them, and he is worried as shit they are going to collect soon. He knows about your non-disclosure, and he is convinced there is more gold out there that you and Stinson are looking for. He's dangerous man, Milt!"

Milt shook his head. "So, he just up and told you all this? Isn't that nice of a dangerous man. He's full of shit!"

"He didn't tell me, Milt. Puppy Powers did."

Milt sat up in his seat. "Puppy Powers? What…what the fuck are you talking about?"

"I got a tip and caught up with Puppy coming off shift in the parking lot over at the hydro dam and told him I was a reporter. At first, he wouldn't talk to me, but I convinced him things were moving fast with Mead looking into these missing people. We got into his truck, and he gave me the Marty Feldman look. That's when I knew he was going to talk."

"And?"

"He told me way more shit than I was ready for. He told me Krylic is responsible for those people that have gone missing. He would follow them up to Yars Lake after stopping them on the highway. He would use his dart gun to tranquilize them and then search their campsite for any maps or information on the gold. The problem is, he would…as Puppy Powers said…sometimes make a mistake. Overtranquilize them. That's where Puppy came in."

"Came in? In what way? He would go up there and help Krylic dispose of bodies?"

"Dispose might be an understatement." Berts said. He took his phone away from his ear. "Did you just hear a beep?"

Milt looked at the display on his own phone. "Shit, my battery is dying. Don't worry about it. Yeah…what about the bodies?"

"Krylic would call Puppy on a night shift and tell him to close all the sluice gates at the hydro dam. Diverts all the water to the turbine water intake valves. Hell of a whirlpool. Krylic would dump a body off the bridge, and it would get sucked down into the intake. Body would go through the turbines like a fucking meat grinder. No body, no evidence!"

Milt shook his head. "And no signs of a struggle at these robbed campsites if the people are drugged."

"You're ahead of me, Milt. All these robberies have been Krylic. There is no Chad DeMello."

"Jesus Christ." Milt replied. He heard the beep on his phone again. "Shit," he said as he looked at the flashing battery icon again. He put the phone back to his ear. "Why the fuck would Powers be in on this? He'd be an accessory to murder."

"That's another matter, Milt, but let's just say his computer-viewing habits were well known by Krylic."

"Shit." Milt said, letting out a long breath. "You better get a hold of Mead about this, Berts. Tell her the full story. She needs to look into this."

"Already did, Milt. She is a cool customer. Took it all in stride when I told her. She is going to track Krylic and Powers down and bring them in for questioning. Wouldn't be surprised if she is headed your way."

"Fucking right, she needs..." Milt paused and looked at his phone as the line went dead. "Fuck!" He stared at a blank screen. "Fucking piece of shit!"

He threw the phone on the passenger seat and started the truck. Slamming it into drive, he sped out of the gravel ditch and headed for Yars Lake.

***

"You got everything?" Silas asked as Blessing strapped on her small hiking pack.

"I've got what I need," she replied. "You know, I did do my own research on wilderness hiking and cave exploration before this trip. Maybe I should be quizzing you."

"Alright, take it easy." Silas slipped his pack over his shoulders and turned to Ben. "We shouldn't be more than a few hours. We'll check out all the jars. Why don't you shoot a flare when lunch is ready?" He laughed.

"You brought flares?" Ben asked.

"Of course." Silas tightened his straps. "One each. How else did you think we are going to celebrate when we find the gold?" He smiled at Blessing as he headed out the door.

She shook her head and followed.

When Silas came up to the ninth jar, he gazed at the contents. "Same!" he said as Blessing joined him.

She looked around at the thick bush. "This makes no sense. All these jars are doing is basically following the shoreline of the lake. Why would anyone go to all this trouble? Is this supposed to lead us somewhere? Maybe it is a practical joke."

Silas released his grip on the jar and let it swing in the wind. "Could be." He pointed to their left. "If logic serves me right, I would say the next nine jars are in that direction. It's just a little after eight now. Ready for one more hour?"

Blessing squeezed a drink of water from her hiking bottle. "Let's do it!"

Soon after, Blessing came upon a slope in the forest and peered down through the trees. "I can see the lake!" she called back. She looked at the jar in front of her. "And number fifteen is a ditto!"

Silas came up beside her, breathing hard. "This is reminding me of our bike ride all over again."

"Keep hydrated, and you'll be okay," Blessing said with a smile. She turned towards the lake. "Three more, and then what?"

"Chad DeMello?" Silas said, raising his eyebrows. "I don't have a clue, but someone must have a hell of a wad of gum in their mouth." He took a drink. "Okay, looks like this arrow is pointing toward the lake, although it's getting hard to tell with the wind picking up. Consensus?"

"Agreed," Blessing replied. "I just hope the last jar doesn't just point the way back."

They made their way down the slope. Finally, Silas broke through the thick trees onto a narrow stretch of beach and was relieved to feel a refreshing breeze coming off the lake. He glanced thirty feet down to his right and watched Blessing emerge. She walked directly to the beach edge, squatted, and splashed water on her face. Then she looked over at Silas. "Dead end?"

He walked over to her as she stood, and then they scanned their surroundings. "Nothing here that I can see. Maybe we did get it wrong," Silas said. He stepped over to a large piece of driftwood and sat on it. "Well, I want a moment of recuperation before we trace our steps back and have to go to battle with the mosquitoes again."

"Rest up, then, my friend," Blessing replied. She spotted a large outcropping of rock jutting out into the lake another hundred feet up the beach. "I'm going to go climb that rock for a vantage point."

"Be my guest, eagle eye," Silas said. He closed his eyes and leaned back to feel the sun. "I'll be right here, getting my vitamin D."

Blessing laughed. "How did you ever survive on all those other trips you went on?"

Silas kept his eyes shut. "I had Sherpas carry me!" he said with a grin.

Blessing smiled. "I'll be back."

***

Milt slowed as he spotted the MNR truck parked on the side of the road. As he passed, he took a look inside and could see it was empty. "Fuck!" he said to himself. "He's already here!"

He drove another five hundred feet and pulled off into a clear area on the side of the road. He shook his head as he stared at the shiny black pickup truck parked near the sign to Yars Lake. *These kids have too much fucking money.* He grabbed his blue windbreaker from the passenger seat and jumped out of the truck. He walked back to the cargo box and lifted out his day pack and rifle. Then he slung the pack over his shoulder, took a drink of water, and looked at his watch, which read 8:10 am. If he pushed it, he estimated he could be at the cabin before nine.

***

Blessing climbed up onto the tall rock and saw that it extended into the distance as a ridge along the shoreline. She shaded her eyes and scanned the nearby bush, hoping to catch the glitter of a glass jar.

"Hey! Lazybones!" she hollered. "Shit out of luck! Time to retrace our steps!"

She sighed when Silas didn't respond. She took a few steps under the shade of a large tree and was about to yell again when she noticed an object out of the corner of her eye. She walked over and examined a collection of dense limbs extending over the rock ridge from the trees below. She bent down and could now see a glass jar hanging from a low-lying branch not more than a foot off the rocky ledge surface. She leaned down further and spotted another hanging jar farther back on the branch.

She stood, stepped back, and cupped her hands. "Silas!" she yelled. "I found some more!"

Silas stood and straightened his shirt. "You found another jar?" he called back.

"Two more!" Blessing shouted. "Come and take a look!"

Silas trotted down the beach and climbed up onto the rock. He walked over to where Blessing was squatting, and he got down beside her and stared at the tangled mess of tree branches and the first hanging jar.

"I think it has everything in it," she said to him. "It looks untouched."

"I think you're right," Silas replied. "Question is, how do we get in there to take a closer look?" He took off his pack. "You know what? Time for a commando crawl."

Blessing lifted the heavy branches, and Silas crawled under. He grabbed the first jar and rotated it. "Yup, everything is in this one!" He let it go and crawled toward the second jar. "Shit, I'm getting covered in mud under here!"

"People pay good money in Toronto for that!" Blessing called out.

Silas made his way to the second jar and peered in. "Same!" he hollered back. "Not sure what it means, but I'm coming out. Barely see in here." He pushed off the rock to turn and then spotted a hanging wire ahead. "Hold on! Think I see something. Think it's more snare wire."

Blessing struggled to hold the heavy tree limbs up. She estimated Silas had already crawled in fifteen feet, and she could now only see the soles of his hiking boots. "The last jar?" she shouted under the branches.

"I'm just reaching for it now. There's a gap… Whooaah… Fuck… Holy shit!"

"Silas!" Blessing yelled. "Silas! You okay!"

She heard tree branches breaking and a muffled thump. "Jesus! Silas!" She tried to push the thick branches aside to get a glimpse of what had happened.

"Goddamn it!" Silas yelled as he lay on his back twenty feet below, sprawled over forest debris and sand. Narrow rays of light penetrated down to him from above. He tried to get up, but then he felt an intense pain in his right shoulder. "Fuck!" he said as he forced himself to a sitting position. He looked up at where he had fallen from and strained to see the dark shadow of the rock ridge.

"Blessing!" he yelled. "Can you hear me?"

Blessing lay down and crawled forward a few feet under the branches. "I can hear you!" she called out. "Where are you? Are you all right?"

"I fell…" Silas tried to discern his whereabouts in the dim sunlight. "Down some sort of crevice, I think. Looks like it might be part of a shaft tunnel or cave. But don't come any closer! It's slippery as hell close to the edge!"

"What do you want me to do? Are you okay?"

Silas flinched as he tried to move his right shoulder. "I banged up my shoulder pretty good!" He felt more pain as he tried to stand, so he sat back down and stared at his left ankle. "And I have a foot here that is pointing in the wrong direction! And it fucking hurts!"

"Did you hit your head!"

Silas felt sand beneath him. "Nope. Got lucky and landed on a bed of sand." He noted some sharp rocks behind him. "And missed the concussion." He looked up at the crevice opening. "B…throw my pack down with my water. I think I'm going to need some help getting out of here." He glanced ahead and could see some light. "I think there may be another way in here down at the bottom, but you're going to need to do some bushwhacking to get here!"

Blessing wiggled backwards and grabbed Silas's pack. Then she crawled back in and positioned herself to throw his gear over the rock ledge.

"Okay! Here it comes!" She slung the pack sideways as hard as she could and watched it disappear off the edge of the crevice. Her throw was quickly followed by a thump.

Silas gently reached over and pulled the pack close. "Got it, B! Now, be careful and climb down the rock and come around. I've got my whistle. I'll guide you to the spot with my voice and the whistle."

"Got it! Hang on. I'll be right there."

Chapter 24

EXPLORATORY OVERDOSE

Rob Krylic walked within thirty feet of the old cabin and gave it a once-over. "Jesus fuck," he said to himself. He looked up at the moss-covered roof. "Fucking Galverson. He built this thing like a brick shithouse!"

He placed his rifle over his shoulder and stepped up onto the porch. He took note of the fresh footprints on the weathered wood and smiled. He knocked on the door. "Housekeeping!" he yelled. He heard movement inside.

"Hey, one sec!" Ben called out. He came to the door, but Krylic pushed it open before he could lift the latch.

"Good morning," Krylic said, walking in.

"Oh, hi," Ben replied. "Hello, officer. How are you?"

"I'm good… I'm good." Krylic replied as he walked to the centre of the room. He brushed the table with his hand. "Bone dry." He looked up at the ceiling. "That's good!"

"Yeah! So far, so good." Ben said, displaying a nervous smile.

Krylic slowly looked around the room and then leveled his gaze at Ben. "You got those fishing licenses yet?"

"Uh…yeah!" Ben said, and he quickly stepped over to his pack and opened it.

"Don't bother," Krylic said. "I'll ask you to show it to me when you have a fish on your line."

Ben stood. "Sure! We'll have them ready."

Krylic walked over to the back window facing the lake. "Where are your travelling comrades? They down at the lake?"

"Uh…no…they went for an early-morning hike. I slept in."

Krylic looked at his watch, which read eight o'clock. "Early risers. I like that." He returned to the centre of the room, swung his rifle off his shoulder, and lay it on the table. "You guys came up here to rock climb, right? That's what you told me when I stopped your truck a few days ago."

"And explore. Hobby of ours."

"Right…explore. And what exactly are you exploring for, again?" Krylic asked, leaning forward with both hands on the table.

"Just the history of the area. The old mine up here."

"Mm-hm…" Krylic said, nodding. "You know what? I think it would be best if you did show me that fishing license. Save me the trouble of bothering you again."

"Sure!" Ben walked over to his pack, and as he opened it, he said over his shoulder, "You might know—"

He felt a stabbing pain in his shoulder. "Ah, shit!" he yelled. "What was that?" He reached back and felt the tranquilizer dart in his left shoulder. He pulled it out. "What the fuck!" he said, staring at the dart. He looked at Krylic. "What the fuck are you doing?"

"Just a little something to settle you down," Krylic replied as he stepped over to Ben. He took the dart from Ben's hand. "Now, you are going to feel a little woozy in a few minutes, so why don't you tell me where your friends really are before I decide to do give you another shot and make things a lot worse."

Ben glared at Krylic in disbelief. He took a few steps backwards and wiped the blood from his shoulder. "You're fucking crazy!" he said. "You're going to be in a lot of trouble for this!"

"Crazy?" Krylic said, smiling. He opened the chamber of his tranquilizer pistol and pulled out a bag of darts from his pant pocket. "I would say you and your friends are the crazy ones for coming all this way to search for gold that ain't fucking yours!" He placed a dart in the pistol and snapped the chamber shut. He raised the gun and pointed it at Ben. "Now, where did your friends go to find the gold, or are they going to be transporting a vegetable back to Toronto instead of a human being? Your fucking choice!"

Ben blinked as the drug started to take effect. He put his hands up. "Okay. Listen, mister. We don't know where the gold is. They are just checking a trail we marked with jars yesterday. It's just..." Ben backed up against the cabin wall and felt his legs becoming weak. "It is just a stupid experiment we are doing." He slid down to the floor and looked up, shaking his head as he tried to keep his eyes open. "We don't know about any gold."

Krylic walked over and stood over Ben. "Jars," he said with a grin. He watched as Ben's eyes started to close. "Don't worry, Mr. Explorer, it was a small dose. Just enough time for me to look around." Krylic squatted down. "And maybe check out your little experiment."

***

Blessing hiked around the outcropping of rock and forced her way through the tangled forest undergrowth to the backside of the ridge. "Silas," she called out, "are you there?"

"I can hear you, B, barely! Can you hear me?" Silas hollered back.

"I can, but this rock face is covered in thick brush! I'm going to follow it. Blow your whistle so I can locate you!"

Silas took out his rescue whistle and started blowing on it.

Blessing climbed over fallen logs as she navigated her way around heavy branches and dead tree limbs, keeping tight to the border of the rock. She heard the whistle getting louder. "Hold on, Silas! I think I'm close. Are you there?"

Silas repositioned himself. "I can hear you! You must be near!" He looked farther down the dark crevice. "Hold on! I see more daylight coming in a ways down! Keep going! I think you can get in that way!"

Blessing followed Silas's directions and pushed forward through the thick bush. She ran her hand along the rock face and felt a break. "I think I found it!" she called out. She ducked underneath a large branch and saw a narrow opening in the ridge. She poked her head in and yelled, "Silas!"

"Yeah! I'm over here!"

Blessing took a small flashlight out of her backpack and entered the narrow gap in the rock. She stopped, shined the beam of light through the darkness, and looked around. She could see the enclosure opened up into a large cave structure. The floor consisted of sand with sharp rocks protruding at various points along its length. She shined the light on either side of her and then above her head. She estimated she was at least two arm's lengths from the jagged walls on either side and twenty feet below the rock ceiling. She looked ahead and spotted the dim rays of sunlight marking the place where Silas had fallen. She carefully manoeuvred her way over and around the sharp rocks as she called out his name.

"I see you, Silas! I'm coming!"

Blessing came up to Silas and fell to her knees. She gave him a hug.

"Ow!" he yelled. "Don't think I'm in shape for that!"

Blessing leaned back. "Sorry." She tried to keep calm as she looked at Silas's ankle. "You really did a number on that, didn't you?"

"Didn't have time to practice my crevice landings before we left," Silas said, wincing in pain.

"You can't walk on that, Silas. We need help to get you out of here. But I can't leave you like this."

"You may have no choice, B. It will be a while before Ben figures we are overdue."

"Wait." Blessing said, standing up and taking her pack off. "The flares. There could be other people up here fishing or exploring, right?" She searched her bag and brought out the flare. "How do you set this off?"

"Unscrew the cap at the bottom and pull the tab, but make sure you have a clear shot through the crevice. Otherwise, we will be having our own flare bonfire right down here."

"Got it!" Blessing said. She followed Silas's directions and set the flare off through the narrow crevice opening. "Wow!" she said, watching the flare glow brightly in the sky. "Someone is going to see that!" She came back to Silas. "Guess we now sit and wait. How are you feeling?"

"I'll survive." Silas gingerly lay down on his back. "Goddamn it!"

"More pain?"

"Nope. Just thinking that this is all my mom needs, another person to care for." He shook his head as he caught a glimpse of the last hanging jar on the branch overhead. "What the fuck is this jar scavenger hunt all about, anyway? Somebody is pretty twisted to lead us to this. It's like a bad version of the Goonies."

Blessing looked around. "It is weird. What do you think this place is?" She stood.

"I think it's some sort of hollowed-out cave system. It's near the lake. Ancient water erosion? Who the hell knows. I'm just glad it has wet sand to break falls."

Blessing took a few steps back into the dark part of the cave and shined her flashlight around. "Well, there is a pretty dark tunnel here to the left that seems to extend along the shoreline under the ridge." She turned and walked to her right. "And another opening over here that slopes downward."

"Be careful, B. We don't need two of us to be rescued."

Blessing bent over and shined her flashlight down the second tunnel. "Silas, I think I see something down there."

Silas twisted his head back to see where she was looking. "Yeah? Like what? Don't be telling me about anything unless it is shiny."

"Just a minute." Blessing looked back at Silas. "I'm going to go down and take a closer look."

"Oh, shit! I knew I should have sent you for help." Silas struggled to stand up. He tried to put weight on his left ankle, but it radiated sharp pain. He took a hobbled step towards the cave wall and braced himself as he watched Blessing disappear down the sloped tunnel. "Don't take chances, B!" he yelled.

"I'm not!" she called back. "I'm already at the bottom!"

"And...?"

Silas waited for an answer, but Blessing didn't respond.

Blessing leaned forward and shined her flashlight over a pile of old wood. She picked up a piece and read the faded lettering of the Stinson mine. "Holy crap..." she said under her breath. She squatted and sifted through more broken crate pieces. She spotted an object and picked it up. "Silas! I'm coming back!"

She scrambled to the top of the tunnel and saw Silas leaning against the cave wall. She hurried over to him. "Shit, Silas, don't try to stand on that ankle." She guided him down to a sitting position on a rock and took a seat beside him. "Look at what I found down there." She handed him a piece of wood.

Silas read the faint Stinson mine lettering and numbers on the wood. "Holy shit!" He stared at Blessing. "Is this a piece of a gold crate? Fuck, is it part of the lost gold? Did you see any?"

Blessing shook her head. "Sorry. Think we struck out on that one. Just a pile of broken crates down there. I figure someone beat us to it long ago by the looks of the pieces. But..." She showed Silas a hat. "I did find this old piece of head protection for you to wear." She grinned as she placed the worn hat on his head.

Silas put the wood down and then pulled the hat off and looked at the ripped and soiled logo. "Brown Airways. Certainly lives up to its name." He tossed it at Blessing, but she deflected it. "Ew...I don't want it!" she said, laughing. She bent forward and picked up the wood. Then she took a deep breath. "Well, at least we found something, and you know what this means, right?"

She didn't wait for an answer. "It means I at least deserve some recognition, wouldn't you say?"

Silas nodded and smiled as he looked at the broken wood. "Yup. You are one smart MBA treasure hunter. This has to be from the plane, alright. And I can't imagine the crash site is very far from here." He studied some of the numbers. "Makes total sense. I guess we can scratch one of two off our list."

Silas looked up at the last hanging jar swinging from a slight breeze. "But who the fuck would want to lead to a pile of empty crates? Now, if we could only make sense of that shit before I have to be stretchered out of here."

***

Milt came up to the cabin and bent over with his hands on his thighs as he tried to catch his breath. "That's it!" he said. "No more fucking bacon and eggs for breakfast." He was lifting his head to take a drink when he was distracted by something in the sky. He watched as a flare streaked skyward. "Christ, that can't be good." He ran over to the cabin porch and hopped up onto it. Then he rapped on the door and pressed the latch.

"Hello!" he said as he swung the door open. "Anybody here?"

He caught sight of Ben lying against the back wall, motionless. "Hey!" he said, running over to him. He threw his rifle onto the floor and kneeled beside Ben. "Hey...are you okay? It's Ben, right?"

Ben slowly opened his eyes. "Yeah...that's me."

Milt ran over to Ben's pack, grabbed his water bottle, and hurried back. "Here," he said. "Drink this."

Ben took a long drink and struggled to open his eyes. "Shit." He tried to focus on Milt. "What the hell happened?"

"I think you were drugged," Milt replied. "C'mon. Let's get you sitting down." Milt helped Ben to his feet, walked him over to the table, and sat him down in a chair. "You alright?" he asked, looking into Ben's eyes.

"I…I'm okay," Ben replied.

"Fuck." Milt said. "Was this done by Rob Krylic? Short, bald guy wearing a MNR uniform?"

"Yeah…yeah, that's the guy." Ben said. "He's fucking crazy. Shot me with a tranquilizer dart." He rotated his shoulder. "Still hurts!"

Milt went over to one of the windows by the door and looked out. "The guy's more than crazy. He's a fucking lunatic." He turned back from the window. "But I'm pretty sure he is gone now. What did he want? And where is the rest of your group?"

"That's the problem," Ben said, rubbing his eyes. "He's gone to look for them by following those hanging jars out there. He thinks we're here to find the gold."

Milt walked over to Ben and stood in front of him. He bent down. "Okay, tell me flat out, Ben. You three have some inside knowledge of where the gold is? That's why you are up here? To find the gold?"

Ben slowly looked up at Milt. "We are actually here to find Chad DeMello, Mr. Tonkin, the lost kid that came after you nine years ago. We were paid money by his father to try and find him."

Milt stood and took a step back as he stared at Ben. "What? What did you say?"

"Marty DeMello. He made a deal with my friend Silas after he sold him a scooter. He paid us good money to come up here to try and find his son. I wasn't supposed to say anything. That's why the jars—"

"Hold on!" Milt said as he put up his hand. "Stop right fucking there! Marty DeMello hired you? To find his fucking son?"

"Yeah. I know it sounds crazy, but that was the deal. He has already paid us some money. I just didn't know we were going to run into some crazy asshole with a tranquilizer gun."

Milt sat on the edge of the table, hung his head, and rubbed his brow. "Jesus Christ." He looked up and let out a long breath.

"Look, we didn't want to involve you, Mr. Tonkin. It was just by chance that Silas bumped in to you the other night."

Milt shook his head. "You didn't want to involve me..." He walked over to Ben. "Are you guys fucking crazy? Marty DeMello and the whole fucking DeMello clan are fucking criminals! Chad DeMello is dead! You understand me? Dead! You really believed his story about finding his son? No fucking way! He has some other fucking angle on this. He might even be working with Krylic. Maybe he is involving you to get revenge on me." Milt slammed his fist on the table. "That fucking piece of shit!"

Ben waved his hands. "Mr. Tonkin, please calm down. All we know is what he told us, and he never said anything about revenge on you. But that crazy Krylic guy is out there right now looking for my friends, and I'm really fucking worried about what he might do!"

Milt paced back to the window. "You kids really know how to fuck up a guy's Sunday, don't you?" He walked back and rubbed his face with both hands. "Okay, you said something about jars. What about them? What does that have to do with anything?"

Ben bit his lip. "Well, it might sound even crazier, but Marty DeMello asked us to hang jars on a trail towards that old mine up here. But when we woke up this morning, they had been moved. Blessing and Silas went to follow them. They are filled with stuff from when his kid, Chad, was growing up. Toys he liked. Even Nazareth tapes."

"Nazareth tapes?" Milt repeated. He walked slowly over to Ben and leaned over the table. "Shit, that's how you knew. That's why you mentioned Chad listening to Nazareth the other day at the Abby."

"Yeah...I guess so."

Milt threw off his pack and took out a pen. He pulled out his hunting guide from his pack, ripped the back cover off, and wrote down a number. "Here!" he said, handing Ben the number. "I'm going to go look for your friends. When you get your legs back, head back to town. Call this number as soon as you get a cell signal and ask for Oakey, the guy you met at the Legion the other night. Tell him I could use his help up here. And tell him to follow those fucking jars to find me!" Milt rushed over and picked up his gun.

Ben looked at the number and then back at Milt. "But what about the police? Shouldn't I call them, too?"

"Don't worry," Milt said as he stopped at the door. "Somebody who likes to write about this shit already did."

***

Silas lay on his back with his pack supporting his head. He looked down at his left ankle. "How big do you think that ankle will get?" he asked Blessing, who was staring up at the crevice opening.

She stood. "We can't wait to find out." She looked at her watch and then walked over to Silas and felt his head. "You're getting hot. That's not good! Maybe I should hike back now."

"I think you may be right. I have food and water. Besides, nobody is going to find—"

"Shhh…" Blessing said, putting her hand up. "I hear someone."

Milt yelled out from the top of the large rock. "Hey! Hello… Blessing, Silas!"

"Down here!" Blessing yelled back. Silas grabbed the rescue whistle from around his neck and blew hard.

"We're right here!" Blessing called out, directing her voice up through the crevice. "We need help!"

Milt pushed some branches up and peered underneath them. "Where are you, guys! It's Milt Tonkin!"

"We're down here in a cave!" Blessing said. "Don't come any closer! You'll fall through a crevice! You have to climb down and come around the side! We'll direct you with the whistle!" She turned to Silas. "Give me your whistle. I'll go back to that opening and make sure he hears it."

Milt made his way along the backside of the rock ridge, following the sound of the whistle. He climbed over logs and under thick brush. "Damn it!" he said as he scraped his hand on a splintered branch. He looked ahead and saw Blessing bent under a large tree limb, blowing the whistle.

"Hey!" Milt said as he approached her. "Everything okay?" he pushed his way past the tree branch and followed her through the rock gap.

"I think Silas has a broken ankle, Mr. Tonkin." she said. "He needs help!" She pointed her flashlight. "He's up there where the sun is shining through."

Silas let out a sigh of relief when he saw Blessing and Milt appear out of the darkness of the cave. Milt came up and rested his gun on a rock as he knelt beside Silas. "How are you feeling, friend?" He glanced at Silas's swollen ankle. "Pain?"

"Painful enough." Silas replied. He raised himself to a sitting position. "I think, with a little bit of help, I can make it out of here." He looked at Milt. "But before we do that, we got something to show you, Mr. Tonkin." Silas stretched forward and picked up the old piece of crate. He handed it to Milt. "You recognize that?"

Milt took the piece of wood and examined it. He read the Stinson lettering and saw the faded crate serial numbers. "Shit!" he said, looking up. "Where did you get this?"

Blessing walked over with her flashlight and turned it on. She pointed the beam toward the darkened sloped tunnel. "There is more down there, Mr. Tonkin, if you would like to take a look."

Milt stood and took a few steps toward the tunnel. Then looked back at the piece of wood. "There is more of this? How much more?" He reached toward Blessing. "Can I borrow that flashlight?"

"Absolutely." She handed Milt the light.

"And take this camera, Mr. Tonkin," Silas added. He pulled his camcorder from his pack and handed it to Milt. "I want everything on film for my documentary, if you don't mind."

Milt took the camera from Silas and strapped it over his shoulder. He turned and quickly edged his way down the tunnel. "I'll be right back!" he called out.

When he reached the bottom, his light revealed a large stack of broken gold crates and pieces of wood. "Christ!" he said, breathing hard. He bent down and started frantically overturning crates and throwing pieces of wood aside. "Got to be something here." he said as he continued to search.

He flipped the last crate piece with his foot but saw nothing. He squatted, dropped the flashlight, and then placed his face into his hands as he gazed through his fingers at the empty crates. *Fuck, none of this makes sense*, he thought.

He stood, picked up the flashlight, and scrambled back up the tunnel. "Lots of empty crates down there!" he yelled up to Blessing and Silas. He reached the top of the tunnel. "But no—"

He abruptly stopped as he saw a figure appear from out of a dark area of the cave.

"Gold?" Rob Krylic finished. He stepped forward with his dart rifle resting across his forearm. "Why would there be, Milt? Because you already took it."

"Hey, Rob," Milt said, glancing at his rifle.

"Don't even think it, Milt. This may only be a dart gun, but I have a big enough dose in here to bring down a moose. Imagine what that will do to your body."

Milt looked at Blessing and Silas as they stared back at him in fear. He turned back to Krylic. "What are you going to do, Rob, dart all three of us?"

Krylic laughed. "You still don't get it, do you, Milt? You haven't explained to these fearless prospectors who is the good guy and who is the bad guy here? I'm here to save them from you." Krylic looked at Blessing and Silas. "This man is a fucking thief, or have you smart Toronto wetbacks not figured that out yet? He took the fucking gold long ago." Krylic glanced up at the hanging jar. "This is all just a big fucking setup to lure you here so he can cover his tracks. Wanted someone else to find the empty crates so Stinson would stop looking and the cops would stop asking questions. Isn't that right, Milt?" Krylic didn't allow Milt to answer. "Turn around and let's go take another look at those crates. Maybe I can match off some numbers."

Milt turned, and as he took a step toward the tunnel entrance, he felt a sharp pain in his back. He instantly realized that Krylic had shot a dart into his back. "Fuck!" he yelled as he stumbled forward.

Blessing screamed as Krylic sat on a rock, watching Milt as he struggled to pull the dart out. "It's barbed, Milt. You won't be pulling that one out without some help." he said, laughing.

"You're not going to get away with this, Krylic!" Milt replied. He made another vain attempt to pull the dart out with his hand.

Krylic smiled. He looked over at Blessing and Silas. "You see, kids, you would think someone smart enough to steal all that gold would know that struggling is just going to speed up the drug." He looked back at Milt and could see his legs were starting to wobble and he was reaching for a rock to support himself. "Works fucking fast, don't it, Milt!"

"Look, officer." Silas said. "We don't know about any gold being stolen, but he was just trying to help us. We don't want any trouble! This—"

Milt slumped to the ground, his back against the cave wall. "Don't waste your breath, Silas." He strained to keep his eyes open as he turned to Krylic. "Powers talked, Krylic. It's over. Mead knows everything. She'll be up here to arrest you soon."

Krylic walked over and sat down beside Milt. He squeezed Milt's face hard with his hand. "Mead ain't going to arrest me and doesn't give a shit about you, Tonkin. You know, I thought you would have figured that out by now."

He looked over at Silas and Blessing. "And I don't need Powers to help me make people disappear." He stood and looked down at Milt. "Get some fucking shut-eye, Tonkin. I have other matters to take care of before I deal with you."

Chapter 25

FAMILY AFFAIR

ilt felt water splash on his face, and he looked up at the fuzzy outline of someone standing over him. They were wearing jeans and a green muscle shirt. "Milt... Milt! Wake up!"

Milt tried to orient himself to the voice. "What...who...?"

"It's me, Milt, Jocelyn. Are you okay?"

"Yeah...just groggy." Milt reached out for the water bottle Jocelyn was holding. "But I could use some of that." He took a long drink and then wiped his mouth. "Shit, guess Krylic is two for two on his dart shots today." He looked around.

"Wait!" he said, looking up at Jocelyn. "Where is the young couple from Toronto? Where's Krylic?" He could see Blessing's and Silas's belongings scattered across the cave, and then he spotted Krylic's tranquilizer gun leaning against a rock. Some unused darts lay on the ground near where he had been shot. "What the fuck happened? You have to catch Krylic, Jocelyn! He's the one who has been responsible for all the missing people! The guy is a fucking murderer!"

"Calm down, Milt," Jocelyn replied. "Take a deep breath. I know all about Krylic."

"Jesus Christ, Sergeant! How can I be calm with all this shit going on?"

Mead walked over, leaned against a rock and folded her arms. "Because it's all under control, Milt." She gazed around the cave. "Funny how you always seem to plan our meetings on my day off."

She looked back at Milt. "Oh and don't worry, the hikers from Toronto are fine. I already helped them back to the cabin and came back to get you. They'll take a little rest there until we are able to get some people in here to stretcher the young man out. You've been out for quite some time."

Milt let out a sigh of relief as he stretched his head back. "Well I'm glad someone knows how to keep calm. That's a relief. And Krylic? You've arrested him?"

"Well, let's just say he was the master of his own fate, Milt." Mead leaned forward and dusted some dirt off the front of her jeans. "Sad, really. But then again..." She looked up and forced a smile. "I'm sure the DeMello's were not far behind."

Milt stared at Mead and slowly nodded his head. "Right... well I guess I leave that in your capable police hands, Sergeant. I figure it was only a matter of time before his own bullshit caught up with him." Milt reached out his hand for a lift up.

Mead ignored Milt's outstretched arm and stared back with a blank face. "Speaking of bullshit, Milt. What about you?"

Milt dropped his arm back to his side. "What about what?" he said.

"The bullshit." Mead responded. "Your bullshit. You seem to have been giving out your fair share for years here in Tear Falls. There a reason you couldn't be straight with me? Your friends? Maybe even your own wife?"

Milt responded with an expression of surprise. He put up his hand. "Okay, look, Jocelyn, I was going to tell you about my non-disclosure but I assumed you already knew. And you don't know the crap I've gone through ever since Rick stole and crashed that plane twenty years ago. The police, the DeMellos. And the promise I made to take care of his mom. Rick and I were like brothers. I didn't need the town to have something else to make my family feel guilty for."

"But you don't feel guilty about placing Rick's mom in a nursing home even though that was against Rick's wishes. You call that family, Milt? You did that after you got all the reward money from finding the gold and maybe a few extra bars on the side from some crooked mine manager?"

Milt creased his brow as he stared back at Mead. "Hold on, Jocelyn, you've got it all wrong. I've been trying—"

"You've been trying to do what, Milt?" She said, cutting him off. "What exactly have you been trying to do?"

She walked over and reached into the shadow of a dark rock shelf. She picked up her service revolver and placed it in her waist band. She walked back to Milt and took out a paper from her back pocket. She thrust it in Milt's face. "Read this before you call yourself fucking family, Milt!"

Milt took the letter and saw it was dated November, 1971. "What the hell is this?" He asked.

"Read it!" Mead said as she kicked the flashlight over to Milt. He picked up the flashlight and turned on the light and read the letter. He reached the bottom of the page and recognized Rick's signature. He looked back up at Mead. "This some kind of joke? Who the hell is Beth?"

"It's no joke, Milt." Mead replied. "Rick's dad killed himself on a snowmobile because of me. He just couldn't stop drinking and bring himself to tell his own wife he had a kid from an affair with my mother on one of his business trips. But Rick knew. He found the letters from my mother after his father died." Mead shook her head. "But he found it too tough to bring himself to tell his sick mother about it. But he did ask me to make sure his mother was well taken care of if anything happened to him. But I just couldn't do that until my own mother died two years ago. Now she is the only family I have left. And I want her back, Milt!"

Milt looked back at Mead in shock. "Wait... wait... you're a half sister to Rick? That can't be true. He would have told me!"

Mead took out a pair of gloves from the front pocket of her jeans and pulled them on. "Hard to take, isn't it Milt. The bullshit and all. But I guess you should be used to that because you were never a true friend to Rick."

"Jesus, you are the one who has been talking to Berts all this time. All the faxes... and... that house. You bought the fucking house all because of Rick's mom. You're B!"

Mead smiled. "That's right, Milt. You should pay more attention to nameplates. Jocelyn E. Mead. My middle name is Elizabeth, or Beth." Mead walked over and picked up Krylic's gun.

Milt tried to stand but his drugged legs gave way. "Okay... Jocelyn... we can discuss this. I did my best with Rick's mom. Everyone said the home was the best place to manage her MS. We can work something out with her care if you're a half sister. I'll talk to her lawyer!"

Mead held Krylic's gun up and looked down the sight. "Already did that, Milt. Got me nowhere. You know he is one hard-ass lawyer and he seems to have one big fucking hard-on for you too." She placed the gun on her forearm and looked up. "He told my lawyer he didn't give a shit if I was a half sister. The will is iron clad with your name stamped all over it and I guess the money for him, wherever the fuck that is coming from." Mead took a few steps forward. "Now do you think that's fair, Milt? That I should be cut out of a family because of you? Someone who felt it was too much trouble to honour Rick's wishes and put his mother away in a nursing home like a fucking criminal in a prison. You betrayed Rick, Milt. You have his blood money all over you. You're not fucking family. You're a fucking fraud!" Mead reached down to the cave floor and picked up a dart and placed it in the chamber of the gun.

Milt's breathing became shallow. "Jocelyn! This is fucking crazy! You will go to jail for this!" Milt shuffled backwards up against some rocks. He moved the video camera to the front of his body to try and protect his chest. "Jocelyn... please... think about what you are doing here!"

"Oh, I have thought about it." She raised the barrel and pointed the rifle at Milt. "That's why I'm holding Krylic's gun."

A figure emerged from the darkness behind Mead. "Put the rifle down, Sergeant! And I can assure you, I have more than darts in mine!"

Mead turned to see Oakey pointing a rifle at her. She laughed. "Oh, another small-town rescue. How fitting. I like it." She abruptly tossed Krylic's rifle at Oakey. "Here, catch!" she called out.

Oakey leapt back and deflected the rifle with his own gun. Mead used the distraction to draw her revolver from her waistband, and she fired a shot into Oakey's leg.

"Fuck!" Oakey yelled as he dropped his rifle and fell back clutching his bloodied leg. Mead walked over and pointed the hand gun at Oakey. She looked back at Milt. "You people of Tear Falls sure know how to make things complicated, don't you Milt!"

Mead suddenly turned her head as she heard music emanating from a dark part of the cave running along the lake. She stared at Milt. "What is that Milt? This one of your jokes?" Mead took a few steps back keeping the gun trained on Oakey. She looked back into the darkened tunnel and strained to see where the music was coming from. She glanced back at Milt. "You better speak up Milt! If you have someone else in here, you better tell them to come out for their own good. What the fuck is that music!"

Milt shook his head in confusion as he looked in the same direction. "I think... that's... Shit, that's fucking Nazareth!" he yelled, as a man burst out of the dark tunnel and tackled Mead. Her gun flew out of her hand as she rolled over fighting the man. She used her police training to deliver a swift knee to the man's midsection. He fell sideways as she rose to her feet and lunged for the gun. The man dove and collared Mead's feet. Mead fell and stretched for the gun. She yelled out in pain as she felt a sharp object stab her thigh.

"Pull it out!" she yelled. "Pull it out, or it will kill me!"

The man kneeled on Mead's back and pinned her down as he pulled the dart out of the back of her right thigh.

Milt struggled to his feet and kicked the gun aside. He looked at the man. "Holy shit!" he yelled. "Who the hell…" He struggled to maintain his balance as he tried to decipher the man's face behind his tangled beard. "Fuck! Is that you, Chad?"

The man looked up. "I…I didn't do it, Mr. Tonkin. I didn't kill any of them!" He rose to his feet as Mead's body went limp, and then he stumbled back a few steps. "I didn't kill the campers, and I never killed Galverson. I only took supplies, but I never hurt nobody! But the cops think I did!"

Milt put up his hands. "Okay…just take it easy, Chad. Just take it fucking easy. Nobody said you killed anyone. It's going to be okay, but I need your help right now." Milt looked over at Oakey, holding his bloodied pant leg. "My friend over there is bleeding, and the sergeant may need some help, too. All I want is for you to help me get them back to the cabin. If you want to disappear again, that's okay with me."

Milt looked at Oakey, who nodded in agreement. "Look, I can vouch for you, Chad. I will tell everyone what happened here. You can count on it."

Chad took a deep breath and backed up a few more steps toward the dark tunnel. Before he could bolt, Milt pointed above Chad's head to the hanging jar. "If you are going to run, Chad, I want you to know something. All those hanging jars you've seen in the bush…it's no trick. They're a message from your dad. He wants you to come home."

Chapter 26

RATED PG

Milt wiped his forehead with a bandana from his pocket as he leaned against his truck in the hospital parking lot and waited for Oakey. Finally, Oakey came out the front doors and limped to the truck.

"I guess you got the worst of it this time!" Milt yelled with a smile.

"Fuck off, asshole!" Oakey yelled back. He came to the passenger door of the truck. "And I'm done with rescuing your sorry ass!" He opened the passenger door and eased himself onto the seat.

Milt jumped in the driver's seat and started the truck. "At least you were just grazed by that bullet and only in the hospital for three days. Shit, I took one nearly clear through the shoulder and spent two weeks in bed."

Oakey looked over at Milt. "It's not a fucking competition."

Milt smiled as he steered the truck onto the main highway. "Home?"

"That would be nice." Oakey looked out the window and then back at Milt. "RCMP took the video camera?"

"Yup. Took everything. I think they have a whole fucking detachment up here. The only people outnumbering them are the press again."

"Figures. Hey, how did you know to turn on that video camera, anyway? You into true-crime shit or something?"

Milt laughed. "Not even close, my friend. I was using that camera to try and protect a dart going right through my fucking heart. I had no idea I turned the thing on." He glanced over at Oakey. "But don't tell anyone. Let's make sure Berts gets the story that I planned everything."

"Well, at least those Toronto hikers are going to get their reward," Oakey said. "It's making national news that Chad DeMello walked out of the bush after nine years. Nobody is going to give a fuck about any lost gold now."

Oakey turned to Milt. "And make sure Berts pays you for anything you tell him this time, alright? No more fucking best-selling freebies."

"How about I do one better and negotiate a part for you in the movie," Milt replied, looking over and smiling.

"That would be good," Oakey said, nodding. "I could handle that."

"Well, it would only be done under the condition that you come with Kristen and me down to Mexico next month. We can discuss your acting salary over some tequila shots."

"Ah, shit, Milt, I can't do that. That's your bag. You go and enjoy yourself down there."

"Oh, no! You're coming, buddy. Mexico awaits, and Eduardo wants to hear all the stories about Rick and see his mom again."

"Fuck, I don't know." Oakey rubbed his leg and stared out the front windshield. He turned back to Milt. "And you are really going to rent an RV? All the way to Tijuana?"

"Damn right, I am!" Milt replied. "Fuck, Oakes, how long before word gets out some gold is still missing? You want to be around for that? They're going to come after you this time, not just me. You want ten Berts breathing down your neck instead of one?"

Oakey laughed as he looked away. "In one month, eh?"

"Four weeks, and Kristen and I are going, guaranteed. Otherwise, I'm getting a divorce. Think about it, wounded man. Cool drinks and warm waters can do wonders for the healing process, and each day is like the one before. No surprises." Milt grinned.

Oakey nodded as he stared back at Milt. "No surprises. I like that." He extended his hand. "Alright. You're on. Fuck Tear Falls. Let's go!"

Milt smiled as the two men shook. "You won't regret it, my friend!"

One Month Later

Milt placed an arm around Oakey and brought him out onto the boardwalk of the Largo Vida Villa resort. "Now, is that a view, or is that a view, buddy?" he exclaimed. He cupped his hand to his ear. "And do you hear that ocean surf? Music to my ears!"

"And Bryan Adams at the beach bar. Not bad." Oakey replied with a smile.

They turned as they heard Kristen say, "Look who we have here!" She smiled as she walked up to the two men with Eduardo by her side. "A Mr. Eduardo Samos, the esteemed owner of this Mexican resort. He has already settled Rick's mom into her room." She gestured toward Milt and Oakey. "Eduardo, I would like you to meet my husband, Milt, and our good friend Oakey."

Milt threw out his right hand and placed his left on Eduardo's shoulder. "Jesus, Eduardo! I've heard so much about you from Rick and his mom. So glad we can finally meet."

"Likewise, Milt," Eduardo said, shaking Milt's hand. "I'm grateful to see Rick's mom here after all these years. She has always been like family to us." He turned and shook Oakey's hand. "And another good friend of Rick's?"

"Right behind this guy," Oakey said, pointing at Milt with a grin. "He's the one who convinced me to visit your beautiful resort, and from the looks of things, for once, he was right."

"Don't mind him, Eduardo," Milt said. "He just needs a fancy umbrella drink at your bar over there under the hut. I promised him days of sunshine, warm waters, and cool drinks."

"That is easy to do here in paradise," Eduardo said with a smile. "Tell the bartender you want three Ricardo specials as a welcome drink and one water, please!"

"That sounds good to me," Kristen chimed in. "I'll come with you, Oakey."

Milt put an arm around Eduardo. "C'mon, Eduardo. Show me some of Rick's favourite spots."

After the quick tour, Milt and Eduardo stood at the beach's edge, near the pier, and stared out. "Unbelievable." Milt said with his hands on his hips. "And you built all of this yourself? And your English is very good."

"Took some time, Milt, but yeah, every bit. And I can thank all my Canadian tourists for the English. Business investment, you might say."

Milt nodded as Kristen and Oakey arrived. She handed a drink to Milt and water to Eduardo. "Think we can move the Abby down here, Milt?" she said, admiring the view and sipping her drink.

"Wouldn't be a bad idea," Milt said, watching the people relaxing on the beach and fishing. He looked to the end of the pier. "Hey, is that a floatplane I see tied up at the end of the dock?"

Eduardo looked in the same direction. "Yes. He is actually from Canada, Milt. He does tourist fly-ins to some of the beach islands. Really nice guy. He's been here for years. He must do well, because I know he is always sending money back to Canada through the resort bank."

"Really?" Milt said, turning back to Eduardo. "That's cool. I have to go take a look. Rick would have got a kick out of that."

He walked up onto the pier and headed for the plane.

Kristen laughed. "Look at him. Comes all this way, and the first thing he wants to do is check out a floatplane."

"Ah…let him be," Oakey said. "First day in a while he has relaxed with nothing to worry him."

As Milt approached the plane, he slowed when he saw the faded Brown Airways insignia on the fuselage. He noticed movement through the small plane windows and could see an older gentleman with a white beard rummaging in the cargo bay. "What the hell…?" he said to himself as he came closer and could make out the plane lettering.

The man spotted Milt approaching and moved over to the back of the plane. He opened the door and stepped on the ladder. "Sorry, buddy. We do all our bookings…" The man stopped speaking as Milt came up to the ladder.

"Jesus Christ!" Milt blurted out as he spotted the initials PG embroidered on the man's shirt. The man stared back. He extended his hand. "Milt…?"

Milt slowly shook the man's hand as his eyes widened. He turned his head back to the beach.

"Kristen!!"

CPSIA information can be obtained
at www.ICGtesting.com
Printed in the USA
LVHW011948080122
708049LV00017B/742/J